Wining and Dying

A COOKBOOK NOOK MYSTERY

Wining and Dying

Daryl Wood Gerber

WHEELER PUBLISHING
A part of Gale, a Cengage Company

Wheeler Publishing, a part of Gale, a Cengage Company.

Wheeler Publishing Large Print Softcover Cozy Mystery.
The text of this Large Print edition is unabridged.
Other aspects of the book may vary from the original edition.
Set in 16 pt. Plantin.

LIBRARY OF CONGRESS CIP DATA ON FILE.
CATALOGUING IN PUBLICATION FOR THIS BOOK
IS AVAILABLE FROM THE LIBRARY OF CONGRESS.

ISBN-13: 978-1-4328-9887-8 (softcover alk. paper)

Published in 2022 by arrangement with Beyond the Page Publishing, LLC

Printed in the United States of America
2 3 4 5 6 26 25 24 23 22

Thank you from the bottom
of my heart to Krista Davis
and Hannah Dennison.
You have been wonderful, supportive
friends on this challenging but
rewarding creative journey.

ACKNOWLEDGMENTS

"You have to keep your bottom on the chair and stick it out. Otherwise, if you start getting in the habit of walking away when you're stuck, you'll never get it done."

— Roald Dahl

I have been truly blessed to have the support and input of so many as I pursue my creative journey.

Thank you to my family and friends for all your encouragement. Thank you to my talented author friends, Hannah Dennison and Krista Davis, for your words of wisdom. Thank you to my Plothatcher pals: Janet (Ginger Bolton), Kaye George, Marilyn Levinson (Allison Brook), Peg Cochran, Janet Koch (Laura Alden), and Krista Davis. It's hard to keep all your aliases straight, but you are a wonderful pool of talent and a terrific wealth of ideas, jokes, stories, and fun! I adore you.

Thank you to the members of the Facebook fan-based group Delicious Mysteries, which I cohost with authors Krista Davis, Lucy Burdette, and Amanda Flower. I love how willing you are to read ARCs, post reviews, and help all of us promote whenever possible. Authors need fans like you. You keep us on our toes.

Thanks to those who have helped make this tenth book in the Cookbook Nook Mystery series come to fruition: my publishers, Bill Harris and Jessica Faust at Beyond the Page; my agent, John Talbot; and my cover artist, Dar Albert. Thanks to my biggest supporter, Kimberley Greene. Thanks to Madeira James for maintaining constant quality on my website. Thanks to my virtual assistant, Christina Higgins, for your novel ideas. Honestly, without all of you, I don't know what I would do. Cry a little more often, I fear.

Thank you to a delightful reader, Nicole Williams, for allowing me to cast her husband Christopher in this book.

Last but not least, thank you librarians, teachers, and readers for sharing the delicious world of a cookbook nook owner in a fictional coastal town in California with your friends. I hope you enjoy this next installment.

CAST OF CHARACTERS IN THE COOKBOOK NOOK MYSTERIES

Alan Baldini, owner of Baldini Vineyards and Hannah's husband
Bailey Bird Martinez, Jenna's best friend
Brianna Martinez, Baily's daughter, almost a year old
Bucky Winston, Cinnamon's husband
Cinnamon Pritchett, chief of police
Cary Hart, Jenna's father
Eleanor Landry, Keller's mother, owner of Taste of Heaven
Flora Fairchild, shop owner
Gran, Gracie Goldsmith, works at Cookbook Nook
Jake (Old Jake) Chapman, friend
Jenna Hart
Katie Casey Landry, aka Chef Katie
Keller Landry, Katie's husband
Lola Bird, Bailey's mother and owner of Pelican Brief
Marlon Appleby, deputy
Min-Yi, Katie's daughter, almost fifteen

months old
Pepper Pritchett, Cinnamon's mother and owner of Beaders of Paradise
Rhett Jackson, Jenna's fiancé and owner of Intime
Tina Gump, culinary student and Brianna's nanny
Tito Martinez, reporter and Bailey's husband
Vera Hart, Jenna's aunt
Zoey "Z.Z." Zeller, mayor and realtor

ADDITIONAL CAST OF CHARACTERS IN *WINING AND DYING*

Candy Kane, artist
Christopher George, tech company owner
Destiny Dacourt, wine rep
Egan Zeller, Z.Z.'s twenty-something son
Ferguson, skinny male cop
Foster, fresh-faced female cop
Ginny, the concierge at Crystal Cove Inn
Hannah Storm, Hurricane Vineyards owner
Harmony Bold, wedding planner
Jaime Gutierrez, artist
Naomi Genet, artist and part-time teacher
Orah, owner and painting instructor at Palette
Quade, artist
Sienna Brown, owner of Crystal Cove Inn
Wayne Alks, Yardley's husband
Yardley Alks, teacher and internet art guru

Chapter 1

Crack! Clatter! I heard the sound of something falling and glass breaking. Then my cat yowled.

"Tigger!" I raced from the master bedroom, cell phone in hand. "Buddy, are you okay?" I skidded to a stop in the living room and my insides snagged. Not for my ginger cat. He was fine and sitting at the top of the kitty condo looking down at me, mortified. "What happened?"

He mewed.

"I can see that," I muttered. The painting I'd been working on for the Crystal Cove 5th Annual Art and Wine Festival competition was lying facedown on the floor. The easel it had been propped upon had tipped over and broken the west window. "Dang it."

Tigger mewed again.

"Don't worry. I'm not mad at you." How could I be? He was the most adorable cat in the world. And accidents happened. But I was angry at the universe. I mean, honestly, what else could go wrong?

"Jenna, are you there?" asked my wedding planner, the source of my other woe. Her voice crackled through the cell phone. "Are you okay? It sounded as if glass broke. Is there an intruder? Do you need me to call —"

"I'm fine. It's not an intruder. It was my cat." I spotted a ball of yarn near the window. Tigger must have been chasing it and run into a leg of the easel.

"I'm glad to hear you're okay. Now, back to what we were talking about before we were interrupted . . ."

I combed hair off my face, tugged my aqua sweater over my jeans, and shuffled to the canvas. Lifting it by the corners, I inspected the painting. Luckily, the oils had dried completely. I worked in thin layers and not impasto, using blobs of paint. I placed it on a chair at the dining room table and then sat at one of the other chairs and signaled for Tigger to come to me. He did. To calm myself as well as him, I stroked his head.

"Go on," I said.

"Regarding the cancellation . . ." Harmony Bold had been arranging Rhett's and my wedding for a number of months. Everything had been going smoothly until she'd phoned minutes ago to tell me the site for our nuptials in June had to bow out. The recent fire in Napa Valley hadn't hurt the inn, but the beautiful gardens were buried in ash and wouldn't recover for a very long time. If Rhett and I were determined to get married at that particular venue, we'd have to wait an entire year. "What do you want me to do?"

"I don't know." I checked my watch. I would be late for my art workshop if I didn't leave in one minute. "I don't have time to brainstorm ideas. Let me consult Rhett and we'll figure something out, okay?"

"There are plenty of lovely inns up and down California. I'm sure I can find you another place that you'll be happy with."

"By June?"

She cleared her throat. "I can do it. If not, by December at the latest."

"Do what you can." I willed the tension in my shoulders to ease. I had my wedding dress and I had my man. The rest would be icing on the cake. I ended the call, made sure Tigger's food and water bowls were set, and hopped into my VW Beetle.

At the top of the mountain above Crystal Cove stood the Crystal Cove Inn, a charming place that like most buildings in town was painted white, with a red tile roof. Calling it an inn was an understatement. It boasted two wings of rooms as well as a dozen private cabanas and exquisite grounds. With its coveted views of the ocean and the town below, the inn was consistently full.

I parked in the lot, grabbed my artwork from the backseat, and traipsed into the lobby. The spicy scent of apple cider greeted me, as did the aroma of a crackling fire. Crystal Cove was blessed with Mediterranean temperatures, and in April the weather was usually mild, but a storm was forecast for tomorrow, not great for a festival's opening night. The weatherman wasn't entirely sure the storm would hit us. A crisp wind current could send it south. Festival planners were probably crossing their fingers and toes. Given the number of guests sitting on the stone hearth of the fireplace, it was the *in* spot. A few patrons were sitting in the wing-backed chairs reading books.

To my right, a group of folks wearing last year's festival T-shirts had gathered around the concierge desk, no doubt looking for somewhere to dine. The festival didn't officially start until tomorrow night, Tuesday, but Crystal Cove was a tourist destination. Many festivalgoers had arrived over the weekend.

I walked through the lobby's archway leading to the grassy expanse outside.

"Jenna," a woman trilled. "Over here!"

Yardley Alks, owner of the Art Institute, waved to me from beneath the covered walkway that led to the private rooms, communal rooms, and cabanas. I strolled toward her, inhaling the heavenly scent of jasmine hanging from the walkway's eaves.

A petite woman in her forties with a sunny disposition, Yardley was in charge of the workshop I was attending with the other finalists. "The rest aren't here yet," she said, pushing a strand of shoulder-length tawny hair behind her ear. "Let me revise that. Keller is, but none of the others."

Over two hundred artists had entered to win the yearly art competition that would put the winner's art on next year's festival poster. Seven of us had made the final cut. All were taking part in the workshop. Yardley, a reputed art teacher, was on hand to give us suggestions as to how to make our work shine. The judging panel would announce the winner Sunday afternoon at Azure Park. I was so nervous I could barely breathe.

Yes, I owned the Cookbook Nook, a culinary bookshop, and yes, operating the shop and the Nook Café was a full-time, satisfying job, but prior to becoming a businesswoman, I'd entertained dreams of becoming an artist, so I'd entered the competition on a lark. To my complete surprise, I had been chosen as one of the finalists.

"The door to the workshop is open," Yardley said. She had negotiated with the inn's owner to provide a communal room where the artists could paint as well as store the tools of our trade. "Easels are set on the verandah. I'll be right there."

The verandah, at the far end of the grassy expanse, provided a beautiful view of the ocean. Tonight, it was lit up by bright floodlights.

I spotted two women my age setting up a wine tasting on the grassy expanse, both of whom I recognized. "Hi, Hannah," I called to the raven-haired one. "Have fun tonight."

"You'll be joining us later. See you then." Hannah Storm owned Hurricane Vineyard. "But *shh.* It's a secret."

During the festival, over one hundred artists and crafters as well as twenty Santa Cruz Mountain and Central Coast wineries would show their wares. In addition, locally made artisan foods would be featured at booths and restaurants throughout the town. Last's years basil olives were a huge sensation. A specialty Kids Zone at Azure Park would feature music while promoting craft projects designed for children. The festival promised a rollicking good time, and I anticipated it each year.

I hitched my art satchel higher on my shoulder and strode down the walkway to the communal room. The door to the room was open. Like the verandah, the room was brightly lit. Yardley believed we needed to see all the flaws of our art. Tonight, however, she'd planned for us to finish our work outdoors, drinking in the evening air for inspiration.

"Hey, hey, Jenna." Keller Landry, an ice cream entrepreneur and part-time handyman, turned to greet me. In his plaid shirt and narrow-legged jeans, he looked even leaner than usual. Had he lost weight? He swept the thatch of brown hair that invariably fell down his forehead to one side. "Just got off the phone with Katie." Keller was married to my good friend, who was the chef at the Nook Café. "She says you're full up on reservations for the night."

"Good to hear." I'd left work at five so I could make tonight's workshop. My aunt, who was co-owner of our thriving business, told me she would handle any emergencies, as if we'd have any. I needed to spruce up the display window tomorrow on my day off, but other than that, we'd been running as smoothly as clockwork for the past few months. No snags. No hiccups.

"Katie said she put one of the specials in a to-go box for me," Keller went on. "Chicken basil parmigiana."

"Lucky you." I'd visited Katie in the kitchen earlier and had tasted it. Major *yum.* "Coming outside?"

"Sure thing."

I removed my paints and brushes from my satchel, set the satchel in a cubby, tucked my work back under my arm, and followed him. Though we could leave all our tools in the communal room — it would be locked every night — I liked having my materials with me in case I wanted to tweak something on my canvas at home.

Keller set his work on one of the easels on the verandah and took off the cloth covering.

"Wow," I said, eyeing his work as I set mine on an easel. "That's getting better and better. I love it. Have you named it?"

"I'm calling it *Humanity.*" Keller enjoyed working with mixed media, which could include anything from paint to paper to pencils, glues, crayons and glitter. Then there were the more obscure media, as I liked to think of them, like hardware items, buttons, beeswax, or even pages from an old book. Everything became a potential item to add to one's mixed-media art.

Using red, green, and blue paint, silver glitter, and strips of beeswax, Keller had created a masterpiece of a raging ocean. Within the waves, in India ink, he had written a quote by Mahatma Gandhi: *You must not lose faith in humanity. Humanity is an ocean. If a few drops of the ocean are dirty, the ocean does not become dirty.*

"How did you get the writing so even?" I asked.

He pulled a tapered burin, an etching tool with a six-inch blade, from a set of tools Katie had given to him as a birthday gift. "This tip" — he tested it with his finger — "can fix anything."

"Looks sharp."

"Sharper than sharp. But . . ." He regarded his work and sighed forlornly. "It's missing something."

The kitchen sink? I thought wryly.

"I'm thinking of adding an origami fish, but that seems trite." He sighed again. It was almost a moan.

"Are you okay?" I scrutinized him more closely. His skin was lax and his eyes were bloodshot.

"Me?"

"There's nobody else here."

"Truth is, I'm struggling."

"With?"

"Selling ice cream is, you know, limited, and being a handyman isn't really stirring my creative juices."

"You're going to finish the work on our house, right?" I asked teasingly. He'd been helping out for a few months, stripping and repainting the walls of the house my aunt had given us. No more out-of-date wallpaper or colors that didn't suit us.

He shifted feet. "Yes, but —"

"Yes, but what?" I did my best not to worry. There were other handymen in town, but Keller had the same sensibilities as Rhett and me. He was nailing every aspect of our remodel.

"I'd like to expand my financial horizons through my art." Keller brandished the burin in front of his painting. "I get that it's a pipe dream, but —"

I patted his arm. "You should follow your dream."

"Except I'm worried about Min-Yi."

Keller and Katie had adopted an adorable

Korean girl a while back. She was nearly fifteen months old.

"She's not going to college any time soon," I joked. "You have plenty of time to save up."

"No, it's not that. It's . . . She's not sleeping well. I think it might be my fault. I've been working on this piece for months, and I pace as I work through ideas. She hears me and wakes up crying. Maybe I should quit and —"

"Hello-o-o." The Fairchild twins, Faith and Flora, sashayed to two easels and set up their artwork. They didn't look or act like twins. Flora wore her hair in a long braid; Faith wore hers in spiky abandon. Flora preferred understated and somewhat boxy beaded sweaters. Faith wore clingy upscale workout clothes and gads of colorful jewelry. Flora was down to earth while Faith, who at one time had been an artists representative but was now hoping to become a full-fledged artist, was a tad brassy and narcissistic.

Faith's work, like her, was a bold array of colors depicting ocean waves. Flora's piece, a pen-and-ink of the mountains and neighborhoods that rose above Crystal Cove, was refined and delicate. For Home Sweet Home, the shop she owned in town, she made all sorts of candles, ornaments, wall hangings, and more. She was quite a talent.

"Jenna," Flora said, in the bubbly way she spoke, "that orange plush cat you ordered has come in."

"Terrific. I'll come by later this week to pick it up."

"Keller, your work is really coming along." Flora contemplated his painting, taking in every corner of it. "It makes such a statement. I can see you've done a lot to it." She studied mine. "And Jenna, that's simply lovely."

Faith chortled. "You do have a penchant for blue, Jenna."

She wasn't wrong. I'd painted Buena Vista Boulevard, the main drag in Crystal Cove, at sunset. Blue and darker blue shadows lined the storefronts. Overhead, strings of party lights cast a luminous glow.

"Is this your van Gogh period?" she asked while fussing to straighten her oversized agate pendant necklace. "Van-go or van-gock? Which do you prefer?"

"I think van-go is the most common pronunciation," I said judiciously. We weren't Dutch. Why pretend to be?

Yardley swept into view, the folds of her floral shawl-style sweater wafting. She clapped her hands. "Are we ready?"

Two other artists slipped in behind her. Each said, "I'm here." I didn't know either of them well. One, a dashing Latino in his fifties, owned a pet store that only sold reptiles. The other, a freckly redhead, made coral jewelry that she sold online.

"Welcome," Yardley said. "Now, let's quiet down and get started. As I approach each of you, I want you to tell me what you hope to accomplish this evening. This is our final workshop. Your finished product will remain with me and will be sent along to the judges. How about a little music?"

She clicked an instrumental jazz playlist on her iPhone. The music piped through a portable Bose speaker. Nice. I could feel my shoulders relax. So what if I didn't win the competition? It was an honor to have made it this far.

For a half hour, Yardley orbited the verandah, giving each of us tips on how to improve this or that. So far, I'd heeded every tip she offered. The last art class I'd taken was in college. After Taylor & Squibb Advertising hired me, I had painted solely in the privacy of my home. I'd meant to take classes once I'd relocated to Crystal Cove — there were a number of fabulous art teachers in town as well as an artists' retreat — but I hadn't found the time.

To Faith she said, "See if you can find a way to add a smidgen of white along a crest of the waves."

"Darlin', I don't do anything a smidgen," Faith bragged.

"Try."

To Flora she said, "I thought you were going to fine-tune this with pastels?"

"I am." Flora giggled and held up a pack of chalk.

"You're going to do it all tonight?" Yardley fought a skeptical smile.

Flora nodded.

"Go for it." Yardley patted Flora's shoulder.

Yardley stopped beside me and reviewed my painting, her chin resting on her hand. "Jenna, how about a dot of red here and there? Liven it up."

I recalled an artist named Rabindra, who drew gorgeous pen-and-ink animals. He'd added a bold red dot to each of his paintings. It had been his signature. I didn't want to imitate him.

"Better yet, what do you think about a splash of yellow on one particular shop?" Yardley suggested. "Draw in your viewers and make them wonder what's going on inside the shop. Mystery matters in a painting such as yours."

"Excellent idea."

"Sorry I'm late." Quade, a roguish mixed-media artist in his late twenties, walked onto the verandah with a cynical slouch, his work covered in burlap. He set it on an easel but didn't remove the burlap. "Traffic," he said with a wry smile while finger-combing his shoulder-length brown hair.

Usually, Crystal Cove had light traffic unless the main street was shut down.

"Don't kid a kidder," Yardley said. "You fell asleep."

"Caught me." Quade offered a cocksure smile.

When Yardley frowned, I got the feeling she didn't approve of his cavalier attitude.

Quade, no last name, who'd come to town two years ago and was known for the two gigantic murals he'd been commissioned to paint in Crystal Cove, had dreams of becoming the most famous artist in the world. Rumors abounded about him. He'd been in numerous relationships. No, he was a monk. No, he'd been married twice. No, he was the child of a drug lord who'd sent him to Crystal Cove to hide. Personally, I thought Quade was spreading the rumors himself to add to his mysterious persona.

"Whoa, Keller, dude," Quade said, eyeing Keller's work. "What the heck is that?"

"Ha-ha, very funny. You've seen it before."

"Nope, don't think I have."

"Sure you have." Keller yukked.

Quade imitated Keller's unusual laugh.

"Don't make fun," Yardley warned.

"Make fun? *Moi?*" Quade's mouth turned up with surly defiance. "All I'm saying is he really messed up his piece. Last week it was good. Sometimes less is more, dude."

Keller's brow knitted with frustration. "You're not the teacher."

"And you're not gonna be the winner."

"Fellas," Yardley said.

"He's a pretender, teach." Quade jutted a hand at Keller's work. "Be honest. He's on a fool's errand." He removed thc burlap from his art, and Yardley gasped.

"What's that?" she asked.

"Something new. *Night Sky.*"

Yardley hadn't gasped because his new work was horrible. In truth, it was incredible. It was bold and kinetic, like nothing I'd ever seen. Black on black with large strokes, sharp lines, and textural grooves. He'd adhered silver aluminum bars to the canvas, which caught the light. It reminded me of death and jail and anger all at the same time.

"But your other work . . . *Morning,*" Yardley said.

Quade's initial submission had been the complete opposite of the new work in tone. It had been done in pale colors and the aluminum bars he'd used had been gold filigree, representative of the way the sunlight bathed the ocean waves at sunrise. The honesty and sensitivity of the work had surprised me, given the artist's temperament.

"Where is it?" Yardley pressed. "That's the one that was accepted into the competition."

"Yeah, about that." He jutted his chin. "It seems to be missing."

"Missing?"

"M.I.A. I think someone stole it." Quade stared daggers at Keller.

"Whoa!" Keller threw up his hands. "Don't put that on me, man."

"Did you report the theft to the police?" Yardley asked.

"As if." Quade shrugged a shoulder. "Police won't help the likes of me."

CHAPTER 2

As the surprise and shock of Quade's announcement turned into muted conversations between artists and as Yardley stepped away from the group to have a serious conversation with one of the judges on her cell phone, Naomi Genet arrived.

"Hello, everyone." She waved enthusiastically as she approached us on the verandah. Naomi was last year's poster competition winner and was now a part-time teacher at the institute and Yardley's assistant for the workshop. Pretty in a minimalist way, her brown hair pulled back and braided loosely, her coffee-colored peasant dress loose on her tall frame, Naomi weaved through the artists to me. She was a regular at the Cookbook Nook, often eager to find a cookbook that would provide recipes for her three-year-old daughter. A few months ago, I'd invited her to the Nook Café to chat about art techniques, and as our friendship grew, she'd coaxed me into entering the competition. "Nice work, Jenna," she trilled. "I love the splashes of yellow."

"Yardley's idea."

"She's incredible, isn't she?" Naomi said, eyes bright, the model of a perfect assistant.

"She has an eye, for sure."

"I wish I had her acumen for business."

I whispered, "Between you and me, I'm pretty sure Wayne is the one who handles the business side."

Yardley and her husband owned Wild Blue Yonder, an internet company named for a basic coloring crayon. Wayne Alks was a social media expert, invariably traveling the country pitching their company, which provided online classes with curriculum for art teachers. Yardley came up with the idea when she realized teachers craved lessons that were easy to teach at any level. Inspiration, she said, was all they needed. Fifteen years ago, Wayne set up their first e-commerce store, as the business was evolving. Now, they sold over five hundred lesson plans every year and employed a staff of twenty who traveled countrywide.

"Have you mulled over becoming one of Wild Blue Yonder's full-time staff?" I asked.

"And go on the road? I could sure use the

money, but, no, I couldn't do it. Not with Nina."

"Right. Nina." Her little girl was the spitting image of her mother. Long brown hair, gorgeous skin, a sweet tentative smile. "How does she like the kids gym class?"

"She adores it. She's fearless." Naomi set her bulging crocheted purse on a chair and it flopped over. Pens, paper, postcard-sized sketches, cell phone, a cellophane wrapper, and keys spilled out. "Crap," she muttered as she bent down to shove it all back in.

"Hey, Naomi," Quade said, his eyes drinking in her backside. "Looking good. How about going out for that coffee you promised me?"

Naomi jerked to a stand, her gaze withering. "I never promised."

I was surprised that Quade was acting so cool. He didn't seem upset that his work had vanished. Was he lying about what had happened? Was he still in possession of it and had simply lost his inspiration to complete it?

"Ladies and gentleman!" a woman said, raising her voice. Sienna Brown, the owner of the Crystal Cove Inn, strode into the center of the verandah in riding gear, breeches that were a tad too tight tucked into boots and a heritage show coat over an untucked white blouse. She raised her arms. "Quiet, please, if you don't mind." She was about five-ten, my height, but she was more formidable with broad shoulders, square jaw, piercing eyes, and hair coiled into a no-nonsense French twist. "When you're done for the night, we are having a soiree on the grassy expanse by the lobby, and you are all invited as my guests."

Each of the artists said, "Thank you."

"Now, if you don't mind" — she swung her gaze around — "I'd like to peek at your work. I won't say a word. I will show no bias. Promise."

Slowly, she roved the verandah, taking an inordinately long time to study my piece. I might have done the same in a gallery and did my best to ignore her stare. She hummed as she neared Quade, rapped him on the shoulder, and crooked her finger, requesting that he follow her to one side. I could see them past the right edge of my canvas. Sienna said something I couldn't make out. Quade's face flushed, his gaze narrowed. Whatever they were chatting about was not making him happy.

Suddenly, Quade aimed a finger at Sienna.

Before he could say a word, a hip-looking middle-aged man with a thick mustache appeared on the covered walkway. "Miss

Brown!"

Sienna made a closing remark to Quade and turned on her heel, chin held high. She met up with the man and together they strolled down the walkway and entered the lobby.

Quade lumbered back to his canvas, stared at it, and uninterested, descended upon Naomi. "Hey, babe," he said.

"Don't call me babe."

"What may I call you then?" He offered a cockeyed grin.

"You know my name. Why don't you use that?"

"Nao-omi," he said, dragging out the word lasciviously.

She frowned and proceeded on to Keller to give him pointers.

Yardley strode to Quade and said, "Please keep your distance from Miss Genet."

"My distance?"

"Yes. Cool it. This is not a hook-up event or one of your chat rooms. This is a group of artists seeking a goal. Act like you care. And FYI, the judges will accept a new submission from you, but this is the last night to put finishing touches on it, so —"

"It's done. It's perfect, as is, teach."

"That's it. Come with me." Yardley tagged his arm.

She marched to the far end of the verandah. Quade followed. The two chatted heatedly for about two minutes, Quade hitting his left palm with the back of his right to make a point, Yardley leaning in to offer a rebuttal. Moments later, Yardley returned to the class and Quade refocused on his art.

"Let's finish up," Yardley said, the epitome of calm. "You have exactly twenty minutes to finalize your work. Then take them to the communal room, along with your easel, and I will make sure they are delivered to the judges in the morning. After you've done that, please convene on the grassy expanse. We'll have a wine tasting, compliments of the Crystal Cove Inn, and I'll make a toast. Paint on!"

The time flew by with each of us, other than Quade, tweaking, polishing, and adding a bit more. I felt like one of the cooks in a baking show hoping my cupcake creation was the best. Tick-tock.

When Yardley clapped her hands, time was up.

Naomi supervised as we placed our art in the communal room, making an effort to steer clear of Quade.

Quade, disgruntled, turned his ire on Keller again. "You. Let's have a chat."

But Keller wasn't in the mood. "Bug off."

He slipped out of the room, offered his elbow to me, and guided me to the grassy expanse.

"How are you?" I whispered.

"Quade. What a joke."

"He does seem to rile everyone." I squeezed his arm. "Hey, whatever happens going forward, we should be super proud of what we produced. By the way, if you want, after the judging, I can hang your art alongside mine at the Nook Café and we'll see if we can find buyers."

Quade caught up to us and snorted. "If you really want to sell your work, you need a representative, and honestly, Keller, I think that'll be hard for you to find, dude. They don't rep amateurs."

"You know what, buddy?" Keller said, a snarl consuming his face. "Stay far away from me tonight, okay? I'm on edge and I don't want to punch you."

"Yo! Tough guy. Okay." Quade held up his palms like he had to Naomi and sauntered away snickering.

Keller was doing all he could to keep his anger in check.

"Wine?" I asked him.

"Yeah, sure."

"This way, everyone." Hannah Storm, who was dressed in black, stood in front of two tables draped with burgundy tablecloths and set with small tasting glasses and various bottles of wine, as well as handblown wineglasses that were for sale. A banner boasting Hurricane Vineyard as the sponsor for the soiree graced the front of the tables.

I drew Keller in that direction.

"Jenna!" Hannah said. "So good to see you. You know Destiny Dacourt, don't you?"

"Sure I do. Hello."

Destiny was a beautiful multiracial woman who owned Tripping with Destiny, a wine tour group that took day excursions from one vineyard to the next. I'd often see her driving around town in her eight-passenger safari-style Jeep accompanied by her black Labrador retriever while narrating on a microphone to her guests. Prior to opening her company, she had been a rising star in the beach volleyball world. According to an article I'd read in the paper, a shattered ankle had ended that career.

"Check out Hannah's handblown wineglasses," Destiny said.

I lifted an Aegean blue raindrop-patterned wineglass and inspected it, front and back. And then lifted a red-splattered glass. I whistled. "These are beautiful. Where'd you get them?"

"They're not mine," Hannah said.

"They're made by an artisan in Carmel-by-the-Sea. We're going fifty-fifty. Each is completely different, though some might bear the same pattern or the same color." Hannah was one of the nicest women I knew. I'd met her over a year ago when she'd become an aficionado of five-ingredient recipes, and then learned more about her during the Renaissance Festival. She'd recently married Alan Baldini, a quirky but delightful vintner who owned the vineyard next to Hurricane.

"Pour you some Hurricane pinot noir?" Destiny asked. "Or I have a Baldini Vineyard sauvignon blanc. It's a new line for —" She paused and looked past me. Her gaze narrowed and her cheeks flamed as pink as the cropped sweater she was wearing.

Quade was hitting on Naomi again. Didn't the guy understand the word *no*?

Hannah placed a hand on Destiny's arm. "Chill, girlfriend. Jenna, if you couldn't tell, my pal here likes Quade a lot."

"He's sort of an egomaniac," I whispered.

"Yeah, but he's hot and talented, and she's smitten beyond belief."

Destiny's mouth curved up in a smirk. "I'm right here. I can hear you."

Hannah giggled. "I've encouraged her to ask him out, but she's nervous about it."

She rubbed Destiny's shoulder. "Let that confidence perfume you're wearing do its magic."

"Confidence perfume?" I asked.

"Mm-hm. One of the artisans in the festival is selling it. Smells like honey mixed with heaven." Hannah gave Destiny a nudge. "Go on. Say, 'Hi, Quade, want to grab a cup of coffee this week?' "

Destiny shimmied to her full height, smoothed the sides and fanny of her tight jeans, lifted her noble chin, and threw back her shoulders. "Here goes nothing."

"Poor Des," Hannah said as her friend sashayed off. "She's been rejected by more guys than any woman deserves. I don't get it. She's stunning and sweet. It doesn't make sense."

As Hannah poured a few tasting glasses of wine for Keller and my workshop mates, I watched Destiny make her move. She had sensuous hips that swayed as she walked. Drawing near to Quade, she said something that made him throw back his head and laugh. The move peeved Destiny. No, it had hurt her feelings. She spun around and, fingers pressed to the corners of her eyes, raced past the tasting table and sought a safe haven in the communal room.

"Blast it," Hannah muttered. "Jenna, can

you man the table while I console her?"

"Sure thing."

Guests started to migrate from the inn to the wine tasting.

I said to Keller, "C'mon, all hands on deck." As he helped me pour, I leaned in and said, "Is it the full moon or the impending storm or what? I feel like we've been cast in a bad soap opera tonight."

Keller didn't laugh. He was scowling at Quade, who was yet again approaching Naomi.

CHAPTER 3

Tuesdays are my one day off each week, although I've been trying to take off every other Friday. Because tourism was the mainstay of Crystal Cove and many visitors planned three-day vacations, the Cookbook Nook stayed open on Mondays.

Today, with no one in the shop, I'd turned on some classical harp music, rearranged the moveable bookshelves, and set out an array of cookbooks on the main display table, including *The Art of French Cooking,* as well as *Modern Art Desserts,* one of my all-time favorite cookbooks, with a picture of a Mondrian-style cake on the front and recipes like Matisse parfait and Kahlo wedding cookie included, and three wine-themed cookbooks: *The Art and Science of Wine, The Wine Lover's Cookbook,* and *The Art of Making Wine.*

Then I turned my attention to the Art and Wine festival display in the bay window. I'd put it together Saturday, but it needed tweaking. Because we were located in the quaint Fisherman's Village shopping center that boasted a retro movie theater, wine bar, and shops, we had lots of foot traffic, so the display window always needed to shine.

So far I'd placed three bottles of wine and faux grapes atop a yellow-and-white-checkered tablecloth. In addition, I'd set out *Plating for Gold: A Decade of Dessert Recipes from the World and National Pastry Team Championship.* I'd browsed it before installing it into the design. Without a doubt, I would be making chocolate banana caramel crunch soon, even if I had to beg Rhett to guide me through the recipe step by step. I'd also included a couple of the arty salt and pepper shakers and hand-painted ceramic cookie jars that artisans had brought in on consignment to sell this week. My favorite was the adorable cat-themed cookie jar featuring a kitten popping out of the top holding a sprinkled cookie.

I was unwrapping the final items to insert into the display when Katie — Chef Katie to her staff and fans — emerged from the breezeway connecting the shop to the Nook Café. No chef's coat, no toque. She was simply dressed in a striped shirtwaist dress. She preferred dresses when she worked in the kitchen. A dress allowed her legs to stay cool. Her curly hair was tied in a messy knot.

"What are those?" she asked, towering over me.

I cast aside the butcher paper and blew dust out of the two glasses I'd purchased from Hannah last night. "Aren't they pretty?" One was gold-and-red-flecked and the other was gold-and-red-striped. Hannah had labeled them companion pieces because the colors were the same. Sunshine spilled through the display window and glinted off the glass.

"They're beautiful." She cocked her head. "Ahem, shouldn't you be spending time with Rhett though? It's your day off."

"We're going on a hike this afternoon. He wanted to sleep in. What are you doing here?"

Katie chortled. "I couldn't sleep if I tried. I'm so excited about our demonstration day."

During the festival, there would be many presentations, from jewelry artisans, *plein air* painters, vintners, and foodies. The Cookbook Nook was hosting a couple of artsy events, including Chef Katie presenting the Art of Plating Food on Friday. She would focus on dessert.

"I'm hoping to have an audience of sixty," she said, "although I know we'll be competing with the other vendors."

In the brochure online, the festival organizers had listed the main events for each day, as well as the smaller events. Many would be conducted on the Pier, a wonderful boardwalk located at the southern end of town filled with shops, eateries, a theater, and games. The majority would occur in Azure Park, the town's largest outdoor venue, which had a terrific stage fitted with a state-of-the-art sound system. Our mayor was over the moon with excitement by the expected turnout.

"So many people don't know how important plating is," Katie said, miming with her hands. "They don't know how chefs use squeeze bottles and decorating spoons and spatulas to create designs." She hugged herself with joy. "It's going to be delicious fun sharing secrets of the trade." She reached into the pocket of her dress and pulled out something wrapped in cellophane and tied with a blue bow. "I almost forgot. I brought you this." She handed it to me.

It was filled with tiny cookies. "What are they?"

"Wine cookies. Aren't they perfect for this week's theme?"

I opened the bag, took out a cookie, and bit into it. "I love the hint of anise."

"I'll be giving them away at the demonstration. Each will have a Nook Café sticker on them so people won't forget us."

"You think of everything."

She beamed. "By the way, Keller said he really liked your painting."

"And I liked his."

"He has a sincere distaste, however, for that guy named Quade. What's up with —"

"Oh dear, oh dear, oh dear!" Pepper Pritchett, dressed in a beaded blue cardigan and trousers, hustled into the shop and skidded to a stop. Her short silver hair was windblown. "I know you're closed, but I'm hoping you have coffee brewing. My machine is on the blink, and —" Tears sprang from her eyes.

I scrambled to my feet and hurried to her. "What's wrong?"

"Nothing," she rasped.

No one said *Oh dear* repeatedly when nothing was wrong.

"Katie," I said, "I have coffee in the back. Pepper, come. Sit."

Katie blazed through the drapes to the stockroom, and I ushered Pepper to the vintage kitchen table where we always had a foodie-themed jigsaw puzzle in the works.

Often our customers liked to sit and take a moment to lose themselves in a puzzle. This week's puzzle, in honor of the festival, featured a carafe and a glass of wine and a beautiful cheese board. One hundred pieces. Not too challenging.

"What's going on?" I asked, wishing I could smooth Pepper's hair for her.

She fitted a corner piece of the puzzle to the unfinished border. "Same old . . ."

Katie returned with coffee in a china cup, a packet of creamer and sugar and a spoon on the saucer, and a handful of tissues. "Here you go."

"Thank you." Pepper poured the creamer into the cup and stirred then mopped her eyes with a tissue.

"Pepper, come on, spill," I said.

Pepper owned Beaders of Paradise, a beading and craft shop cattycorner from ours. She was an inspired beader and often taught classes. When we'd first met, the day I'd stepped foot in the Cookbook Nook and had decided to change the course of my life, Pepper had barged in, as angry as a rhinoceros, and had verbally assailed me. Over the years, we had made peace and even admittedly liked one another now.

"Cinnamon," she whispered. She wasn't asking for the spice to add to her coffee.

Her daughter, Cinnamon, was the chief of police for Crystal Cove, and one of my good friends. When we'd first met, Cinnamon had believed me guilty of murder, but over the years, we'd bonded. Last year she had even temporarily deputized me to help her with a case.

"What about Cinnamon?" I asked.

"The baby," she droned.

I motioned, encouraging her to continue. Cinnamon had been pregnant but had lost the baby a few months ago.

Pepper started to hyperventilate.

"Breathe," I said. "Cinnamon is okay. She's coping." Cinnamon was nothing if not stalwart. She was handling the loss better than anyone could.

"No, she's not. She cries a lot."

"When you're around."

"Yes."

"Sometimes people cry to console the other person." I wasn't a therapist, but I'd consulted a shrink after my husband's death and recalled many of the things she'd said to me. "Is it possible Cinnamon is crying to make you feel better?"

Pepper's lashes moistened with tears. She blotted them again with a tissue. "Do you think?"

"Yes. She and Bucky are going to try

again," I said. Cinnamon had married the most adorable fireman. "And again and again, if necessary." I felt a laugh burbling up inside me and stifled the urge to say, *They like to do it and often.* I wouldn't reveal a pal's secret. "You will have a grandchild. I promise."

Cinnamon did want to have a child. Girl or boy, it didn't matter. I wasn't sure if I wanted to become a mother. Rhett and I had been talking.

"Oh dear," Pepper repeated and tears started up again.

Katie, who looked close to tears herself, sniffed.

I peered at her. "Would you fetch a bag of wine cookies for Pepper?" I motioned for her to return to the kitchen. We didn't need everyone collapsing into tears.

As she bustled off, I petted Pepper's shoulder. "There, there," I said. "It's going to be okay."

She didn't believe me. She wailed.

At half past one, I approached the front door of Rhett's cabin. It was ajar. A second later, his black Labrador retriever bounded through the opening, down the steps, and nearly knocked me over. "Rook, sit!" I ordered. The dog obeyed. I rubbed him under his chin. He nuzzled my hand with his snout. "No treats. We're taking a walk." He rose to all fours and rounded me, sniffing the back pocket of my jeans. "Okay, found me out, you big lug. You can have *one.*" I handed him a crunchy bone. He downed it merrily.

Rhett, looking ruggedly handsome in jeans, Pendleton, backpack, and hiking boots, strolled outside, closed and locked the door, and then enveloped me in a hug and kissed me.

"Mm," I murmured. "You taste like bacon."

"Did you eat?" he asked.

"A light lunch. You know me. I hate to hike on a full stomach."

"How's Tigger?"

"At home, with free rein."

He clasped my hand, ordered Rook to heel, and we were off. The sun was brilliant in the cloudless sky, but beneath the canopy of trees, the temperature was mild.

"How's the house coming along?" he asked.

"Only the guest room to go. Keller is on track to finish in a few weeks."

"He's done with the master?"

Once I'd completed the seascape mural behind the king-sized bed, I'd decided that the other walls needed to be more exciting than eggshell white and had opted for a pastel blue. Keller hadn't balked, though he had lightheartedly said that he wouldn't redo all the walls in the house.

"You should come see it," I said in a come-hither tone.

He wrapped an arm around me. "How about tonight after the festival kickoff?"

"I was hoping you'd say that."

I broke free and we walked side by side for an hour, drinking in the scent of pines, listening to the various creatures chatter and flit. Occasionally, Rook would wander off but quickly return. He loved his master.

"How did the workshop go last night?" Rhett asked as we settled on a flat rock near the small lake we frequented when hiking. He pulled a bottle of water from his backpack and filled a small travel bowl with it for Rook, who settled at our feet. Then he withdrew a chocolate-caramel bar. He wiggled it under my nose. "Snack time."

"A man after my own heart."

Rhett unwrapped the candy, broke it in half, and handed me a portion. I bit into it, loving the ooze of caramel, and followed it with a swig of water.

"So, the workshop?" he asked.

"It was good, and I'm pleased with my piece."

He tilted his head. "You're holding back."

"Okay, at one point I said to Keller that it felt like we were in a soap opera."

"How come?"

"Quade was hitting on Naomi. Destiny tried to ask Quade on a date, but he rebuffed her. And Sienna and Quade argued. Come to think of it, so did Yardley and Quade."

"Okay, hold on. I don't know most of these people. Start with Quade."

I described him and how confrontational he could be. "What do we know about him?" I asked. "Nada. Nothing. He showed up in town and has no history. I mean, c'mon, who is he really?"

"You don't like him."

"I'm not sure anybody but Destiny does. You know her. The wine tour gal? She's smitten."

"Hey, speaking of her, maybe she could come up with a vineyard venue for the wedding."

During the wine tasting after the workshop, I'd texted Rhett about the cancellation. He'd texted back *Stay calm.*

"Great thought," I said. "She knows all the vintners. She could have connections.

I'll have Harmony touch base with her."

"In the meantime" — he turned to face me, his expression grim — "we have to discuss something very serious."

Emotions caught in my throat. "What?"

"When am I moving in?"

We'd agreed to live separately until we married.

"What do you mean?" I asked.

"I don't want to wait any longer. I want to wake up beside you every morning." He ran a finger along my jawline. "I want to see this beautiful face first thing. What do you say?"

"Yes!" I cried and threw my arms around his neck, pulling him into a kiss.

"Yeah," he murmured. "I'm crazy about you, too."

CHAPTER 4

At exactly six p.m., Mayor Zoey Zeller — Z.Z. to her friends — hoisted a microphone and said, "Welcome, everyone, to the Art and Wine Festival Opening Night at the Inn!" Z.Z. was short and squat, but standing next to her lanky, twenty-something son Egan, she appeared even shorter. His father had been equally tall, my aunt had told me.

"Is everyone warm enough?" Z.Z. asked. "Hopefully, we'll get to enjoy all of tonight's festivities before the storm hits. *If* it hits."

Nervous laughter burbled from the attendees.

The weatherman had reiterated that the quickie in-and-out storm might miss us entirely, but wind was kicking up and clouds were convening in the night sky. I shivered and pulled my shawl tighter.

About fifty of us were standing on the grassy expanse behind the Crystal Cove Inn, which the staff had decorated with glossy banners and twinkling lights. Near the verandah, arranged in a horseshoe, stood tables draped with white tablecloths. Hannah and two other vintners milled behind the one that had been set up for wine tastings. Destiny, there in her capacity as a wine maven and not associated with one particular vintner, stood in front of the table, prepared to chat up each of the wines. In addition, there were a variety of food vendors.

To the right of the food and drink stations, beneath a white protective awning, stood the seven finalists' artwork on easels. Artistic spotlights allowed the guests to view the work in detail. Seeing a few people studying my work made me anxious. Did I have thick enough skin to hear a bad critique?

"This evening is the official start of the festival," Z.Z. went on. The other opening night events on the Pier, on Buena Vista Boulevard, and at Azure Park would begin concurrently, with others from the mayor's office making the announcements. "In a half hour, once all the guests have arrived . . ." The guest list for each opening night event was by invitation, although I had seen a few inn guests mingling at ours. Sienna hadn't roped off the area. "Yardley Alks and her lovely assistant, Naomi Genet, will introduce our artists." Z.Z. signaled to the women.

Yardley, braving the cool temperature in a cap-sleeved yellow-and-blue floral sheath, and Naomi, in a long-sleeved pink lacy number, appeared perfectly suited to hostess an art gathering.

"Are you ready to get this party started?" Z.Z. shouted.

The crowd cheered.

"Here we go. Ten, nine, eight . . ."

Egan joined in. "Seven, six, five . . ."

Z.Z. had hoped to set off fireworks to mark the occasion, but fire laws in California had become much stricter in the past year. Instead, she had opted for the firing of a starter's pistol.

"One."

Bang! A similar sound resounded in numerous parts of town. The crowd erupted into applause.

Bailey, my best friend and colleague at the shop, was standing to my right. She clinked her wineglass to mine. "To your success! This should be fun. I love, love, love having a night out with adults, you in particular." Bailey adored her nearly one-year-old daughter, but she needed adult stimulation outside of work hours. "Tina is super happy with the extra sitting money." Tina Gump, a former clerk at the Cookbook Nook, was now attending culinary school and working part-time as a nanny. Bailey sipped her wine. "Mm, loving this. What are you drinking?"

"A Hurricane pinot noir." I surveyed the crowd.

Rhett was off to one side chatting with Keller and Katie, who had taken the night off from the café to celebrate her husband's moment in the limelight. Rhett and Keller had dressed similarly, both in white shirt and jeans, but Keller had donned a cowboy hat, making him look as rakish as a good guy in a western. Katie radiated joy in a white dress and glittery earrings.

My dapper father, Bailey's mother Lola, and my aunt Vera, wearing a luminous caftan that only she could pull off, joined them. Lola, who was an older version of Bailey, with spiky hair, a penchant for colorful jewelry, and a flair for style, instantly launched into conversation, probably weighing in on which restaurants would be serving what delicacies during the festival. My father, his silver hair gleaming in the glow of the lights, listened to her attentively. Rhett bobbed his head as Lola spoke. He owned Intime, a French bistro, and Lola owned the Pelican Brief, which featured fish dishes. Both had opted out of participating at festival venues and had chosen, instead, to offer specialty prix fixe dinners at their respective restaurants. They would leave the fun food, like dipped pretzels, pistachio meatballs, and drunken olives, to the visiting vendors.

I caught Rhett's eye. He winked at me, sending a delicious shiver down my spine.

"Tito would have loved this," Bailey said. Her husband, a reporter for the *Crystal Cove Courier,* had been summoned to Southern California to help with his ailing grandmother.

"How long will he be out of town?" I asked my pal.

"At least a week. I'm a single parent. *Oof.*" She grunted. "So . . . tell me more about you and Rhett moving in together."

I'd shared the news the moment I saw her. I hadn't been able to contain my excitement.

"How will it work out between Tigger and Rook?" Bailey asked.

"Actually, they're at the house now and having a good old time. Tigger likes to chase Rook, and Rook is all for it. They . . ."

I paused as my attention was drawn to Quade approaching Naomi again. Clad in all black, swaggering like a panther, he looked menacing.

"What are you staring at?" Bailey whispered.

I pointed.

Naomi, who was distracted by a loose thread on the sleeve of her dress, didn't see Quade coming. He raked his hair with his fingers and tapped her shoulder. She turned and let out an *eek.*

Keller, like a protective big brother, swooped to her side. He said something to Naomi. She nodded.

Quade shoved Keller in the chest. "Out of my way, hack," he said loudly enough for all to hear. His words were slurred. Had he been drinking prior to the party? "I was having a private conversation."

"You're the hack," Keller said, unwilling to be cowed. "Stealing everyone's technique, including mine."

"Stealing? Did you accuse me of stealing? You're the thief."

"I didn't steal anything. You probably dumped your artwork in a Dumpster because it was so bad."

Quade hauled back.

In the nick of time, Yardley grabbed his arm. "Cut it out. Both of you."

Quade tried to wrench free of her grasp but couldn't. Either Yardley was stronger than she appeared or he was relenting.

"Tonight is a joyous occasion," she said, releasing him. "Why don't you fellas mingle?"

Katie trotted to Keller and steered him into the lobby of the inn.

"Wow," Bailey said, "that was something."

My gaze remained riveted on Quade. Growling, he tramped past Bailey and me, heading in the direction of the artwork. Did he intend to sabotage it? I started after him, but paused because Destiny, who had left her post at the wine tasting table, cut in front of him.

Flirtatiously, she fluttered the flounce of her black dress and caressed the chain of her ebony perfume bottle necklace. "Hey, Quade, buy you a drink?"

"Can it," he muttered.

Destiny's smile turned to a frown of concern. "Is something wrong? Has something upset you?"

"I don't want to talk about it."

"C'mon. You know me. I'm a good listener."

"Babe, don't you get it? I'm not into you. I never will be."

"But . . ." she sputtered, her newfound confidence waning.

"Bye-bye," he said.

If Quade wasn't so horrid, the two might have made a handsome pair, but he was downright mean. What attracted her to him?

He stomped toward the artwork again, came to a halt and stood, arms folded, head cocked, as if studying it. Even so, I kept a steady eye on him.

"Jenna, my mother is beckoning me," Bailey said. "I'll be back in a bit. Can't wait for the announcement!" She squeezed my arm and scurried to her mother, her dangling earrings tinkling in her haste.

At the same time, Cinnamon Pritchett and her handsome husband Bucky Winston drew near, wine tasting glasses in hand. "Well, well, that was something between Keller and that artist," Cinnamon said. "I've never seen Keller lose his cool like that. Is fatherhood getting to him?"

Bucky threw her a look. Cinnamon returned a saucy smirk.

"I think it might concern his finances," I said. "It's hard to be an entrepreneur. He's hoping his art might open new opportunities for him."

"And well it might," Bucky said. "His stuff is good. I like it."

Cinnamon snorted. "Meet my husband, the fireman art critic."

Bucky laughed. They had a wonderfully

easy relationship.

"Quade, on the other hand," I said, continuing my line of thought, "rubs people the wrong way. He has a thing for Naomi Genet, the assistant art teacher, except she wants nothing to do with him, so people around her are acting protective."

"Yardley Alks seems to have the situation under control," Cinnamon said.

"Want me to freshen your glass, honey?" Bucky asked.

Cinnamon thrust it at him. "Yes, please. Let's try the Nouveau pinot."

Bucky sauntered off, stopping to chat with Rhett and my father on his way.

I touched Cinnamon's arm. "Hey, your mother came into the shop earlier today."

"What did she have to say for herself?"

"She's concerned about you because, you know . . ."

"I'm fine." Cinnamon fingered the collar of her navy jacket. "I'm holding it together."

"Really?"

"Fake it, you own it." She forced a smile and tucked the right side of her hair behind her ear. She'd let it grow, which softened her appearance. She no longer resembled a camp counselor. "I will fake it until happiness returns."

"And Bucky?" I asked.

"He's not as good as I am at faking it. He wants it to happen ASAP." Cinnamon frowned. "And if I don't get pregnant, he wants to adopt. I'm not so sure about that."

"Katie did and her little girl is adorable."

"I know. I know." Cinnamon brandished a hand.

"What has Bucky decided about joining the police force?"

"Ha! I knew he wouldn't follow through. He did the academy and everything, but in the end, he loves being a fireman. And with all that's been going on in California, we need guys like him."

"Do you worry —"

Cinnamon held up a hand. "Don't. Say. It." She dropped her arm to her side. "Yes, I worry. But he worries about me, too. We're both in dangerous professions. We do what we have to, to make this a better world."

Bucky returned with the wine and handed one to Cinnamon. "I saw Deputy Appleby come in," he said. "He looks nervous."

Cinnamon grinned. "Let's make him welcome. Arty affairs make him uncomfortable. Jenna" — she turned to me — "have a good show."

As I was making my way to Rhett, I spotted Quade chatting with Sienna Brown near the communal room. *Chatting* was a stretch.

She was aiming an accusatory finger at him, and he was throwing his arms wide, as if he was clueless to whatever it was she was alleging. Her cheeks were flushed, as were her upper chest and neck, the color appearing that much brighter because she was wearing a white jacquard dress.

Oh, to be a fly flitting about listening in. So many set-tos. So many underlying stories. Bailey's husband Tito would have had the courage to move closer. Not I.

Movement to the right caught my eye. The guest with the thick mustache who'd hailed Sienna yesterday was making a beeline for her. In his beautifully tailored suit, he didn't look quite as hip as he had before, but he was dashing. Proceeding at a brisk pace, he brushed something off his shoulders and straightened his gray tie, and then suddenly pulled up short. Why? Because he'd realized Sienna was in a heated conversation? Was he savvy enough not to intrude?

Standing alone, frozen in place, he looked familiar to me. Had I seen him on television or in the newspaper? He wasn't a reporter. He didn't have a recorder or pad and pen at the ready. Maybe he was a vintner or an artist, although he didn't look like an artist. On the other hand, neither did I.

Working his jaw side to side for a moment,

the man regrouped and began again, his pace slower, more deliberate. He approached the wine tasting table, and Destiny tried to engage him, but he ignored her. That was when I realized his mark wasn't Sienna Brown, who had left Quade and was striding along the walkway in the direction of the lobby. No, like Quade earlier, the man seemed to be fixated on Naomi.

Naomi, who was chatting with a patron near the artwork, had her back to the lobby and was oblivious to the man's searing gaze.

A frisson of fear spiraled up my spine. Quickly, I pulled my cell phone from my evening purse and took a photograph of him. Then I boldly strode toward him. He caught sight of me with my cell phone raised and blanched. I wasn't scary, but given my height and the few self-defense classes I'd taken, I'd learned to appear somewhat intimidating.

The man veered left, hurried down the walkway, and vanished into the lobby of the inn.

Sensing this guy was a stalker and way worse than Quade, I searched the crowd for Cinnamon. She was nowhere in sight. So I sought out my father. A former FBI analyst, he would know how to pursue this. He was still conversing with Lola and my aunt.

"Hi, everyone," I said.

"Jenna, dear, are you excited?" my aunt asked. "Five more minutes until you're introduced."

"Very excited, but right now, I need to ask Dad a favor." I showed him my cell phone image. "I think this man might be stalking Naomi Genet. I've seen him twice now, yesterday and tonight. When he caught me photographing him, he hightailed it. Can you ask one of your *friends*" — I cleared my throat for effect — "to identify him?"

My father took my cell phone and shared the photo to his phone.

"Heavens," Aunt Vera said, her forehead pinched. "I was doing a reading for Naomi the other day. You know how she wanders in from time to time. Her daughter was keen on seeing Tigger. Knowing she had a moment, I offered to do a free reading. I was feeling rusty."

My aunt, who was my partner at the Cookbook Nook and café, loved to give tarot card and palm readings. Sometimes she charged for them; other times, she didn't. She was a big believer in the supernatural. Me? Not so much.

"And?" I asked.

"I divined a new man was coming into her life." Aunt Vera fingered the phoenix amulet she always wore. "Hopefully not a dangerous one."

My father gave me back my phone and put a hand on my shoulder. "I'll have an answer inside a day, and I'll alert Cinnamon."

"I looked for her before coming to you, but she and Bucky must have gone."

Dad winked. "I think they took a romantic stroll through the gardens."

The gardens were down a path beyond the rooms and cabanas and reminded me of something out of a Jane Austen novel, filled with azaleas and crape myrtles.

"Aha. Good for them. In the meantime, I'll have a chat with Naomi."

Questions for her cycled through my mind. Why was Quade so intent on pursuing her? And who was the man with the mustache? I found her talking with Yardley near the easels.

Naomi checked her smart watch. "Almost time," she said to her boss.

Yardley smiled. "I'll alert Z.Z."

As Yardley moved away, I drew near. "Hey, Naomi, I have a question for you."

"Sure."

"Do you happen to know this man?" I opened the camera app and held up my cell phone.

She took one look at the photograph, gasped, and raced away while stabbing her smart watch.

CHAPTER 5

When Yardley returned, she asked where Naomi had gone. I started to explain that I'd spooked her but stopped when Z.Z. spoke into the microphone.

"Ladies and gentlemen, it is now my proud honor to introduce Yardley Alks, brilliant art teacher, innovative internet businesswoman, and the inspiration for the Art and Wine Festival poster art competition. Yardley, take the mic."

As Z.Z. handed off the microphone, she whispered, "Yardley, where's Naomi?"

"The impending storm has her rattled," she improvised. "She hates thunder. Would you mind looking for her?"

Z.Z. said, "I'll send Egan in search."

"Bless you." Brandishing a dazzling smile, Yardley turned to the crowd and, speaking slowly and clearly, said, "I hope all of you have had the chance to view the artists' works. The winner will be announced Sunday at Art in the Sunlight at Azure Park. Meanwhile, let me say, I have had the greatest time getting to know our artists and foster their fine work. As you can see, each is unique, expressing the individual's vision of Crystal Cove. Bravo to all of you. And now, it is my sincere pleasure to announce the finalists. Would you all make your way to the art display, please?"

I was standing closest and took a spot next to Yardley. The other six weaved through the crowd, Quade lagging behind, grinning to each guest as though trying to schmooze the judging panel.

"They are, in no particular order, Jenna Hart, Flora Fairchild, Keller Landry, Faith Fairchild, Jaime Gutierrez" — the pet store guy — "Candy Kane . . ." The redhead's name drew a few laughs. "And Quade," Yardley continued when the laughter died out. "Give them a round of applause."

The hoots coming from my father, who usually remained subdued, were over the top. Even so, pride swelled within me. My mother, may she rest in peace, had been the artist in the family, but she'd taught me that art came from the heart, and in order to be an artist, one had to paint with abandon and not judge what ended up on the canvas. In all my creative ventures, I'd tried to follow her lead.

"Enjoy the remainder of the festivities," Yardley said, "and feel free to chat with the artists."

Over the course of the next half hour, at least ten guests told me how much they'd enjoyed my work. Another twenty offered congratulations.

When I was alone, Rhett sidled over to me and brushed a finger across my forehead. "You look worried. About the weather?"

"No." I told him about Naomi running off and Z.Z.'s son having gone in search. He'd come up empty.

"Do you have her phone number?"

"Good idea." I tried calling her, but she didn't answer. "Do you mind if we go to the concierge and ask about the man with the mustache?"

Rhett offered his arm. "I'm all yours."

In the lobby we approached a cheerful woman in the inn's green uniform, standing at the concierge's podium. Her name tag read *Ginny.*

I described the man. She said she was pretty sure he was a guest, but she didn't know his name. He hadn't asked for directions or reservations so far. Then I asked about Naomi, describing her.

She pointed. "I saw her heading out the front door, valet ticket in hand."

"The man I described didn't accost her?"

"No, ma'am. Not that I saw."

Rhett rubbed my shoulder. "There you go. She must have driven home."

I breathed easier.

At eight, as Hannah and Destiny were wrapping up the wine tasting, Rhett and I helped Yardley and the others move the art into the communal room, and then we called it a night and headed back to the house.

On the drive, as the clouds opened up and rain poured down in sheets, I checked my cell phone for messages. I'd received a text from Naomi. *Sorry I ran off. Had to tend to Nina.* Relieved that she was okay, I made a mental note to phone her in the morning to touch base.

When we arrived, we found Tigger and Rook asleep in the bed I'd bought for Rook. Tigger didn't like storms.

Rhett slung his arm around me and kissed the side of my head. "One big happy family," he whispered. "Did you eat anything at the party?"

"Barely."

"Want me to rustle up something?"

"You bet I do."

Rhett was an incredible chef. In less than a half hour, right after the quickie storm had passed, we were dining on shrimp tossed in a remoulade sauce, toast points topped with avocado and crisp bacon, and a selection of cheese and jams. Divine.

Just past eleven, as I was in bed drifting off in Rhett's arms, my cell phone rang. I wriggled from his grasp and grabbed the phone off the bedside table. Yardley's name was illuminated on the screen, and my stomach plummeted. I stabbed Send. "Hello?"

"Did I wake you?" she rasped, out of breath.

"No," I lied. "What's up? Is everything okay? Is Naomi —"

"I'm not calling about her. It's . . ." Yardley sucked back a sob. "It's Quade. He's dead."

"Dead!"

"In his cabana at the inn."

His cabana? I was puzzled. He was staying at the inn?

"He's been stabbed," she went on.

"Stabbed?"

"Please come to the inn. Help me sort this out."

"You need to call —"

"Please, Jenna. You've been through something like this before. I've never . . ." She cleared her throat. "If Wayne were here, I'd call him, but he's in New York. Thank you. Bless you." She ended the call abruptly.

Rhett was already on his feet and dressing. He refused to let me go alone and offered to drive. I was glad he did. I was shaking all over. Another murder? Of someone I knew? Admittedly, Quade had not been my favorite person, but he didn't deserve to die.

As Rhett negotiated turns on the rain-slick road, I phoned 911. A murder was police territory, not mine. With Yardley's husband out of town, I was going to the inn to give her moral support. That was all.

We arrived at our destination in less than ten minutes. A few guests were in the lobby, most warming themselves by the fire, all apparently unaware there'd been a murder on the property.

Ginny the concierge signaled me. "Mrs. Alks told me to expect you."

"Where is she?"

"At the cabanas." The cabanas were located past the wing of suites. Six faced the ocean; six had mountain views. "What's going on?"

"When the police arrive, send them around," I said.

"The police?" Ginny blanched.

Rhett and I hurried on. The left side of the walkway was dry but water dripping from the jasmine kept the right side wet. We found Yardley outside unit five, a mountain-view cabana. She'd changed into jeans and a sweatshirt and was quivering. Tears were streaming down her face. The door was ajar.

Rhett put a hand on her arm. "How are you doing?"

"I'm shaken to my core."

"Do you need to sit down?"

"No, I'm —"

A siren pierced the silence. Yardley flinched.

I peered into the room but didn't step inside. The lights were low and the drapes closed, but one glance revealed an expansive layout with a well-appointed living room, an adjoining kitchen area, and what I imagined was a bedroom to the right. Quade was lying on the brocade sofa, naked, his heavily tattooed backside facing the door. I didn't see blood. He hadn't been stabbed in the back. A mixed-media work — not his competition entry — stood on an easel beyond the sofa. Washed dishes had been left to dry on a towel on the kitchen counter. A scrap of paper lay on the floor beneath the sink and a couple of wads of paper were near a small trash can, as if he'd tried to shoot free throws from the sofa and missed.

I turned to Yardley. "Why was Quade staying here? He told me he was renting a place on Poinsettia until he figured out where he wanted to buy."

"He is . . . *was.*" She blinked back more tears. "But his place needed to be fumigated, so Sienna was gracious enough to give him a few room nights on the house. She believes in supporting artists."

Was that what Sienna and Quade had been arguing about? Was she commenting about the state of his quarters? Had he played music too loudly or mistreated the staff?

I inhaled. "Do you smell tar or something leathery, like a men's cologne?"

"I'm picking up all sorts of odors." Yardley wrinkled her nose. "Quade brought many of his media with him. Paints. Oils. Metal chips. When he's feeling creative, he can't . . ." She gasped. "*Couldn't.* He couldn't rest." She covered her mouth with the back of her hand, as if she'd said too much.

"Why were you here?" I asked. "I mean, why were you the one to find him?"

"I received a text from him around nine saying he didn't feel well. He had an upset stomach. He ended the text with the word *Naomi.* But there was nothing after that. Do you think —"

"He was accusing her of something?" I finished.

"I don't know."

"He liked her. Maybe he wanted you to call her, but he passed out before he could finish the message. He had been drinking earlier."

She wrapped her arms around her body. "I was talking to Wayne, long distance, and responded to Quade that I'd be over soon."

"Why would Quade text you?" Rhett asked.

"Because I'm his mentor?" Her tinny voice skated upward with doubt. "I do know a thing or two about dealing with sore tummies, having been a grade school art teacher. Quade knew —"

"What's going on!" Sienna Brown bellowed from a distance. She'd changed out of her white jacquard dress into a black pantsuit. She marched toward us, her gaze riveted on Yardley. "I heard sirens. Ginny said we're to expect the police. Why?"

Yardley sputtered, "Quade . . . is dead. He's been murdered."

Sienna paled. "What?" She started for the room.

I held her back. "Please, Sienna, don't. It's a crime scene."

She peered past me. "For heaven's sakes, Jenna, he's not dead. He's sleeping."

"No, Sienna, he's dead." Yardley's voice cracked. "I entered because he'd texted me. The door was open. I thought he'd left it that way. He's been stabbed."

A housekeeper and a hospitality deliveryman carrying a covered tray drew near.

The housekeeper yelped. "Stabbed?"

The hospitality guy whispered loudly enough to be heard, "Miss Brown entered the cabana at a quarter to ten."

I turned my attention to Sienna. "You went into the room?"

She squared her broad shoulders, looking cool under fire. "Yes. I was making rounds, as I often do before retiring for the night, and I noticed the door was open. I poked my head in and saw him asleep on the couch, as he often was."

"You've found him asleep before?" Rhett sounded skeptical.

"Three nights in a row. He was a furious and passionate artist. He would often exhaust himself after an hour of work. He was lying like that" — Sienna motioned to the room — "nude, curled on his side."

"He loved painting au naturel," Yardley said.

"That's what he told me, too," Sienna went on. "Anyway, as I was leaving, I saw that he'd left dishes on the counter, so I washed them, as I would for any negligent guest, and I left. I didn't know that he was . . ." She shuddered. "Maybe he wasn't . . . dead. Maybe . . ." She folded her hands in front of her.

"He never did dishes," Yardley said idly. "It was beneath him."

I wondered how she would know such a personal thing about one of her students and again questioned why Quade would have contacted her when he'd felt sick, grade school teacher credentials notwithstanding. Why hadn't he contacted his doctor? That would have been my first instinct. Or 911.

"All right, everyone, please back away from the door." Chief Cinnamon Pritchett, not in uniform and wearing no makeup, clearly roused from sleep as I had been, strode to us.

Deputy Martin Appleby, a largish man with a moose-shaped jaw, and two uniforms — one a fresh-faced female, the other a skinny male — trailed her.

Cinnamon gazed at me and frowned.

"Again?"

"I wasn't the one to find him," I said, as if that exonerated me from earning her wrath.

Rhett said, "Mrs. Alks found him and reached out to us." I liked how he'd used *us.* "We came to give her emotional support."

"The coroner is on his way," Appleby said to Cinnamon while inserting his cell phone into his pocket.

"He's been stabbed," Yardley murmured. "I . . . I went in. I'm sorry, Chief Pritchett. I didn't know it was a crime scene. I —" She begged with her eyes for me to finish.

Rhett cut in, offering that the hospitality deliveryman had witnessed Sienna entering the room at nine forty-five.

I quickly recapped Yardley's account to Cinnamon and added what Sienna had told us about washing dishes.

"So that sets the murder sometime between nine and nine forty-five?" Cinnamon stated. "A narrow window."

"If he was dead when Miss Brown entered the room. Otherwise, the time frame could be around ten to eleven, when Yardley arrived. Also a narrow window."

"Foster," Cinnamon said, "get any staff statements, please."

"Ma'am," the fresh-faced female cop replied.

"Ferguson," Cinnamon said to the skinny male cop, "establish a perimeter, and get me the security videos."

Sienna cleared her throat. "I'm sorry, Chief Pritchett. The security cameras have been glitching. The company has promised to fix them, but they keep resetting the appointment."

"Swell."

I wondered about Sienna's story. Why had she changed out of her white dress? Because there was blood on it? Were the security cameras really glitching? They had to be. The police would check even though she'd said they needn't.

On the other hand, stabbing wasn't a typical murder method for a woman. I weighed what the hospitality guy had said, or in this case, what he hadn't said. He hadn't mentioned hearing any loud noises around the time he'd seen Sienna enter the room. Quade would have screamed if Sienna had stabbed him, wouldn't he?

"Chief," I said, "the text to Yardley ended with the name *Naomi.* No message following."

"Got it."

"I'm not saying Naomi Genet did this.

She couldn't have."

Cinnamon threw me a wry look. "Why not?"

"She . . ." I paused. She *what*? Was too nice? Too fragile? "She went home. The concierge saw her leave before eight."

"She could have come back."

Cinnamon donned Latex gloves and stepped into the cabana. Appleby followed. Cinnamon switched on the overhead recessed lights and continued to the body. She felt for a pulse and then moved to the opposite side of the couch and peered down. Her face turned grim. Carefully, she reached between the body and the back of the couch. She lifted something and inspected it. She showed it to Appleby.

Cinnamon crossed to the doorway, carrying a tapered tool with a wooden knob handle. "Does this look familiar?" She held it out to me. Blood clung to the burin's shaft.

"You didn't . . . pull that out of . . ." I gagged.

"Don't be ridiculous. It was lying on the couch."

"He was stabbed with it?"

"Yes."

"While he was lying in that position?" I couldn't figure out how the killer would have been able to do so.

"Doubtful. There's —" She shouted over her shoulder, "Deputy, do not move the body."

"Do I look like a rookie?" Appleby replied sarcastically.

Cinnamon addressed me. "I'll leave the where and how to the coroner. Back to the matter at hand, do you recognize this tool now?" She turned it so I could see the top of the handle.

The initials *KL* were stamped on it.

My insides roiled with worry. It was Keller's burin. The one he'd shown me from his tool kit during the workshop. Why would he have —

No, no, no. He didn't kill Quade.

"What's wrong?" Rhett slipped up beside me.

"The weapon," I said. "It's Keller's tool."

"Keller Landry had a fight with Quade," Sienna said from behind the crime scene tape that the policeman was unfurling.

"It wasn't a big fight," I countered, sticking up for my friend.

Cinnamon said, "I saw the set-to, Jenna. Remember? You said Keller was concerned about finances. Did he feel Quade was his competition? Did he think Quade might impede him from achieving his goal?"

"No!" The word flew out of me.

"Of course he was," Sienna said. "They both used mixed media. With Quade out of the picture, Keller Landry could shine."

I turned on the woman, my gaze blazing with indignation. "Keller would not do this. He is a gentle soul. A passive man. And why would he have left his tool behind if he'd killed him? Someone is framing him, Cinnamon . . . I mean, Chief. Were there any defensive wounds?"

"You know I can't answer that."

I gazed past her into the cabana as I replayed events earlier in the evening. Quade dogging Naomi. Quade rebuffing Destiny. Quade having a heated conversation with Sienna. He'd been tipsy, slurring his words by then. I flashed on the text he'd sent Yardley saying he didn't feel well. Was it possible he'd passed out before the murderer stabbed him?

"Did you notice the wads of paper?" I asked Cinnamon.

"I'm not blind. I'll check out everything. Don't you worry."

I searched the burgeoning crowd and saw Sienna chatting with a few guests. My thoughts returned to the set-to between her and Quade. She had given him a costly gift by allowing him to stay in a cabana for free.

Granted, it was her inn. She could do whatever she pleased. What had they argued about? Had Sienna added something to one of his drinks earlier in the evening to ensure that he would pass out so she could slip in later and kill him? Did she wash the glass to hide the evidence?

CHAPTER 6

I didn't sleep well. Rhett tried to comfort me, but I tossed and turned. Images of Quade on the couch and Keller wielding a bloody etching tool pervaded my dreams. I rose early, tamed my unruly hair, splashed my face with water, and threw on running clothes. A jog on the beach, listening to the ocean rhythmically lapping the shore, the sand still wet from last night's rain, helped clear my head. Keller was innocent. I knew that at my core. Cinnamon would figure it out soon enough.

When I returned, I decided to make an omelet using herbs from my garden . . . *our* garden. Though I hadn't learned to cook until I'd moved back to Crystal Cove — and for the first year, five-ingredient recipes were the only ones I could master without breaking out in a panic — I was really enjoying cooking these days. Rhett slipped up behind me as I was turning the omelet onto plates and kissed my neck. A delicious shiver of joy swizzled through me.

"Smells great," he said as he set the table and poured coffee.

After we ate, rather than go back to sleep, Rhett left with Rook for a long hike, and I threw on my favorite coral sweater, denim skirt, and bejeweled sandals, and drove to work with Tigger.

Once I'd set up the cash register and roamed the Cookbook Nook to make sure titles on spines read from top to bottom, aprons hung smoothly on their hooks, and all the gift items were turned to their most advantageous angle, I queued up instrumental jazz music and dialed Naomi on my cell phone.

She answered after one ring. "Hello?"

"Naomi, it's Jenna. I was worried about you."

"Didn't you get my text?"

"Yes."

"The sitter contacted me to say my daughter missed me. I don't go out much at night."

"What about the picture of the man I showed you? Did you recognize him? You left so abruptly that I thought I'd upset you."

"Upset me?" Her voice cracked. "Of

course not. I'm sorry, Jenna. I have another call coming in. Thanks for checking on me." She ended ours.

I noted that she didn't say a word about Quade being dead. That had to be a good sign.

"Is everything all right, dear?" Aunt Vera asked. She was wiping down the craft table in the children's corner before setting out new supplies. From the outset, we had decided a corner featuring children's cookbooks as well as utensils and food-oriented games would be a great lure. Parents and grandparents often came into the shop with children and needed something to occupy the young ones' attention while they browsed.

"Talking to Naomi was weird."

"How so?" Aunt Vera asked.

"It was almost as though she couldn't wait to get rid of me." I explained about the man I believed was stalking her. "When I showed Naomi the picture I'd taken, she gasped and ran off."

"Maybe her cell phone buzzed in her pocket at the same time you displayed the photo."

"Or perhaps her smart watch did," I murmured. That might explain why she'd been stabbing it while racing away.

Whistling cheerily, my aunt ambled to the vintage table, picked up the turban that matched her emerald green caftan, and set it on her head. "So what else is on your mind?"

I hadn't told her about the murder and didn't intend to. Why spoil her good mood?

"I'd like to pull all cookbooks with the word *art* in the title from the shelves and put them on sale for one day. *The Art and Soul of Baking. The Art of the Cheese Plate. The Art of Vintage Cocktails.* I think we stock about ten books with similar titles." I rounded the sales counter and traveled from bookcase to bookcase selecting books.

"Any special reason we're having a sale?"

"For the charity."

"Oh, yes, silly me, of course. All the proceeds will go to the charity."

During each festival, the mayor selected a charity that the festival would sponsor. This year's was the Boys and Girls Club of America. They planned to expand art programs for kids.

"In a half hour" — I checked my watch — "the artisans who have made the specialty cookie jars and salt and pepper sets are coming in to be available to customers to talk about their wares. It'll be casual. They'll roam the shop. They're donating twenty-five percent of their proceeds to the charity, too."

"Marvelous."

"Katie made cookie-jar-shaped treats for the occasion."

"Adorable." My aunt began whistling again. Ever since she and Deputy Appleby had become a couple, she'd been light on her feet. I was so happy for her.

Two hours later, after we'd sold more than half of the discounted books and all of the specialty decorative items — the artisans had departed utterly thrilled with the customers' enthusiasm — Bailey flew into the shop pushing her daughter in a stroller, the tails of her turquoise scarf flying behind her.

"Sorry I'm late." Typically, she brought Brianna to work in the morning. No one minded. The girl was so easygoing. Later, Tina, after her morning classes, would pick up Brianna and tend to her for the afternoon. "I got caught up on a call with Tito. He heard about the murder. Fill me in. That artist is dead?"

My aunt gasped. "Which artist?"

I motioned for them to hush. I didn't want to scare away the few remaining customers.

"The one with the single name," Bailey said. "Quade. He did the mural on the side of the junior college. With all the sea creatures."

"Jenna, did you know?" Aunt Vera asked.

"Yes. I didn't want to ruin your upbeat mood."

My aunt clucked her tongue with dismay. "Murdered."

"Stabbed in one of the cabanas at the Crystal Cove Inn," I said. "Yardley Alks found him."

"How do you know so much?" she asked.

"She phoned me."

My aunt raised an eyebrow. "Why you?"

"Because she knew I'd had experience finding, you know . . ." I twirled a hand, not uttering the words *dead bodies.* "But don't worry," I hastened to add, "Rhett went with me and we dialed 911 right away. Cinnamon showed up. So did Marlon."

"Ah. That's why he went out so late last night."

My aunt and Deputy Appleby had eloped last year in Las Vegas. No one quite understood why, at their age, they'd wanted to marry rather than live together, but they were blissfully in love. Appleby had moved into my aunt's house on the beach. His daughter had been supportive; his son, from whom he'd been alienated, was coming around.

"He didn't say anything to you?" I asked.

"No, and he was out of the house before I awoke. Go on."

"Someone stabbed Quade." I paused. "With one of Keller's art tools."

"No," they gasped in unison.

"Although the police might want that kept secret for now. I think the killer planted it to implicate Keller."

"Why do such a thing?" Aunt Vera asked.

"Keller and Quade have been squabbling lately. The killer probably thought the feud and the fact that they were sort of rivals, both using mixed media in their artwork, would be enough to incriminate him."

"Did Cinnamon say that?" Bailey asked as she disappeared into the stockroom and returned with the sit-me-up, owl-themed floor seat for Brianna. The baby was the spitting image of Bailey with short spiky hair and had an affinity for colorful outfits, today's matching her mother's red-and-turquoise getup.

"I'm sure she's keeping an open mind," I said. "She didn't go right out and arrest him, if that's what you mean." At least I hoped she hadn't. "I should check in on Katie." I started toward the breezeway.

"Don't go yet, Sunshine," my father said as he entered the shop with Lola. Both were dressed in white shirts and jeans, though Lola looked way more stylish, her jeans studded with silver stars and her blouse formfitting.

"Why are you here?" I asked.

Lola crossed to Brianna and unbuckled her from her stroller. "Hello, sweet thing," she cooed, lavishing her granddaughter with kisses.

"You sent me on a mission," my father said, "and I always complete a mission. The man in the photo you showed me is Christopher Michael George. A self-help guru from Silicon Valley. He runs the Believe You Can Foundation." He scrolled to an internet page on his cell phone and showed me the screen.

"I know him." Lola rose with Brianna in her arms. "He's hugely popular. I've seen him interviewed on a number of the daytime talk shows. His talks are all about believing you can find love and a sense of self."

"Oh, him," my aunt said. "I've seen him. He's covered virtually every topic under the sun."

"Mm-hm," Lola said. "He's witty, albeit pompous, if you ask me. He's also a collector of fine art."

"That might explain why he's in town," my father said. "The festival."

"But why was he pursuing Naomi?" I asked.

"Because she's pretty," my aunt suggested.

"More than pretty," Bailey said. "Naomi is —"

"Hello-o!" Gran, aka Gracie Goldsmith, breezed in, her cheeks rosy from sun exposure despite the broad-brimmed hat she was wearing. Having an extensive knowledge of cookbooks, she had offered to work part-time as Tina was making her career switch. "What's this about Naomi?"

Aunt Vera *tsk*ed. "Gracie, you have the ears of an elephant."

Gran chuckled. "I've been told that many times."

Bailey said, "Jenna is worried that a man might be stalking Naomi."

"Interesting." Gran stored her purse beneath the register. "Minutes ago I saw her at Azure Park with her adorable little girl. They were browsing the various Art in the Sunlight festival booths. A man was ogling her."

"Are you sure?" my father asked.

"Yes. I have to admit I was worried on Naomi's behalf until she and her daughter met up with a group of women, their play group, I think, at Squiggles."

"Is this him, Gracie?" My father flashed

his cell phone in her direction.

"Yes. Oh, my!" Gran pressed a hand to her chest. "There he is."

"Who?" I asked.

"The ogler. With the mustache. He's entering the Nook Café."

I whirled around and saw Christopher Michael George striding through the café's door. As before, he was striking yet casual, in dark gray corduroys, a striped shirt, and a light gray sweater slung around his shoulders.

Not wasting a moment, I hurried down the breezeway and into the café. The place was busy. Nearly all the tables were filled. The hostess was seating Mr. George at a table by the window with a view of the ocean. He was being quite chatty with her.

"I've got your six," my father said from behind me.

I glanced over my shoulder. Dad's gaze was humorless. I knew he did not approve of me barging ahead. On the other hand, he had not grabbed my arm and held me back.

"Mr. George," I said as I drew near to his table. The hostess had returned to her post. "I'm the owner of the café, Jenna Hart." I extended my hand.

"Is there a problem?" He set aside his menu. His eyes were dark but warm, exactly the kind of eyes that would draw in viewers.

"This is my father, Cary Hart."

"Christopher George," he replied. "Everyone calls me Christopher. Never Mr. George."

"Big fan," my father said, lying through his teeth.

"Really?" Christopher asked. "Which seminar is your favorite?"

"The one on confidence."

"There are three."

"All of them," Dad tried.

Christopher George smirked. "Haven't seen any, have you?"

Dad snickered. "Not a one."

"Sir," I said.

"Christopher. Please." He directed his attention back to me.

"Yes, Christopher, forgive me, but I spotted you last night at the soiree at the Crystal Cove Inn, and I didn't get the chance to say hello."

His warm eyes cooled. "You're the one who took a photograph of me."

I nodded.

"Are you a fan, too?" he asked.

"No, sir. I was one of the artists last night. I was taking photos of everyone at the party and hoped to greet each personally."

"Uh-huh," he said skeptically.

"You were particularly interested in the assistant art teacher, Naomi Genet."

Christopher squared the edges of his menu with the place mat. "Is that what she's calling herself these days?"

"You know her?"

"As a matter of fact, I do. Or should I say I *did*?"

My father pulled out a chair and motioned for me to sit, and then he sat beside me.

The waitress swung by the table, saying, "I'll be right back."

Christopher said, "Don't bother. I'll be leaving in a sec." He nudged the small vase holding a daisy to one side, leaned forward on his elbows, and folded his hands. "She's my wife. She disappeared three years ago."

I frowned. Naomi had told me that her husband had died.

"I was heartbroken," Christopher added.

"I presume you asked the police for help," my father said, mirroring Christopher's pose, his tone light but his gaze direct.

"Of course."

Naomi hadn't elaborated about her past, and I hadn't pressed because I'd never appreciated when people had questioned me about David, my husband who had supposedly died in a mysterious boating accident until I'd discovered that he hadn't. When he'd turned up alive, I'd been shocked. When he'd revealed his deceit, it had broken my heart. When he'd died of real causes a short while later, I'd let the memory of the two of us fade. But not once had I ever lied about him being my husband. What had made Naomi leave Christopher George? Had he —

"Foul play was not suspected," he went on. "There was no body. No crime scene."

I winced, flashing on Quade, dead in the cabana.

"And then, a month after she left, she sent me a note of goodbye. Through the mail. No explanation. No mention of reconciliation. The police verified that she'd written the note and closed the case. I employed a private detective agency," he added. "For six months. They came up empty. Ultimately, I gave up. People who don't want to be found have plenty of ways to stay off the grid. However" — he raised his head to meet our gazes, tears gracing his eyelashes — "when I saw posters for the festival with last year's winning entry, I couldn't believe my eyes. I recognized my wife's style as well as her distinctive initials, *NG.* Of course, when she was married to me, she was known as Nancy George."

Nancy. Naomi did not look like a Nancy.

I said, “Sir, you were stalking her last night and then again at Azure Park this morning.”

“I wasn’t stalking her. I’d seen the program for the festival. I’d expected she’d be at the inn on opening night, seeing as that was where they were honoring the new competitors. Congrats, by the way.”

I thanked him.

“I was hoping to get a word with her,” he continued, “but she ran off. As for this morning, it was a fluke. I went to see the van Gogh on stilts paint *Starry Night* on the LED screen.”

“There’s a van Gogh on stilts?” I asked.

Christopher splayed his hands. “Look, all I want to do is talk to my wife. Find out why she ran away.”

My father coughed.

“I didn’t abuse her, sir. I never laid a hand on her.”

“There are many kinds of abuse,” Dad said.

I picked up a spoon and traced circles on the tablecloth. “She told me she’d moved to Crystal Cove to start over with her daughter.”

Christopher’s mouth dropped open. “The child is hers? How old is she?”

I swallowed hard. “Three years.” It suddenly occurred to me that Naomi might have left Silicon Valley because she'd been pregnant with another man's child. Quade's perhaps? We didn't know much about him. Had he presumed the child was his? Was that why he had been hounding Naomi? Had she killed him to stop his endless pursuit?

Christopher rubbed the back of his neck. "Is it mine?"

Mentally, I smacked my forehead. Yes, that could be a possibility, too. *Duh!* "I have no idea," I said lamely. "Sir, you're an art collector, I hear."

"I dabble."

"Is the name Quade familiar to you?"

I could feel my father staring at me, but I couldn't take a moment to explain that I was fishing, trying to find some connection between Christopher and Quade. Had Naomi met Quade through her husband's business contacts? Had Christopher George come to town to have it out with Quade?

"No. Doesn't ring a bell." Christopher aimed his finger at me. "Wait. Isn't he one of the finalists for this year's poster art competition?"

He'd used the present tense, as if he didn't know Quade was dead. Was he being cagey or truthful?

The door to the café opened and Cinnamon Pritchett, in full uniform, her hat firmly on her head, and Foster, the fresh-faced female officer who'd accompanied her last night, entered. Cinnamon caught sight of me and I reddened, feeling guilty for merely talking to Christopher George. But neither he nor I were the targets of Cinnamon's visit. She and the officer made a hard left toward the café's kitchen. To talk to Katie?

Not without me being present. My café. My kitchen. I touched my father's arm. "I've got to go."

Christopher started to rise.

"Sir, please stay," I said. "Have a meal on the house. Dad, will you make sure that happens?" I bussed his cheek and got to my feet.

Christopher settled into his chair. "Would you please tell me where I can find Naomi? All I want to do is talk."

"I'll have to ask her," I said. "You're staying at the inn under your own name?"

"Yes."

"I'll do what I can."

When I entered the kitchen, my heart sank. Keller was sitting at the chef's table with his daughter Min-yi, who had the most beautiful jet-black hair and dark eyes. He often brought her to visit her mother in the mornings. His ice cream business didn't pick up until late afternoon. Both were wearing overalls and nibbling grilled cheese sandwiches.

"Keller Landry," Cinnamon said officiously, "I have a warrant to search your house."

"Wh-why?" he stammered.

"We have it on good authority that a painting of Quade's has gone missing, and word is that you might have stolen it."

"No way!" Keller's voice rattled.

Katie, in her white chef's coat and toque, rushed to her husband's side and looped her hand around his elbow. "Who told you such a lie, Chief?"

"We got an anonymous tip."

"Anonymous?" Katie hissed. "What kind of coward sends an anonymous tip?"

"Why would I steal his work?" Keller rose to his feet and opened his hands.

"Apparently you were jealous of his talent," Cinnamon answered.

"Not so!"

Min-yi squealed.

"Sorry, sweetheart." Keller kissed her. "Daddy's a little upset." Lowering his voice, he said, "Chief, my art is every bit as good as Quade's. Better, even."

"If you haven't stolen it, Mr. Landry, then there's nothing to worry about."

"Can't you call me Keller?" he pleaded. "I mean, c'mon, you buy double scoops of my chocolate pistachio ice cream."

Cinnamon stiffened. "Mr. Landry —"

"Jenna, do something!" Katie cried.

What could I do? This was police business.

"Go with him," Katie said. "In my stead. I can't leave here. We have forty charity donors coming for a specialty luncheon."

"Jenna, no," Cinnamon cautioned.

"I won't get in the way," I stated, "and I can see to Min-yi, if necessary."

"Min-yi can stay here," Katie said.

"Then I'll be emotional support for Mr. Landry," I tried. "Please, Chief."

Cinnamon sighed. "Fine. Let's go."

CHAPTER 7

Katie and Keller lived in a modest two-bedroom house in the hills, surrounded by a gorgeous array of white azaleas. The place belonged to Katie's uncle, but ever the adventurer, he'd decided to take a world-wide sailing trip and had rented it to Katie and Keller for a song. Cinnamon made Keller and me stand outside while she and her officer, both wearing Latex gloves, inspected the premises.

"I didn't do this, Jenna," Keller said, pulling dead blooms from an azalea.

"I know."

"Why would I take Quade's work? So I could copy it? I don't even like his work."

Birds twittered merrily in nearby trees even though we fell into a gloomy silence.

Twenty minutes later, the garage door opened. Cinnamon stepped into the sunlight. "Mr. Landry, please join us."

Keller had turned the garage into his

studio, which consisted of a workbench, a wall fitted with a peg board to hold tools, padlocked storage cupboards, and an easel upon which stood an oversized canvas — Keller's work in progress, I presumed. In addition, Keller's tricked-out ice cream bike, fitted with a freezer at the rear, stood by the window.

Keller shuffled inside, visibly shaking. "Yes, Chief?"

"Can you explain this?" She signaled the officer to remove the oversized canvas from the easel.

Beneath stood another canvas. Quade's *Morning.*

I gasped.

"Chief, I don't know —" Keller sputtered. "I didn't put that there. I don't even know where Quade lives. How would I have been able to steal it?"

"Chief," I said, doing my best to calm my fear, "wouldn't he have hidden it better if he had truly stolen it?"

"There aren't many places to hide it," she said. "There are only two closets and a few cabinets in the house. We found no hidden compartments beneath the flooring. What better place than to hide it in plain sight?"

Keller moaned. "Why would I steal it?"

"As I said earlier, Mr. Landry, because

you were jealous, which is probably your motive for killing him."

"He's dead?" Keller gawked at me.

I said, "He was stabbed last night with one of your —"

"Jenna!" Cinnamon exhaled sharply. "Mr. Landry, he was stabbed with one of your art tools. A burin."

"No way. It couldn't have been one of mine. I'm meticulous about my tools. I put them back in their cases, and I keep them under lock and key."

"Where?"

"I'll show you." Keller grabbed a ring of keys off the pegboard of tools, strode to the rightmost cabinet, and unlocked the padlock.

"Mr. Landry, is that where you always keep your keys?" Cinnamon asked.

"Well, y-yeah," he stammered.

"Pretty easy for a thief to find them."

"We use padlocks because of our daughter. We don't want her to get into anything."

"She's not even two," Cinnamon said wryly. "I doubt she could reach that cabinet."

Keller said, "It's more for us. We're parents-in-training. You must have noticed that all the cupboards inside have been baby-proofed." He opened the door and brandished a hand. "So, you can see my tools are right —" A hiss escaped his lips. "I . . . I can't believe it. My tool kit isn't here."

"As a matter of fact," Cinnamon said, "I knew it wasn't. We found the remainder of the kit in the communal room at the Crystal Cove Inn."

"But I didn't leave my tools there. I wouldn't."

"Why not?"

"Because, as I said, I keep them here. Whatever you found can't be mine." He gazed into the cupboard as if willing his tool kit to magically materialize.

"The initials *KL* are on the handle of the burin."

Keller winced. "Someone must have broken into my garage. Must have stolen my —"

Foster snorted.

Keller glowered at her and refocused on Cinnamon. "Chief, I didn't do this. I have an alibi."

"Mr. Landry, I haven't even told you where or when this happened."

"Keller," I said gently, "where were you last night at —"

"Jenna, stop. I'll ask the questions." Cinnamon's glare was steely.

I blanched.

"Where were you last night between the hours of nine and eleven p.m., Mr. Landry?"

Keller scratched the back of his neck. "On the beach. Painting."

"It was dark," she stated. "And wet."

"Ma'am, it may've been wet after the rain, but it was bright. The moon was full. I go there a lot to clear my head. I took Katie home after the soiree, paid the sitter, and then set off."

"With this painting?" She gestured to the oversized work in progress that the officer had set at the foot of the easel.

"No, ma'am, the one in the bed of my truck."

"Show me."

Keller had parked his truck at the end of the driveway. I'd pulled up behind him in my VW.

Keller trudged to the truck, opened the tailgate, which had a storage compartment to hold his paint supplies, and removed a wide waterproof-covered container. He slid it onto the tailgate, unzipped the cover, and removed the contents, which was a three-by-four canvas featuring a partial image of the Pier.

"Did anyone see you on the beach?" Cinnamon asked.

"I remember spotting a few people, but they won't remember me. See, they were wrapped in blankets and totally focused on what they were doing."

"Which was?"

"Scouring the area with a dowsing tool."

Crystal Cove had some avid dowsers who would search for jewelry and coins dropped by beachgoers. Most came out at sunrise. A few daring souls braved the elements at night.

"Chief?" I raised my hand as if I was in school.

Cinnamon scowled, clearly peeved by my presence. "What?"

"Might I ask who gave you the tip about the missing artwork? It wasn't really anonymous, was it?"

She hesitated then conceded, "Yardley Alks."

I tilted my head. Had Yardley, who claimed she was Quade's mentor, put the artwork in Keller's garage and then alerted the police? To what end? To throw suspicion off herself for killing Quade? No, I couldn't believe it. Yardley wasn't a killer.

"Who else do you suspect of murdering Quade, Chief?" I asked.

"I believe I've found my guy. We have the weapon, the stolen art, and the motive."

"I'm being framed!" Keller cried. "The killer must have known where I keep my tools, and . . . and . . ." He fought for breath.

"Chief," I said, a theory springing to mind, "what if Quade stole Keller's tools and put his art in his garage to mess with him — to prank him — but before the prank played out, Quade was killed, using the very same tools? It was common knowledge that he wasn't happy with Keller. He deemed him his competition. Both worked with mixed media. He was constantly harassing Keller about his work."

"Constantly?" Cinnamon folded her arms. "Sounds like motive."

"That's not what I meant," I said hastily.

"Look, Jenna, I have spoken with a number of people who believe Mr. Landry had it in for Quade."

"Like who?" I asked. "The other competitors?" Flora and Faith were gossips. Had Candy or Jaime said something?

Cinnamon turned to Keller. "Mr. Landry —"

"Chocolate pistachio!" he blurted.

"Keller." Cinnamon softened her voice, leading me to believe that she, too, didn't think him capable of murder. "I'd like you to come into the precinct for questioning."

"Now?"

"Now."

"Do I need a lawyer?"

"For the moment, no. If you come willingly, it will go much easier for you."

By the look on Keller's face, I was certain he didn't believe her.

I drove back to Fisherman's Village, parked, and rushed through the café into the kitchen. Bailey was sitting at the chef's table with Min-yi, who had fallen asleep on the banquette. Katie was busy supervising her staff as they served up the lunches of crispy duck salad, white fish sliders, and shrimp pizza for the forty charity donors.

Bailey said, "Mom took Brianna for a walk and then she's going to give her to Tina so I could come here, sans child, to bolster Katie."

At the mention of her name, Katie caught sight of me and hurried over. Wiping her hands on her apron, she whispered, "Keller phoned me. He said he might have forgotten and left his tool kit in the communal room because he's been so tired."

I'd been afraid of something like that. He hadn't been robbed. On the other hand, someone had stolen Quade's painting and had planted it in Keller's garage.

"I told him not to say anything else," Katie

added. "Not until —"

"Not until Mom gets there," Bailey cut in. "She's going to represent him until she finds him a suitable defense attorney." Before opening the Pelican Brief Diner, Lola Bird had worked as a lawyer. During her lucrative career, she had challenged some of the state's staunchest attorneys.

"We can't afford an attorney," Katie said.

I rested a hand on her arm. "Don't worry. My aunt will cover the payments."

Although Aunt Vera and I had brought Katie and Bailey in as limited partners a while ago, that minimal amount of extra earnings, above and beyond salary, wouldn't help pay for an attorney. My aunt, who had made a load of money thanks to keen investments in the seventies, could afford to pay for the lawyer and would do so willingly. She adored Katie.

"Who do you think set Keller up?" Bailey asked.

On the drive back to Fisherman's Village, I'd tried to come up with suspects, but I couldn't fathom who might want to make Keller the patsy for the crime. Yardley Alks? Why, for heaven's sake?

"Katie," I said, "who might have access to your house?"

"Anybody here, I suppose. I hang the

house keys on the loop over there." She indicated the dressing room at the back of the kitchen. "But I can't imagine anyone that works here has it in for my husband."

The dressing room was not easily accessible for a customer dining at the café. What about one of the workmen? I wondered. We often had a technician on-site to fix an appliance or a painter touching up the walls in the café.

"What about one of your uncle's friends?" I asked.

Katie frowned. "He had one. She died. That's why he's sailing around the world."

I said, "I had no idea. I'm so sorry."

"He wasn't in love with her, but they were quite close. Both geeks. Both loners."

Bailey said, "Did your uncle employ a housekeeper?"

Katie bit back a sob. "As if! You should have seen the place before we moved in. Dust bunnies abounded."

Bailey mouthed, *Do something.*

I slung an arm around Katie's shoulder and said, "Don't worry. We're going to find out the truth. Keller is not guilty."

Chapter 8

Bailey and I returned to the Cookbook Nook. While she helped Gran unpack a new shipment of *The Great Cook: Essential Techniques and Inspired Flavors to Make Every Dish Better,* by James Briscione, a terrific cookbook that I referred to often for learning about everything from sautéing to setting up a pantry, I moved to the children's table to organize tomorrow's cookie art event.

First, I gathered palettes and art supplies from the stock room. Tigger trailed me, his tail a question mark. "I do it every year, fella." Next, I gathered a set of cookbooks that adults who attended with the children might enjoy. One featured a silver frame around a plate of pasta, which made me flash on Keller, so vulnerable, so scared, swearing he'd been *framed.* Who would do that to one of the nicest guys in the world? He loved his family. He would do anything for a friend in need.

I paused. Had my earlier theory been correct? Had Quade, as a prank, hidden his art at Keller's, intending to call him out on it? But before he could, he was killed?

"Jenna?" my aunt said, sneaking up behind me. "You look lost in thought."

I turned. "It's so sad. Cinnamon has brought Keller in for questioning in the Quade murder."

"I heard."

"He . . ." I paused. Saying Quade's name, which could have been either a first or last name, caught me off guard. Which was it?

"He what?" my aunt asked.

"He didn't do it, of course."

"Of course. On that note, I heard that one of Naomi Genet's works went missing a few days ago."

"Who told you that?"

"The receptionist at the Art Institute. She's a client." My aunt plucked at the folds of her caftan. "Is it possible someone is stealing art around town? Someone who doesn't want the festival to be a success? I haven't mentioned it to Z.Z. I don't want her to suspect anyone out of hand."

"Do you think the thief could be one of the festival participants?" I asked. Tigger nudged my ankle. I bent to tickle his neck.

"I don't know what to think, but it does seem suspicious that there have been a rash of thefts within days of people arriving."

"Two stolen paintings is hardly a rash." I picked Tigger up by the scruff and cradled him. His purring helped calm my unsettled nerves. "Why steal Quade's art? Why steal Naomi's?"

Bailey and Gran joined me and my aunt, the four of us creating a conference circle.

Bailey said, "Did I hear that right? Another piece of art has gone missing?"

"One of Naomi's pieces. Stolen from her house," my aunt replied.

"When was it stolen?" I asked.

"Naomi couldn't put a date on it. She believes it must have been recently, but she couldn't recall the last time she'd gone through her work. She noticed because Shari Gregory asked her to hang a piece in Latte Luck Café." Shari enjoyed featuring local artists' work.

"Jenna," Bailey said, "we should track down Naomi and get the scoop. We need to suss out whether the thief is one person. For Katie and Keller's sake."

"Good idea." I set Tigger on the floor and faced my aunt.

"Go." She flapped a hand. "Gracie and I have things under control now that the hoopla has died down. Don't be long, however. We'll all need to chip in, in order to close up quickly so we can attend the Wearable Art event tonight."

The Art Institute was located in the hills, not far from the Crystal Cove Inn. Whenever I visited, I felt a sense of peace. The one-story building was tucked into a cove of trees, which gave it a sort of secret haven look. Perhaps that was why Naomi had sought a job here, to escape the real world and hide from her past.

I opened the heavy oak door and allowed my pal to go in first.

"I've never been here," Bailey whispered, acting as if we'd entered a holy shrine. "It's beautiful."

Art hung on all the walls of the foyer, except for the glass wall behind the receptionist's art deco rosewood desk. Classrooms were down the corridor to the left. Conference rooms were to the right. Through the glass behind the receptionist's desk, I saw Yardley sitting in the equally arty business office. She was facing a computer, her back to us. The screen was lit; the cursor was moving.

The receptionist, a stout middle-aged woman, set aside the *ARTNews* magazine she was reading and regarded us, her brow furrowed. "Help you?"

"Yes, please. I'm Jenna Hart. You're a client of my aunt's."

Her brown eyes grew warm. "Dear Vera. She gave me the most wonderful tarot card reading this morning. She said I'd find a world of inspiration in the near future."

"Are you a painter?" I asked.

"No, I'm a poet, and do you know, suddenly I'm feeling as creative as I've ever felt."

"Good for you." I didn't know much about tarot except what I'd heard my aunt convey. I knew the images on the cards and their basic meanings. "Is Naomi Genet here?"

"She's teaching."

"When will the class be over?"

"In two minutes. You can wait there." The receptionist pointed to a pair of arty but uncomfortable-looking chairs.

"May we browse?" I asked.

"Please do. If you need any literature, Mrs. Alks has created a pamphlet explaining each of the pieces."

"Thanks."

In college, I'd minored in art history, so I guided Bailey to two of the works that I recognized, copies of Diego Rivera's most famous paintings. His style featured large characters with simplified lines and luscious colors. As we were moving on to another famous reprint, teenaged students wearing or slipping on backpacks suddenly flooded the foyer, each chatting in a lively fashion.

"Can we go in?" I asked the receptionist.

"Please do."

Bailey and I weaved through the throng until we reached a room where students were exiting. I peeked inside. Sunlight streamed through the windows on the far side of the room. Easels fitted with sketch paper stood haphazardly about the room. Naomi was wiping off a chalkboard behind a sturdy desk.

"Naomi," I said.

She turned, her face flushed, her hair loose around her face. "Oh, Jenna and Bailey. Hi. Nice to see you."

I glanced over my shoulder. No students had made a U-turn and were headed this way. We had a moment of privacy. "May we come in?"

"Sure. Class just let out, but you probably deduced that." She set the eraser aside and smoothed the front of her checkered apron. "What brings you this way?"

"You."

"Me?"

"We heard you're missing a piece of art."

"How did you hear about it?"

"The receptionist here" — Bailey hooked her thumb over her shoulder — "told Jenna's aunt, who told us."

Naomi's eyes misted over. "I think it was stolen. I reported it to the police, but theft isn't high on the department's priority list, I gather."

"When did it go missing?" I asked.

"I'm not sure. It was in a closet with the rest of my work. I was going through it all because Shari Gregory asked me and a few other artists if we wanted to display one of our works at Latte Luck Café during the festival. It was a great opportunity."

"Which piece was stolen?" I asked.

"A sixteen-by-twenty acrylic of the ocean on a stormy day. Lots of blue upon blue with swipes of black and gray."

It sounded similar to Quade's newest work, I noted.

"I suppose I shouldn't miss it," Naomi went on. "My daughter never liked it. She wanted me to paint something sunnier. I gave Shari another piece."

"I haven't been in Latte Luck for a few days," I said. "Which painting is yours?"

"The gardens behind the Crystal Cove Inn at sunset. It's lovely yet docile. Nina approved."

"Do you have a clue who might have stolen the painting?"

"No." Naomi frowned.

"Where did you say you store your art?"

"At my house. It's probably my fault it's gone. I might have left the door open. I have a tendency to do that. I'm such a scatterbrain sometimes." She swept her hair over her shoulders. "The police didn't find prints or anything like that. Nothing to go on. I figure whoever stole it either liked my work or will try to sell it elsewhere."

I said, "Your signature will be on it."

"You mean my initials? I suppose so. Although the thief might be able to claim they're his or hers."

"Right," I murmured. "Especially someone named, say, Nancy George?"

"How did you . . ." She sputtered. "How did you find out . . ."

"I met your husband, Christopher George, the man I thought was stalking you the other night."

"Where? How?"

"He showed up at the Nook Café. He wants to talk to you."

"No." She covered her mouth with her hand.

"He's staying at the Crystal Cove Inn,"

Bailey added. On the drive to the institute, I'd told her about my conversation with Naomi's husband.

I said, "When I showed you his picture, Naomi, you ran."

She peeked at the door. Was she pondering running now?

I pressed on. "So I asked my father to do me a favor and figure out who the man was. I was worried."

"He . . ." Her eyelids fluttered.

I held out a hand. "You ran away from him. You changed your name. Why?"

She breathed high in her chest. Her face turned ashen.

"Sit," Bailey said. "Do you need water?"

"No, I . . ." Naomi settled into the chair behind the desk.

"Did he hurt you?" I asked, concerned.

Naomi shook her head but the shake turned into a nod. "Yes. Once. He knew I was running away. He grabbed my arm. Yanked it from the socket. He apologized. He said he thought I was going to fall down the stairs. He was lying." Her lower lip trembled. "I shook free and continued to run. Out of the house and into an Uber waiting for me outside the gate."

"Why did you need to escape?" I put a hand on her shoulder.

She shivered. "He was so controlling and mistrustful. Everywhere I went, his security people followed me. They kept an eye on me even when I slept."

"He has security people?" Bailey asked. "Why?"

"Because he has a lot of followers," Naomi said. "Some aren't stable. He's received death threats. In fact, that's the reason he gave me for keeping an eye on me, but I knew better."

"How did you hide once you left?" I asked.

"My mother helped me change my identity. Her father, my grandfather, used to work for WITSEC. He'd taught her some tricks of the trade. Now she's . . ." Naomi chewed her lower lip. "She's dead."

"I'm sorry. Did she live here in Crystal Cove?"

She worried the heart-shaped locket around her neck, which was similar to the one I wore. "No, in San Luis Obispo. She sold art and stained glass. The business was flagging, but she did everything she could to help me. When she got sick and knew she was dying of lung cancer, she suggested I move here. She'd always loved Crystal Cove." She splayed her hands. One started to shake. She tucked it into the other. "She didn't have much money. A small savings.

That helped me start anew. She found the house I'm renting. It's small. Two bedrooms. All I have left of her are this necklace" — she tapped it — "and a few precious stained-glass panels. She's the one who encouraged me to make my own stained-glass works."

"I didn't know you made stained glass."

"I dabble. It's hard to make a living as an artist or a teacher's assistant. I've sold a number of panels thanks to my site on Etsy. You know what Etsy is, don't you? An e-commerce website for crafts and such."

"Yes."

"The panels are a popular item."

"And your father?" I asked. Even given all of our dates for coffees, I hadn't heard much about Naomi's family, though I'd told her nearly everything about mine.

"Also deceased. He left when I was four. I didn't know him well."

"I'm sorry."

"It's okay."

"About Nina," I said, returning to our earlier discussion. "Is Christopher the father? Or was Quade?"

The tremor that had started in her hand shimmied through her entire body. "Quade?" Her voice crackled with tension. "Why would you ask about him?"

"He was hounding you. At class and at

the party. Was there more than a passing familiarity between you two? Did you two date at one time?"

"No . . . Yes." It took her a long time to continue. "We did date. Briefly. Until I realized he was an egocentric narcissist. 'My art is the best,' " she said, mimicking Quade's voice. " 'Nobody can match me in talent.' It became tiresome." She huffed. "So I broke it off."

"Was he the father?"

"No." The trembling subsided. "We met a year after Nina was born. If he —" She slung an arm across her body, protectively hooking her hand on her shoulder. "If he continues to pursue me, I warned him I'd get a restraining order."

"You won't need to do that," Bailey said.

"Don't tell me." Naomi held up a palm. "He finally decided to quit this sleepy town, as he dubbed it. In the middle of the festival. What a jerk! He realized he wasn't going to win the competition and didn't want to suffer the humiliating bruise to his ego."

"Did he know you'd changed your identity?" I asked, not ready to broach the matter of his death.

"I might have told him I'd changed it, for artistic purposes. I never told him more. I guess I'll have to, now that Christopher has surfaced."

"No, you won't." I shared a look with Bailey, who motioned to continue. "Naomi, I hate to break the news, but Quade is dead. He was murdered last night."

She gasped and once again her hands started to tremble. Watching her process the information, I wondered whether she might have killed him in order to keep her identity a secret.

CHAPTER 9

Bailey and I returned to the shop and helped Gran reorganize everything before closing for the day. We had no last-minute shoppers because there were so many evening events planned around town. My aunt had left to prepare for the evening's wearable art event.

At six, I took Tigger home. Rook was eager to see his buddy. Rhett had left at three for Intime. While the two animals played chase in the backyard, I filled their water and food bowls, and then I dressed for the event. Wearable art was the theme, so I threw on the most sparkly outfit I had, a silver sequin mesh cardigan and shell over tapered black satin pants. I added a pair of dangling silver earrings to finish the ensemble and applied a thin sliver of smoky gray eye shadow.

"Inside, you two," I said to the pets before

heading out. "Love you and miss you already."

The Aquarium by the Sea was a beautiful establishment endowed by a widow. It featured floor-to-ceiling windows and a wave-shaped roof. An artist had carved images of sea lions, manta rays, sharks, and more into the walls of the edifice. A moat of steadily flowing water surrounded the site.

The Wearable Art event was being held in the expansive courtyard at the rear of the building. A banner hung above the site's entrance. A woman in a Monet-esque gown was accepting tickets. Aunt Vera had treated all of us at the shop to the event. I handed the woman my ticket and strolled into the roped-off area. The elaborate fountain, which usually featured water shooting straight into the air, had been reduced to a modest burble. Sounds of chatter and laughter filled the air, as did the strains of a string quartet playing chamber music. Festive lights, in a crisscross design, sparkled above the venue.

I roamed past the various displays, all of which were open air, no booths or tents that might make the area feel crowded. As I strolled past table after table, I admired artistic brooches, ornate necklaces, T-shirts, ties, and more. I scanned the crowd for family and friends but was quickly distracted by the aroma of toasted cheese. A waitress wearing a Renoir-print apron over her white shirt and black slacks was offering hors d'oeuvres. I hurried to her.

"You're a saint." I took a melted brie on a whole wheat cracker topped with drizzled honey from the tray and popped it into my mouth. Heaven.

"Jenna!" a woman called.

Sienna Brown beckoned me. She was admiring a display of crystal necklaces at a booth named Shimmer. Beyond her, at the next stall, Naomi was fingering colorful diaphanous dresses on a clothes rack while chatting up the saleswoman. She didn't look torn up about Quade. She didn't look anything at all, as a matter of fact. From the side view, her face was a blank slate.

I joined Sienna. "You look nice." Her gold couture dress with a loosely draped duster coat went well with her coloring.

"Thank you. As do you. I dropped by for a moment. To say hello. I have to head back to the inn. The dessert and wine pairing event is about to start." She set down the hexagonal-shaped necklace she'd been studying. "What a shame about Keller Landry."

"He's innocent," I stated.

"Of course he is. He's such a sweet man. I adore him. He supplies much of our ice cream at the inn. It's . . . Well . . . What's the world coming to?" She fingered the stylish curls hanging from her updo. "Quade murdered. Keller arrested."

"He's not arrested." Not as far as I knew. Katie would have touched base with me, wouldn't she? Or Lola?

"My mistake."

I said, "How are you holding up? Having a murder at the inn can't be good for business."

"Actually, it's lured a few new guests. Ghoulish, if you ask me, but I haven't turned them away." She held a multicolored beaded necklace in front of her chest and assessed it in the vendor's mirror then put it back. "Business is business, after all. One needs to balance the books."

"I heard you gave Quade the cabana for free. Did you know him well?"

"I didn't. No. Not well at all. But I feel it's my duty to help out artists whenever I can. I haven't an ounce of creativity in my pinky, but I do admire talent. That's why I allowed Yardley to stage the event at the inn. In retrospect, perhaps that wasn't such a good idea." She peeked at her watch. "I'm sorry to cut our chat short, but I must be going." Without further ado, she weaved through the crowd toward the exit.

I spotted my father and Lola near the first of the vintner tables, he in a tweed sports jacket over blue shirt and trousers, she in a shimmery aqua sheath and shawl. "Hey, you two," I said as I drew near. "What are you snacking on?"

"Touvelle cheese on French bread topped with fig jam." Lola held hers up for inspection before eating it.

"It isn't quite a cheddar and it's not quite a jack," my father said.

"Scrumptious," Lola added, polishing fig jam off her fingertips.

My father kissed my cheek. "Flying solo?"

"Rhett had to work."

"What'll it be?" He gestured to the two-ounce pours of white wine, which included a sauvignon blanc, chardonnay, and Riesling.

"I'll try the sauvignon blanc."

"Good decision," Lola said. "By the way, Keller has not been arrested. They do not have nearly enough evidence."

"Yay!" I accepted a tasting glass from my father.

"I proposed that since the murder weapon could have been planted," Lola continued, "so could the artwork. Cinnamon knows she'll need additional cold hard facts to make the case, starting with motive."

I raised my glass in a toast. "I'm happy to hear that. Cheers!"

"But he's not out of the woods."

"Don't tell Katie that. She's a nervous wreck." I sipped my wine and set the glass down. *Everything in moderation,* I reminded myself. "If you don't mind, I'm going to wander through the courtyard and see what's for sale."

"Don't miss the crystal necklaces," Lola said. "They're splendid."

"I saw them. They're lovely."

As I roamed, Hannah Storm called to me. "Jenna, come try our latest wine! It's called Lightning." She was once again working alongside Destiny.

In her signature black, Hannah looked decidedly plain standing next to Destiny, who was wearing a strapless black dress and a stunning stained-glass necklace that reminded me of a Picasso painting.

I accepted a glass of the wine and took a sip. "Mm, very nice."

"This is our first release of this pinot blend," Hannah said. "Destiny says it will be a real draw on her wine tours."

"Destiny, I think you're right," I said. "It's a winner in my book." Despite her pretty getup, her face was glummer than glum. "It looks like you've heard about Quade. How are you doing?"

She stemmed tears with her index fingers. "I can't believe —" She jammed her lips together. "I can't believe he's gone. If only I'd stuck around and hadn't gone home to do PR for my stupid business. Maybe I could have helped him. I could have —"

"Saved him? And fought off a killer?" Hannah fisted her hands on her hips. "Girlfriend, we've talked about this. Get real. You could not have stopped —"

"I'm strong. I'm quick on my feet. I'm —" Destiny covered her mouth, lowered her head, and hurried through the crowd toward the restrooms.

"Destiny!" Hannah cried, but Destiny kept running. Hannah swept her hair over her shoulders. "Poor thing. She was going to stay home tonight, but I told her that she shouldn't be alone and to come and help me."

"You're a good friend."

"Not so good if she has to disappear into the restroom all night." Hannah served another customer then faced me. "Destiny has had quite a sad life. At the age of eleven, losing her mother in that horrible accident. Nana said the woman was a saint. One of the finest antiques dealers in California. And then, losing her father last year to a heart attack?" Hannah placed a hand on her chest. "He, like his wife, was a lovely man. A fairly well-to-do home builder. And, now, losing her business partner?"

"Oh, no, how'd he die?"

"He's alive," Hannah said, relieved. "But he wanted to press the reset button on his career choice, so he quit the business and relocated to New York. Needless to say, heading up an operation that needs two partners to run smoothly all by oneself is tough to do. That's why her self-esteem is at an all-time low. She thinks she's the root of bad luck. According to her, all the bad omens of walking under a ladder, breaking a mirror, or tipping over a saltshaker don't hold a candle to her getting involved with someone. She thinks she's a pariah." Hannah winked. "She hoped Quade would —"

"Fall for her and turn the tide," I finished.

Hannah drew in a deep breath and let it out. "But look what happened. Luckily, that black Lab of hers adores her."

"I've seen it riding with her on tours."

"He's so sweet. Alan and I have been discussing getting a dog."

A group of four approached and asked Hannah for a sample of Lightning.

I bid her goodbye and sauntered across the courtyard to where my aunt was standing with Gran and Bailey. All were clad in cobalt blue.

I snorted as I approached. "Did you three get a dress memo or something? If I'd known, I'd have worn my blue sheath."

Bailey grinned. "Completely by accident."

"Jenna, dear." Aunt Vera held out both hands. I grabbed hold. She drew me into a hug. "How did it go with Naomi?"

"You didn't tell them?" I asked Bailey.

She plucked her short hair. "I was going to."

I recapped the conversation and how we'd learned about Naomi's estranged relationship from her husband.

"They never divorced?" Gran asked.

"I don't think so."

"Is it possible Naomi revealed her history to Quade and killed him to keep it a secret?" Aunt Vera asked.

"I'd wondered the same thing, but I can't imagine Naomi stabbing someone. Like Keller, she's so sweet and kind."

Gran said, "Who else do you suspect, Jenna?"

"That's the police's job."

"Yes" — Gran winked — "but you often have thoughts on the subject. After all, you were at the crime scene."

I glanced over my shoulder at Hannah's wine venue and recalled Destiny running off. "I have to admit I've got my doubts about Destiny. She was infatuated with Quade, but he rebuffed her repeatedly."

My aunt said, "They were once an item."

"Really?" I hadn't picked up that vibe.

"Yes. When he first moved to town, they were locked at the hip. What a handsome pair they were. Equal in height. Gorgeous faces. Back then, Destiny held her head high. But he ended it."

"Do you know why?"

"At one of our readings, Destiny said he thought she would hold him back."

"Huh." Bailey frowned. "I had no idea she was your client. I don't believe I've ever seen her in the Cookbook Nook. Have you, Jenna?"

"A couple of times, but not for a reading."

My aunt whispered, "I give hers to her privately. She didn't want it to be public knowledge that she'd consulted me because her father —"

"He died," I said.

"He was not a fan of anything paranormal. He was a realist, much like your father, Jenna."

Dad could put a damper on mystical things for sure.

I sipped my wine. "You know, being dumped is a good motive for murder, especially given Destiny's sad history." I filled them in on what Hannah had told me about Destiny losing her mother and father and then her business partner. "Plus, the night Quade was killed, she saw him pursuing Naomi with a vengeance."

Gran said, "Jealousy is another powerful motive."

"She's quite strong," Bailey said. "And a wine tour guide knows her way around sharp tools."

I agreed. "On the other hand, she didn't have access to the communal workshop where Keller mistakenly left his tool kit."

Aunt Vera clucked her tongue. "You can't possibly think one of the artists in the competition is the killer. Are you a suspect?"

"Of course not."

"Flora and Faith are harmless," she went on. "Candy is a love, and Jaime supports every peaceful movement on the planet."

"And we know Keller didn't do it," Bailey chimed in.

"Wouldn't Destiny have killed Naomi instead of the man she loved?" Gran asked, eager for agreement.

"Good point," Bailey said. "I sure would have."

"You know —" I glanced over my shoulder to see if Sienna Brown was near; she wasn't. I turned back. "Sienna Brown and Quade argued the other night. She resides at the inn. She could have easily accessed his room as well as the communal room."

"What were they arguing about?" Bailey asked.

"I'm not sure. It happened more than once. Quade was staying at the inn. For free."

"Free?" my aunt echoed.

"Sienna enjoyed supporting artists. I imagine their beef had to do with his entitled behavior or his treatment of the staff."

Gran's eyes twinkled. "Vera and I are heading to the inn for the dessert and wine pairing. Do you want us to do some sleuthing? We could chat up Sienna."

"Gracie." My aunt clucked her disapproval.

"We'll simply ask a few questions," Gran went on, undeterred. "We'll see if something is afoot."

Aunt Vera swatted Gran's arm. "Listen to you."

Bailey said, "I see my mom waving at me. Back in a bit."

As she strolled away, Z.Z. yelled, "Vera!" She was walking between her boyfriend, Jake Chapman, and her son Egan. "I thought we'd missed hooking up with you."

"Jake and Z.Z. are joining us at the dessert and wine pairing," my aunt offered in explanation.

"Isn't everything wonderful?" Z.Z. gripped a fold of her op-art dress and swayed to and fro, clearly pleased. "Aren't you impressed?"

"Very." My aunt kissed her cheek. "Jake, Egan, are you enjoying yourselves?"

"It's quite a spectacle," Jake said. "Z.Z. has outdone herself." In his leather jacket and jeans — Jake never dressed up — he reminded me of Clint Eastwood in his sixties, craggy and wryly handsome.

"Egan?" my aunt repeated.

"Yes, ma'am," he mumbled. He was wearing a nice suit but it hung on his thin frame.

"How's life now that you've graduated college, Egan?" I asked. His mother not only served as mayor but also as one of the area's premier realtors, a job she took up two years ago to help pay for the extra college courses Egan had needed to get his degree.

"It's cool." His Adam's apple rose and fell.

Z.Z. beamed. "He's going to become an entrepreneur."

"Is that so?" My aunt smiled encouragingly. "Doing what?"

Egan rubbed his chin with the back of his hand. "I'm thinking about becoming an artists representative." With his shy demeanor, I couldn't see that being a good fit for him, but perhaps with grooming, he could grow into the career.

"Because the festival has inspired you?" I asked.

"Uh-huh. I love art. All kinds." His gaze darted evasively to the right. Did he hope he could escape this idle chatter and find people closer to his own age?

"Ready to go?" Aunt Vera asked Z.Z. "I'm looking forward to learning which wine goes with a strawberry tart."

"I'm starved," Z.Z. said.

"Hon," Jake said, "do you mind if I beg off? I'd like to go to the Pier for the shellfish tasting."

Z.Z. patted his arm. "Of course not. You're not going to that unless you go alone." She said to the group, "I'm allergic."

He bussed her cheek and bid us good night. Z.Z., my aunt, and Gran followed in his wake.

"Bye, sweetie. Have fun," Z.Z. said over her shoulder to her son.

Egan lingered.

"So, being an artists representative sounds interesting," I said. "Faith Fairchild used to be one. She could give you some pointers. How are you as a salesman?"

"I think I'll be pretty good."

"Your mother does well with real estate."

"Yeah. Mom says . . ." Egan hesitated, studying the tips of his fingers.

"What does she say?" I prompted.

"Truth?" He met my gaze and jutted a hip. "Mom's been driving me nuts the last few days. Always asking where I'm going and when I'll be home."

Okay, I hadn't been ready for that kind of honest share, although people often did this with me. My aunt said it was because I had an open face and came across as trustworthy. "It's because she cares."

"She's hovering. I'm feeling caged in."

"Have you told her?"

"And break her heart?"

"Your mother is one tough cookie," I confided. "She can take criticism. If she's crowding you, tell her you need some alone time." Bailey had had to do the same with her mother a few years ago. Reluctantly, Lola had given her the space she'd needed. Now, the two of them were fast friends.

"Actually, I took some alone time," Egan said. "The other night. And . . ." He scratched the back of his neck, stalling.

"Talk to me."

He winced. "I have to confess something."

The word *confess* caught me up. "Confess what?"

"I was sleeping on the beach the night of the murder. I couldn't stay at the house any longer. I slipped out the window."

"It must have been very cold and wet."

"Yeah, it was, but I didn't mind. I'm mentioning this to you because I know you like Keller, and I know you've helped people on the wrong side of the law." He guffawed. "That's not what I meant. You've helped innocent people prove themselves innocent. Anyway, I know Keller said he was on the beach painting, and well, I saw him."

"Really? That's wonderful." I touched his shoulder. "You can be his alibi."

"Yeah, uh, no." He inched backward. "Because if I say anything, I'll hurt my mother's feelings. She'll think I'm ungrateful for the roof over my head."

"She's not like that." I grabbed both his arms. "Egan, you have to talk to the police. A man's life is at stake."

He lowered his head. "Okay, I will."

As he shuffled away, hands plunged into the pockets of his oversized jacket, a feeling slithered up the back of my neck. Was he lying about seeing Keller? Why? To give himself an alibi? For —

No. Egan was no killer. He was simply a young man trying to figure out his future without his mother hovering over him every step of the way. Right?

CHAPTER 10

Feeling hopeful that Keller would be exonerated once Cinnamon heard Egan's account, I went to sleep with Tigger nestled on the bedspread by my feet and Rook curled on his dog bed next to the window.

In the middle of the night, Rhett tiptoed into the room. I'd learned early in our relationship that he kept odd hours. At first, when he'd owned Bait and Switch Sporting Supply Store on the Pier, I was shocked to find that he woke at three a.m. so he could catch fresh fish to sell to restaurants or to give early-morning deep sea fishing tours. Now that he owned Intime, he kept quite the opposite hours. He came in sometime between two and three a.m. and crashed for six to eight hours.

Rook yelped. Rhett shushed him.

I stirred and turned onto my side, one eye open. "Hey," I murmured.

"I didn't mean to wake you."

I patted the bed. "Come talk to me. Good night?"

"Terrific." He sat beside me. "Plenty of customers. Only a few snafus."

Rook padded to Rhett and settled onto his feet.

"No fires?" I said, a tinge of panic in my tone. Fire was the fear of any restaurant owner, but more so for Rhett, who'd lost his job as a chef at the Grotto after an arsonist burned the place down.

"None unless you count the shrimp flambéed with Pernod and garlic or the flambéed crêpes Suzette, all on the menu." He kissed my temple. "How was your night?"

I told him about Egan verifying Keller's alibi.

"That's great," he said. "It means you won't need to investigate." He swept a strand of hair off my face.

"By the way, the wedding planner left a message. She's found a few other locations that are available this summer, if we're interested in seeing them."

"Absolutely. How about the end of next week? After all this hoopla with the festival dies down."

"Perfect." I yawned. "Will you take Rook on a walk when you get up? There's only so much game of chase Tigger can play with him."

"Sure will." He kissed me on the lips. "Good night. Sleep tight."

By nine a.m. Bailey and I were moving at full speed in the shop, Bailey setting out paintbrushes and disposable aprons while I distributed paper plates. I was perspiring profusely and grateful I'd worn a short-sleeve sweater and capris. Bailey had dressed in an adorable paint-splatter print dress. Tigger sat on his cat condo studying us. I could imagine his inner thoughts, *Crazy ladies.*

"The kids are coming in less than a half hour," I said. "What were we thinking scheduling this so early?"

"We thought parents would appreciate having an early-morning event before the rest of the day got underway." She stood, arms akimbo, staring at the crafts table. "What's missing?"

My aunt swept into the shop in a magenta caftan, her turban under one arm. "Jenna, dear, could I have a word —"

"Not now, Aunt Vera. Sorry. We're behind."

"Yoo-hoo!" Katie warbled as she emerged from the breezeway pushing a food cart.

"Cookies are here! And lots of tubs of icing, all colors."

"Perfect," I said. "Set them in the middle of the table."

"Sure thing, but before I do," she said, "I have some news." Her eyes were glistening with joy. "Keller is officially exonerated of killing Quade!"

"Woo-hoo!" I shouted.

"Hurrah!" Bailey cheered.

"Z.Z.'s son Egan came forward," Katie went on. "He was sleeping on the beach, it turns out, but it was so cold and damp and the full moon so glaring that he barely slept a wink, and he saw my adorable husband painting."

"Great news." I did a mental jig, happy that Egan had followed through. Had he spoken to his mother, as well? If not, that was his next challenge.

"What about the theft of Quade's painting?" I asked.

"So far, the police are taking Keller's word that he didn't steal it. He's so relieved that I was hoping he'd feel inspired to paint, but he's not ready."

"He will be. Soon. Buck up." I clasped her shoulders. "I'm sorry to cut your celebration short, but let's get cracking for the cookie painting party."

"Right-o. Of course."

As Katie set the plate of cookies down, I *ooh*ed. "How cute. They're shaped like miniature palettes and crayons."

Katie's eyes gleamed with happiness, then her mouth turned down in a frown. "Hey, Vera. You promised me a reading."

My aunt had moved to the vintage table to prepare for tarot readings. She intended to offer one-card readings free to anyone who attended with a child. One-card readings went quickly. A client, or in this case a parent or guardian, would draw one card from the deck, and Aunt Vera would tell them something positive, no matter which card the person had chosen.

"Come. Be my first." Aunt Vera fanned the cards. "Pick one."

Katie skirted the food cart and selected a card.

"Which one did you pull?" I asked as I set a cookie on each of the paper plates.

"The High Priestess."

"Oh, good card," I said. "You're to listen to your intuition, and —"

"Jenna, dear," my aunt chided, her tone crisp. "I do the readings."

Uh-oh. Was she upset that I'd cut her off as she'd entered the shop? I tried not to worry about it. "Yes, ma'am. Have fun, Katie."

Within twenty minutes, parents, grandparents, and children started to arrive at the shop. The children made a beeline for the craft table. Bailey oversaw them as I pointed out the display table filled with cookie-themed cookbooks I'd set out for the adults, each artful yet fun. One of my favorites was *The Cookie Companion: A Decorator's Guide.* The author was a true artist and an incredible resource for color matching and more. Another was *The Complete Photo Guide to Cookie Decorating* with over five hundred full-color instructional photos. Soon, I was going to attempt a batch on my own with no help from Katie.

I spotted Naomi and her daughter Nina entering the shop trailing a woman with carrot-orange hair that matched her son's. Naomi was dressed in a sunny yellow frock, belted at the waist. Nina was wearing a pale pink dress and party shoes.

I crossed to them and said, "Welcome. What a nice surprise to see you." Bending at the waist, I braced my hands on my knees and addressed Nina. "Do you want to paint?"

"I can't."

"She means she doesn't know how to,"

Naomi said. "We're barely into crayons at this point."

"We have a crayon-shaped cookie, Nina," I said and held out a hand. "Want to see?"

Nina pressed her lips together. Naomi gave her a nudge. Guardedly, Nina put her hand in mine, and I guided her to the table.

Seating her beside another girl, I said, "Bailey, give Nina a hand. She's a beginner."

Bailey bent forward so she could meet Nina eye to eye. "I can help with that, young lady. I was a beginner once myself."

I turned back to Naomi. "How are you holding up?"

"Honestly? I haven't been able to sleep a wink. With Quade dead and Christopher out there. Lurking."

"You haven't contacted him?"

"No. I can't. I . . ." She toyed with the belt of her dress. "Do you think it's possible he killed Quade?"

"Why would you think that?"

"You said he was following me. Maybe he, like you, suspected Quade was Nina's father, and he got jealous, but he needn't have been because —" She jammed her fist against her mouth.

"Because Christopher *is* the father," I finished.

Naomi bobbed her head. "I'm afraid of what he'll do when he finds out. Will he try to take Nina away from me? Will he sue me in court? I can't afford an attorney."

The door to the shop opened and Cinnamon Pritchett entered with Detective Appleby, both in uniform. My aunt approached them, doing her best not to kiss her beloved while he was on duty. "Help you?" she asked.

Cinnamon said, "We've got this, Vera."

They weaved through the crowd of customers until they reached us. Appleby removed his hat. So did Cinnamon. She ignored me and faced Naomi.

"Ma'am, you may have heard that the artist named Quade was murdered."

"Yes, Jenna told me. It's so s-sad." Naomi's voice quavered.

"You were seen outside his room at the inn that night."

I stiffened. Had Cinnamon specifically come into the shop after Naomi? How had she known she was here, or had she lucked upon her?

"That's not true," Naomi said, her voice thin. "I wasn't there. I was home. With my daughter."

"Ma'am, we found a scrap of paper, what appears to be the remnant of a note, on the floor of the crime scene. The initial *N* is on it. Did you enter the deceased's cabana and leave a note?"

"No!" Naomi turned to me for help.

I said, "Chief —"

Cinnamon held up a hand. "Back away, Jenna. Ma'am, I'd like you to come with me to the precinct." She could be coldly officious when on duty. It was one of her worst traits.

Appleby, looking as stony as a statue, kept mum.

I gazed at my aunt, who was standing behind Cinnamon and Appleby, looking helplessly at me, hands splayed.

Beyond her, I caught a glimpse of movement outside the shop. Christopher George, in a dark blue sweater over jeans, was standing beside a Mercedes in the parking lot, staring in the direction of the shop. The driver's door was ajar. Had he steered the police in Naomi's direction? Had he put the scrap of paper with the initial *N* in the crime scene? He pompously grazed his shoulders with his fingertips, and then pushed up his sleeves.

Suddenly, I felt protective of Naomi. She was an innocent, doing her best to start over. Despite my conversation with Rhett about not needing to investigate, I knew at that moment that I would do whatever it took to help my new friend.

"My daughter," Naomi rasped.

"She may come with us," Cinnamon said. "We'll have one of our people tend to her while you and I chat."

Chat. Yeah. *Not.* Cinnamon would grill her. I hoped Naomi wasn't lying. Even if she weren't, how could she prove her alibi if she'd been home alone with merely a three-year-old to vouch for her?

Cinnamon and Appleby left with Naomi and Nina, and I went to the craft table, trying to quell my angst.

I drew up short when I glimpsed the boy with carrot-orange hair dueling with Tigger using a paintbrush dipped in red icing. Tigger's paws swiped left and right to fend off the attack.

The animated exchange made me think of the crime scene. Were there any defensive wounds on Quade's hand, or had he been too out of it to defend himself? Quade had texted Yardley that he hadn't felt well. The text had ended with the name *Naomi.* Had she drugged him to make certain he couldn't fight back and then killed him?

The cookie painting event was a success. We sold all of the cookbooks on the display table and a couple of children's aprons, to boot. After Bailey and I cleaned up the mess and I washed Tigger's feet within an inch of his fur, I dialed the precinct and asked for Cinnamon. She answered sweetly, which astonished me. Too often she sounded like she wanted to snap my head off.

I started tentatively. "Um, I was calling —"

"To find out if I'd released Naomi Genet."

"Yes."

"I did. It turned out the witness was not reliable."

"Who was the witness?" I asked, expecting her to say Christopher George.

"A waitress at the inn. As it turned out, Miss Genet wasn't the right height and she had the wrong hair. We did a lineup."

"A lineup!" I squawked. "You didn't tell Naomi you were bringing her to the station for that. You invited her for a chat. You persuaded her to accompany you under false pretenses."

"Cool your heels, Jenna. To our surprise, the witness showed up at the same time."

"Uh-huh." I grumbled loudly enough for her to hear. "What about the scrap of paper with the initial *N* on it?"

"It turned out it wasn't her handwriting." Cinnamon chuckled. "Jenna, relax. Miss

Genet is merrily on her way to Azure Park to take charge of the Art Institute display. Happy?"

"Ecstatic."

She chortled again.

"Since you're in such a jovial mood," I said, "would you answer one more question for me?"

"No."

"C'mon. After all, I did help you solve the last murder in Crystal Cove."

"Jenna . . ." Cinnamon took a sip of something. "I mean this with all the love in my heart, back off."

"But —"

"Keller is innocent. Exonerated."

"Yes, but I'm worried for Naomi. What if her husband thought Quade was the father of the child and —"

"Hold it. What husband? She didn't mention a husband."

Quickly, I filled her in about Naomi running away from Christopher Michael George and changing her name.

"I know that guy," Cinnamon said. "I've tuned in on one of his talks. He's here? In town?"

"Yup. I thought he might have been the one who'd witnessed Naomi outside Quade's cabana."

I could hear the clacking of a keyboard. She was typing something.

"He's staying at the Crystal Cove Inn," I added.

"Got it. I'll be in touch."

"Hold on!" I cried. "I want to ask another question. The wadded-up papers. What was on them?"

"For criminy sake."

"Please," I begged.

"A few sketches."

"By Quade?"

"By Naomi Genet. Of her daughter. Bye."

"Wait. Last one. Yardley Alks said Quade wasn't feeling well. Did you check her cell phone records to corroborate that?"

"Of course."

"Because she's the one who gave you the tip about the art in Keller's garage."

Cinnamon huffed, her exasperation clear. "Mrs. Alks was talking at great length to her husband, who happened to be in New York at the time. She is not a suspect. Since we're playing twenty questions, it's my turn. Have you gotten your investigator's license yet? Oh, no? Big shock." She let loose with a scornful laugh.

"You're hilarious."

"I'm not kidding."

Cinnamon and I had been friends for a

long time now; she tolerated when I overstepped, and I ignored when she dismissed me out of hand.

"I have a theory," I went on, seeing as she hadn't ended the call. "You said there were no defensive wounds on Quade's hands."

"No, I did not."

"But there weren't, were there?"

She grumbled.

"What if the killer drugged him and then stabbed him? Or" — I recalled smelling the scent of tar or cologne at the crime scene — "better yet, what if the killer poisoned him earlier, but it didn't work, so the killer returned and stabbed him? What poisons might smell like tar?"

"None, but . . ." Her voice trailed off. She was holding something back.

"But what?"

"We found arsenic in his system."

"That could explain why he'd texted Yardley about not feeling well."

"Yes."

"So my assumption could be correct. The killer might have laced something Quade ate or drank with the poison, and then left. When the killer came back, he or she expected Quade to be dead, only to discover he was still alive."

"Why did the killer come back?" she asked.

"Because —"

She hung up. She didn't want to hear any other theories.

Chapter 11

Bailey took a lunch break with me, and we strolled to Azure Park to check out Art in the Sunlight. The sun was shining. The salty aroma of the ocean hung in the air. Most people we passed were wearing shorts or short-sleeved tops.

On the way I brainstormed with her, telling her everything I'd mentioned to Cinnamon and then some. I needed fresh eyes on my thoughts.

"This Christopher George sounds like a creep," she said.

"He's definitely a force to be reckoned with."

As we rounded the bend and Azure Park came into view, I gasped. "Wow! It's amazing."

Last week the park had looked like it usually did, trees and greenery and an unadorned event stage. For the festival, the park had been transformed into a spectacle.

A massive arch of crisscrossed silver bars strung with colorful ribbons formed the entryway. A banner with the words *Art in the Sunlight, celebrating Crystal Cove's 5th Annual Art and Wine Festival* was slung from one side of the arch to the other.

As we strolled beyond the arch, the strains of rivaling music — kids songs to the west, rock and roll to the east — assaulted us.

"Whewie," Bailey said. "It's loud."

"It's lively, for sure."

Signs at the entry listed the names of the myriad sponsors of the décor, including restaurants like the Pelican Brief, Intime, and Mum's the Word. Crystal Cove Realty had subsidized the construction of booths. The Crystal Cove Inn as well as Nature's Retreat had funded the Kids Art Zone. And Recology of Crystal Cove, an eco-centric group, had paid for the reimagining of the event stage at the north end of the park, where most of the major announcements for the festival, other than those given at individual venues, would be broadcast. Booths rented by artists, crafters, food providers, vintners, and art-themed carney game sites stood along each side of the park, leaving the center free for visitors to convene at a variety of white weather-resistant tables.

On Monday night, Yardley had reminded

the competitors that the Art Institute booth would be located at the south end of the park.

As Bailey and I headed in that direction, I drank in the rest of the activities. A group of dancers in big cat-themed unitards at Kids Zone were jiving to the music "The Lion Sleeps Tonight." Children and adults were standing in a semicircle applauding in time to the music.

Across the way, a man on stilts and dressed like van Gogh, as Christopher George had described, was pacing in front of a twenty-foot-wide LED scoreboard-type screen painting *The Starry Night,* over and over as the image would appear and disappear. A crowd stood nearby, fascinated.

At the Paint Your Selfie booth, a young woman in a getup covered with cartoonish faces was putting out easels and paints. In front of the booth stood a pushcart and two chairs, one chair for the face-painting artist and the other for her subject. Children with adults stood in line. A few kids were examining the poster board filled with the artist's design ideas, which included cats, dogs, princesses, fairies, and superheroes.

Ding, ding, ding rang out as we passed a carney balloon game with paintbrush-shaped darts as the missiles. "We have a winner!" the man in charge yelled. A teenage blonde squealed with delight.

"Wow," Bailey said. "Look at that." She indicated the Sliver of Silver jewelry booth, where an artist was demonstrating how to hammer silver. *Wham* went the head of the mallet. "I'd be afraid I'd whack my thumb."

"Me, too." I'd tried a jewelry class a couple of years ago when I'd lived in San Francisco. I'd ended up with calluses and some ugly earrings.

At the Art Institute booth, a number of people had queued up to view the paintings mounted on easels. A temporary stage, named the South Stage, equipped with microphone and speakers had been constructed next to the booth, to be used at Sunday's finale celebration.

Naomi, who had donned a floppy sunhat adorned with a yellow bow to match her dress, was chatting with a frizzy-haired woman. She handed the woman a business card. I searched for Yardley but didn't see her. The seven finalist paintings were on easels in a semicircle, as they had been at the soiree, so a viewer could see all in one sweeping glance. I had to admit that Keller's *Humanity* was really good, but Quade's *Night Sky,* even though it wasn't as good as his first submission, was spectacular. The world had lost a talent. My heart snagged, remembering my last image of Quade, nude on the couch. Who had killed him? Why?

"Hi, Jenna. Hi, Bailey," Naomi said as the frizzy-haired woman moved on. "What are you doing here?"

"Taking a lunch break," I said.

"Try the fish tostadas at Holy Guacamole." She motioned to the right. "They're really good."

I drew near. "Hey, I spoke to Chief Pritchett. I'm so glad the witness made a mistake."

Naomi heaved a sigh. "Me, too."

"Where's Nina?"

"With a friend for the afternoon. I have to oversee this booth. Yardley was going to manage it, but a pressing issue persuaded her to return to the institute."

"I hope it's nothing serious," I said.

"No. Simply a matter that had to get settled."

Bailey said, "It's good to have friends to help out, isn't it?"

"You have no idea." Naomi adjusted her sunhat, which had listed a smidge.

"Oh, but I do," Bailey said. "If I hadn't hired Tina as a part-time nanny for Brianna, I'm not sure what I would have done."

"I should look for a part-time sitter," Naomi said, "but I do so much work out of my home, it seems senseless."

"By the way, Naomi," I said, "you have an amazing Etsy presence." I'd checked it out after she'd mentioned her stained-glass collection. In addition, she'd turned many of her artworks into prints, greeting cards, and tea towels. "I imagine maintaining it requires nonstop attention."

"Constant, but it's been fabulous for me. I'm thinking of adding mugs and such, but they're more costly to ship." She aimed a finger at me. "You should think about having an Etsy presence, Jenna. Your work is quite commercial."

"I don't have enough work to even consider it," I said. "And mine is nothing compared to yours. You have such flair." She used broad, impressionistic strokes and bold colors.

She blushed.

Bailey said, "Don't you need a sitter when you teach at the institute, Naomi?"

"I'm there two days a week. My friend sits Nina whenever I need her to. She's a homemaker and has a daughter the same age."

"How perfect." Bailey rolled her eyes at me. "My friends all work."

I knuckled her arm.

Naomi gestured to the art on the easels.

"Jenna, I meant it when I said your work is quite commercial. It's pleasing to the eye."

"But it doesn't compare to Quade's."

"Each is unique," she said judiciously.

Two more event goers entered the booth.

"We'll let you get back to chatting up the customers, Naomi," I said. "Bailey and I had better grab our lunches and return to the shop."

"Have fun."

As we exited the booth, Bailey said, "She's nice, isn't she?"

"Yes."

Bailey tilted her head. "But . . . ? You hesitated. What aren't you telling me?"

"I forgot to tell you earlier that she didn't cue in Cinnamon about running away from her husband."

"Maybe she wants to put the past behind her."

"Or she doesn't want Cinnamon to check into her past." I really wanted Naomi to be innocent, so why hadn't she come clean to the police?

We stopped at Holy Guacamole, waited in the eager line of customers, and ordered two tostadas in a cup, extra guacamole. It was scrumptious, with exactly the right amount of spice. While eating our lunch, we sauntered around the park, checking out all the booths. My favorite was the Potter's Wheel. The artist was selling whimsical animal sculptures as well as pen holders and business card holders. At Bailey's favorite, Art Fusion, which sold beautiful dichroic glass jewelry, she purchased a stunning pair of shimmering blue drop earrings.

"Hey, there's Keller," Bailey said as she was swapping out the new earrings with the ones she'd worn to work. "Pedaling his ice cream contraption. Want a scoop?"

"You bet."

We hurried to him and ordered two scoops of the day's special pecan caramel swirl in a cup. He climbed off the bicycle and started to prepare our order.

"How are you doing?" I asked

"Okay. Katie's worried about me, but she shouldn't be."

I narrowed my gaze.

"Okay, she should be," he admitted, "but I'll be fine. I'll paint again. Soon."

"Like the inside of my house?"

He offered one of his yuk-yuk laughs. "Yeah, that might inspire me. Next week soon enough?"

"Perfect."

As Bailey and I walked back to work, she said between bites of ice cream, "Tell me more about Yardley Alks."

"What do you want to know?"

"You said Quade texted her on the night of the murder. Why?"

"Because he wasn't feeling well."

"Got that. But why *her*? She's married. They weren't having an affair, were they?"

"No way. Yardley is a straight arrow. And I told you Cinnamon has ruled her out as a suspect because she was on a long-distance call with her husband. Not to mention she's quite petite. I can't imagine her having the strength to kill Quade."

"But if Quade was incapacitated, as you theorized to our chief of police, which she must have appreciated . . . *not.*" Bailey cocked her hip with attitude. "If Yardley drugged him, then she could have killed him."

I recalled Yardley and Quade on the last night of the workshop. Learning that *Morning* was missing had upset Yardley. Later, when she'd confronted him about hitting on Naomi and steered him to a private corner to chat, she'd been angry, too. Her eyes had blazed with fury. Had Bailey landed on something? Had Yardley and Quade had more than a teacher-student relationship? Had they been lovers? Would Yardley have killed him to bury that secret?

If Cinnamon's timeline for the murder

was off . . .

"Bailey, I want to speak with Yardley."

"Jenna," she said cautiously. "Cinnamon won't be happy."

"I need to clarify something. C'mon. Yardley phoned me when she discovered the body. *Me.* That puts me in the center of things. I'll tell Cinnamon anything I learn. Scout's honor."

Reluctantly, Bailey agreed.

I texted my aunt to say Bailey and I would be late getting back to the shop. She replied that all was calm. Gracie had arrived and the two of them could handle everything. But she added that she really did need to talk to me when I returned. Worry coursed through me. I promised I'd make the time.

As I pulled the VW into a parking space at the Art Institute, I caught sight of Yardley in a pastel blue pant suit, slightly hunched, scurrying to a car while glancing repeatedly over her shoulder, as if she didn't want to be seen leaving. I ducked down in my seat and ordered Bailey to hide as well.

"Why?" my pal rasped while obeying.

"Yardley is getting into her car. Something's not right."

When Yardley pulled out of the lot in a silver Prius, I shoved the Beetle into gear and followed at a reasonable distance.

"Where do you think she's going?" Bailey asked, easing higher in her seat.

"No idea, but she's acting cagey."

When Yardley pulled onto Poinsettia and parked in front of a narrow two-story building with a fumigation tent wadded in front, as if ready for pick up, I knew where we'd come. Quade's townhome. I told Bailey.

"The plot thickens," she said.

Yardley climbed out of the Prius and hurried up the slate path to the porch. Keys in hand, she slotted one into the front door and twisted. The door opened.

"Why does she have his key?" Bailey asked.

"That's what we're going to find out." I clambered out of the car and jogged to the porch. Bailey trailed me. "Yardley," I called.

She startled and wheeled around, hand shielding her eyes from the sun. "What are you doing here?"

"I'd like to ask you the same thing."

"I . . ." She peeked over her shoulder into the loft and back at me. "The police found a black book in Quade's items at the cabana."

"What kind of black book?"

"They aren't sure. It's in code. I came here" — Yardley licked her lips — "to find the key."

"Speaking of keys," Bailey said, folding her arms, "why do you have a key to his place? Were you and he having an affair?"

"What? Don't be absurd!" Yardley's cheeks flamed red. "How could you possibly think . . ." She breathed sharply through her nose. "If you must know, I'm his mother."

"His mother?" I gawped. "You're too young to be his mother."

"I was sixteen when I had him. Come inside. I'll explain everything."

Earnestness oozed out of her. I didn't think she was dangerous. Besides, Bailey and I were two against one. I liked our odds. I suggested Yardley enter first. We followed and she closed the door. The scent of oil paint and paint thinner permeated the place.

Yardley flipped on a light switch and the four-pronged chandelier overhead illuminated.

Bailey gasped. I understood her reaction. Numerous paintings hung on the two walls of the foyer. Some were traditional. Others were mixed media. All were exceptional.

"Man, he was talented," Bailey murmured.

Yardley agreed. "His talent is . . . *was* mind-boggling. He was preparing to have a solo exhibit later this year."

Beyond the foyer was the living room, outfitted with spartan furniture. Build-it-yourself Ikea items, if I were to guess. To the left of the foyer, a staircase led to a loft above the living room. I could see pedestals holding metal sculptures at the railing and paintings hanging on the walls. To the right of the foyer, a hall led to the rest of the modest unit.

Yardley said, "Like I was saying, I had Quade at sixteen. I've told the police this."

"You have?"

"Yes, when they questioned me. In high school, I made a huge mistake with a boy who turned out to be a scam artist. He ran so fast when I told him I was knocked up. My parents forced me to put the baby up for adoption, but I always wondered how he was faring, so I posted my profile on Ancestry dot com. Quade found me two years ago and reached out."

"Does your husband know about your relationship?" I asked.

"He does now. I told him the night . . ." Tears pressed at the corners of her eyes.

"The night Quade was killed," I finished.

"Mm-hm." She nodded numbly. "The last day of the workshop, Quade made me promise to reveal everything. He was adamant. Two years was long enough, he said."

That could explain their heated exchange after Quade had made a pass at Naomi as well as the lengthy chat Yardley had had with her husband on the night of the murder.

"Quade wanted to get to know his stepfather. He was growing impatient with me, and now, he never will." Yardley stowed her key ring in the pocket of her jacket. "Wayne and I couldn't have children. He was sterile. So, to protect his feelings, I kept my secret all these years. Not to mention, I didn't want him to be ashamed of me for being careless as a teen. Wayne can be quite proper. But Quade hated sneaking about behind Wayne's back."

Yardley ambled into the living room. Bailey and I followed. Quade had tried his hand at art deco, post-impressionism, cubism, and contemporary. He'd turned out a few abstract metal tabletop-sized sculptures as well.

"Do the police think the black book they found could help solve his murder?" I asked.

"They were cryptic." She orbited the room, opening drawers and sorting through the array of art books Quade had owned, an eclectic collection including Klee, de Kooning, Picasso, and more.

Not finding what she'd hoped to, she tramped down the narrow hall. We trailed her.

"Did Quade text you the night he died because you were his closest kin?" I asked.

"Yes. How I wished I'd rushed over."

As we entered the white-on-white kitchen, which was cluttered with unwashed dishes in the sink as well as on the stove top, I flashed on something that had bothered me at the crime scene. The clean dishes in the cabana. Sienna had washed them, but Yardley had remarked on them. Now I understood why. She'd known the kind of housekeeper her son was.

Yardley continued to search, opening drawers, pawing through papers. Coming up empty, she proceeded into the bedroom. It also consisted of build-it-yourself-style furniture. No bells and whistles, only Quade's unique art on the walls. Man, he'd been prolific.

Failing to discover the key in his bureau, closet, or adjoining bathroom, Yardley stood in the middle of the bedroom and ran a hand through her hair. "Upstairs is his workroom. He might have stowed it in his desk."

She climbed the stairs to the loft, her heels clicking on the hardwood steps. I padded after her.

Upon arriving at the top of the stairs, I paused to take in the room. Bailey flanked me and whistled softly.

The walls, like those in the foyer and living room, held a variety of darkly dramatic art that was rich with emotion. A desk with multiple drawers and a cabinet stood to the left. The area by the plate glass window was protected by a tarp splattered with paint and covered in metal shavings, clearly the spot designated as Quade's work space. The remainder of the room was filled with metal sculptures like the ones in the living room, each set on a pedestal.

"I didn't know Quade was a sculptor," I said.

"I didn't either until he invited me here. A year ago, he rented a warehouse so he could make these three-dimensional objects, but soon after, he gave it up. Too much overhead and too hard to market. Oh, how he'd loved including metal and other media in his work." Her face radiated pride. "He'd wanted to experience the full spectrum of art. He'd —" Yardley's voice caught. She didn't continue and moved to the desk to resume her search.

Bailey edged ahead of me to study the sculptures. "Wow," she said under her breath. "They're so unique. Each has a title. This one has a curious name, *Ancient Household.*"

"Hold on, what?" In college, because I'd pursued a major in marketing as well as design, I'd taken a number of art history classes. One, titled "Cubism to Modernism," focused on the talents of Pablo Picasso, Georges Braque, and more. One section included the study of David Smith, an abstract expressionist known for creating huge metal sculptures. But he'd made smaller works, too, and *Ancient Household,* which resembled a harp of sorts, happened to be one of them. Smith had trained as a painter and draftsman, but he'd worked as a welder during World War II.

I hurried to where Bailey was standing and examined the statue. If it wasn't a David Smith sculpture, I'd be surprised. It even had his unique signature using the Greek letters delta and sigma to signify the initials of his name.

"No way," I whispered. "I saw this in the Hirshhorn Museum in D.C. a couple of years ago. Did they sell it?" I turned to Yardley, who was digging through one of the desk drawers. "Was Quade wealthy?"

"No," she said over her shoulder. "Like I said, even the warehouse was too much overhead. He sold a few paintings, and the town paid him handsomely for his murals, but he was by no means well-off. That's why he was planning his own exhibit."

"You know, Yardley, I don't know much about him. There were so many rumors about his past, including one about being the child of a drug lord who'd sent him to Crystal Cove to hide. Was he?"

Yardley stopped her search. "That's a good one. No, his adoptive family are farmers in upstate California, though he was at odds with them because he was an artist and his father had wanted him to go into the family business." She clasped a hand to her chest. "The police have reached out to them."

Intrigued by Quade's collection, I checked out another of the small sculptures that reminded me of the wiry inner workings of a television set with the basic name *Title Unknown.* Like David Smith's comparative work from the 1940s, it was made of steel. Beyond that I found a piece that reminded me of a stick figure man doing a balancing act. *Australia,* it said on the plaque, as I'd expected.

Standing in one spot, I spun in a circle. All of the sculptures in the room, at least a dozen, were David Smith's work. Where had

Quade gotten them?

"Jenna, *psst.*" Bailey beckoned me. She was on the tarp studying some kind of paper on the floor.

I crouched down. "What are you looking at?" I whispered.

"Photographs."

"Of . . ."

"All of these statues. But in other locations. Isn't this *Ancient Household*?"

"Yes. At the Hirshhorn, like I said. I recognize the room it was displayed in."

"Did he steal them?"

I reflected on the sculptures again as a disturbing theory formed in my mind. "What if Quade had rented the warehouse so he could copy Smith's works? Maybe he'd done so because he'd been a devotee or, like Yardley said, he'd wanted to experience the full spectrum of art. On the other hand, why add Smith's unique initials?"

I crossed the loft to where Yardley was searching. She'd emptied out the drawers, setting stacks of items on the desk, including notepads, yellow Post-its, scribbled notes, and miniature sketches. "Any luck?" I asked.

"No."

"May I help?" I gestured to the pile on the right.

"I've sorted through those."

"Perhaps you missed something."

"Be my guest."

I started skimming the pile, looking for some key or code list. "Yardley." I hesitated. How could I broach the subject? "Was Quade a fan of David Smith's work?"

"Who's he?"

"An artist who made metal sculptures. He was very popular mid-twentieth century."

"I'm sorry, but I've never learned about sculptures. I was strictly a student of oils and acrylics."

As I explained the artist's popularity, I landed upon a pink-colored receipt for *Smith statue, value $50,000.* The receipt was made out to a well-known billionaire in the Bay Area who had been in the news a month ago, having donated a wing to a museum. I spotted the edge of another pink receipt and pulled it free. It was for an additional sale to a wealthy dowager who happened to be friends with my aunt.

"Jenna, you're gaping." Bailey drew alongside me. "What did you find?"

"The key?" Yardley exclaimed, grabbing the receipts from me.

"No, wait." I tried to take them back, but she kept hold.

"What are these?" she demanded.

"I'm afraid I have bad news. I think Quade was forging David Smith's work and selling the pieces to unwitting victims." I gestured to the room. "I believe these are all forgeries."

"No." Yardley wagged her head. "No, no, no. He wouldn't. He couldn't. He wasn't like him."

"Like who?" I asked.

"Like his father. His birth father. A scam artist who's been in and out of prison for fraud." She started to sob. "Please tell me it's not true. Please —"

She clutched her chest and fainted.

Chapter 12

The EMTs, with Bucky Winston in charge, arrived within minutes. Not long after, they transported Yardley to Mercy Urgent Care. I drove Bailey back to work, and then I sped to the medical center. The emergency area was buzzing with activity. Many people had imbibed too much wine at the festival. A few had suffered minor scrapes or bruises. Yardley, given her condition, was whisked into a room for observation.

Her heart hadn't failed her, but she had suffered an anxiety attack. A half hour later, she was transferred to a private room, gently sedated.

Informing the head nurse that her husband was out of town and I was a friend, I asked if I could accompany her in the room. The woman granted me access. I was sitting in the chair by the bed, checking messages on my cell phone, when Cinnamon entered.

"Well, well, you're at the center of it yet again, Jenna," she chided. "Bucky touched base with me. So, why, pray tell, were you with Yardley at Quade's townhouse when this all went down?"

I had prepared a harmless fib. "Because I'd gone to the Art Institute to chat with Yardley about the poster competition, but right as I arrived —"

"With Bailey Bird Martinez," she stated.

"Yes, with Bailey. We'd gone to Azure Park to have lunch and stopped by the Art Institute booth, and while there, it dawned on me that since Quade's original poster competition art was recovered from Keller's garage, perhaps that should be the official work under consideration and not his second submission. Yardley would have needed to make that determination." My mouth went dry. I was not a good liar, but the answer did sound reasonable. And I didn't want to mention my errant theory that Yardley and Quade had been lovers. "Anyway, Bailey and I went to the institute, and as we arrived, Yardley was ducking out. Believing her demeanor to be suspicious, Bailey and I followed her and discovered Yardley had a key to Quade's place."

I filled her in on Yardley's reveal about being Quade's mother, which she'd claimed to have told Cinnamon. Then I told her about Yardley hoping to find the key to crack the code in Quade's black book, and while we were there, we discovered that Quade had forged many of David Smith's lesser-known works.

"He forged them? You're sure."

"Almost positive. There are some bills of sale. Needless to say, Yardley was quite shocked. He'd told her they were his works. On the way here, I was questioning whether the forgeries might have been the reason he was killed."

Cinnamon frowned. "Quade's desire to keep his forgeries a secret would have given *him* motive to kill someone, not the other way around."

"Yes, but what if another artist wanted to take over his business? It could be lucrative. Ruling out Keller, of course," I rushed to add. "I texted him. He had no idea Quade made statues."

Yardley stirred but didn't wake.

Cinnamon glanced at her and back at me.

"I was wondering . . ." I began.

"I hate when you do that," Cinnamon ribbed.

I twitched my nose with displeasure.

"I was kidding. I do like the way your

mind works." She rotated her hand. "Go on."

"How did Quade get people to believe him? Unsuspecting wishful thinkers?" I raised my shoulders and let them drop. "How do scam artists pick their marks? You know better than I. FYI, Yardley said Quade's birth father is a scam artist and he's in and out of prison."

She arched an eyebrow.

"On another note," I continued, "have you touched base with Christopher George?"

"As a matter of fact, I have. He didn't know Quade."

"Easy to say, harder to prove," I countered. "He'd hired detectives to look for Naomi."

"He told me they didn't find her but he did, because he'd recognized her art on this year's festival poster."

"What if that was a lie?" I asked. "What if his goons located her before now? What if Christopher George has been in town longer than he claims? What if he saw Quade hitting on Naomi earlier than this week and decided to have a chat with him to set ground rules, and things got out of hand?"

Cinnamon pursed her lips. "Except there wasn't a struggle."

"Which leads you to believe Quade knew his killer?"

"Or the killer, as you theorized, laced something Quade ate or drank with arsenic, eliminating the possibility of a fight." She rose to her feet.

"Do you still suspect Naomi?"

Cinnamon turned to leave without responding.

"Before you go," I said, "may I ask what was in Quade's black book?"

"We don't know. Discovering a key would be useful." She turned her gaze to Yardley. "If only she'd been successful."

As I entered the Cookbook Nook, Keller swooped by me, leaving Katie, looking woeful dressed in her chef's coat, toque in hand, sitting at the vintage table.

"Sorry, Jenna, in a hurry," Keller said. "I've got to help Mom at Taste of Heaven. There's been a snafu. So long, Katie!" He waved goodbye as he walk-jogged out the door.

I hurried to my friend. "What's wrong?" I perched on the chair opposite her. Tigger sprinted to me and circled my ankles, mewing. I lifted him and nuzzled his nose, then set him back on the floor. He scampered away.

"Keller." Katie heaved a sigh. "He's still neglecting his art."

"So you told me this morning."

"I thought he'd take my gentle nudging, cave in, and go home and paint."

"Instead, he went to sell ice cream," I said. "That's his job."

"Yes, but afterward, he could have gone home. He didn't. He took a walk."

"Walking is good for clearing one's head. And there's plenty of art in town that might inspire him."

My friend puffed her cheeks and then released the air she'd gathered. "He went walking in the woods. To practice bird calls."

"Oka-ay." I dragged out the word. I couldn't see anything negative about taking a walk in the forest and communing with nature.

"He doesn't know any bird calls!" she cried. "He was stalling."

"Hey, pal," I said in a reassuring tone. I clasped her hand. "Give him time to find his equilibrium. He was recently a suspect in an art theft as well as a murder. Let's be glad that he was seen at the beach and the police bought the theory that Quade put his own piece of art in your garage as a prank."

She rose to her feet. "You're right. You're always right."

"I am not always right. Merely this time." I rose to a stand and gave her a hug. "I've got a great idea. Go to the kitchen and make something super chocolaty and bring me back a piece."

She saluted half-heartedly and shambled down the breezeway, shoulders hunched.

Bailey finished with a customer and skirted the sales counter, cutting me off before I could enter the storage room to stow my purse. "How's Yardley?"

"She woke up and is under observation. I texted Naomi and she promised she'd see to her when her stint was done at the Art Institute booth. She said she'd contact Yardley's husband, too. By the way, Cinnamon showed up to ask me a few questions."

"Uh-oh."

"Get this." I planted a fist on my hip sassily. "She didn't like hearing that we'd been at Quade's place."

"No way," Bailey clowned.

"Way!"

"Doesn't she know we're doing all we can to help her?"

"Oh, she knows," I said with attitude.

We shared a smirk.

"Is my aunt here?"

"She went to the bank. She'll be back shortly. And Gran had to take one of her granddaughters to Azure Park for a school art project." Before returning to the sales counter to ring up our next customer, Bailey added, "Put your purse away and then those two might need your help."

Two elderly women were showing each other pairs of salt and pepper shakers. One held giraffes necking. The other was partial to the cat and fishbowl set. Both sets were on consignment from local artists.

I slipped into the storage room, tucked my purse into the desk, and came right out. As I headed for the customers, Pepper Pritchett steered a mini wooden pushcart with a purple-striped awning into the shop.

"Ladies, step right up!" she cried like a circus barker. "Anyone in the mood for a beautiful necklace?"

My customers abandoned the salt and pepper shakers and made a beeline to Pepper.

I stopped in my tracks and grinned. "What's going on, Pepper? You're not getting enough foot traffic at Beaders? Now you have to hawk your wares in my shop?"

"Ha-ha." She slipped a hand under the exquisite sapphire-colored handblown glass necklace she was wearing. "I'm selling these for my friend, who happens to be an Etsy marvel. She couldn't attend the festival. She has a sick child." Like a display model, she flourished a hand in front of the pushcart vendor's logo. "Each pendant from Purple Unicorn Crafts is scrolled with silver. Take a peek."

Moving closer to investigate, I noticed the top of the pushcart was divided into a variety of labeled and colored slots, each holding a different-shaped necklace. The elven forest slot was painted green to match the color of the oblong pendant. The steampunk's slot was black to match its bell-shaped necklace.

I lifted one of the aqua blue mermaid's tears pendants and *ooh*ed. "The shapes are quite pretty."

"Each pendant is filled with magic," Pepper confided, pronouncing the word *magic* with an aura of mystery. "The pink are filled with crystal potions to boost confidence, the red to help with self-esteem. Some hold potions to invite love or wealth. They're marked accordingly. I've sold quite a few. Hannah bought one. Flora and Faith, too. The young are loving them."

I didn't regard the Fairchild twins as young, but I didn't quibble.

My aunt traipsed into the shop. "Pepper, what have you got there?"

"Magic," I said with Pepper's breathy intonation.

"Pfft." My aunt made a dismissive gesture.

Pepper scowled. "Oh, sure, Vera, *you* can tell people's fortunes, but magic can't be bottled?"

"Magic isn't in the potion, dear." Aunt Vera placed a hand on her chest. "It's in the heart. One must believe."

"True," one of the elderly customers murmured.

Gran scurried into the shop. "So true, Pepper." My aunt was right. Gran did have elephant ears. "One must believe." She whisked past me. "Sorry I'm late, Jenna. Vera, did you tell her?"

"Tell me what?" My pulse kicked into high gear as I remembered my aunt had wanted to talk to me earlier. Oh, no. Was she sick?

"I get to tell my news first!" Pepper announced. "After all, it's the main reason I stopped in. I think Cinnamon might be pregnant again!"

I blinked. "I just saw her at Mercy Urgent Care. She didn't mention a thing."

"What were you doing there?" Gran asked. "Are you all right?"

"Yardley Alks had a fainting incident. She's fine." I refocused on Pepper. "Are you guessing about your daughter's condition?"

"She was glowing this morning when we

met for coffee."

"Glowing, schmo-ing," my aunt said. "I glow after exercise. Don't spread rumors."

Pepper huffed. "Fine. But I'll bet I'm right."

Cinnamon would have told me, wouldn't she, given our conversation about getting pregnant at the soiree the other night?

One of the customers bought a love potion necklace for her daughter, and Bailey bought a self-reliance one for Tina. Then Pepper, satisfied with her sales, left the shop, and the customers returned to view the salt and pepper shakers.

Before I went to them, I needed answers. "Gran. Aunt Vera." I gathered them into a huddle. "What is going on?"

"What I wanted to tell you earlier, dear," Aunt Vera said, "was that we didn't learn anything from Sienna last night."

"But" — Gran cut in — "on my way to work, I saw her starting to enter a doctor's office. An ob-gyn's office. But she released the handle and went immediately next door to the pharmacy. I phoned your aunt and looped her in."

"Now, Gracie," Aunt Vera said, "be honest. You aren't certain it was an ob-gyn's office. You said you were standing quite a distance away and your eyesight —"

"My eyesight is fine. I was wearing my glasses."

"But Sienna is too old to have children," my aunt argued.

"She's forty-two," Gran countered. "That's not too old."

"Do you think she's pregnant?" I asked.

"No." Aunt Vera shook her head.

"Plenty of women get pregnant in their forties nowadays," Gran said.

"Not someone single and as levelheaded as Sienna. Besides, a woman does not need to be pregnant to go into an ob-gyn's office."

Gran sniffed and turned to me. "Have you noticed that Sienna has been putting on weight?"

"Gracie, please," my aunt said sharply. "Don't rumormonger like the Fairchild sisters."

"Vera, you said it yourself last night. She was wearing that duster coat to cover the fact she was a tad plump. Sienna has always prided herself on her trim figure."

"And that's it?" I asked. "That's the news you were going to tell me?"

"Gracie thought it might be worth the telling."

I grinned. "Got it. I'll put it in my hopper."

"Add one more thing for your hopper." Gran poked my arm. "While I was with my granddaughter at the Paint Your Selfie booth at Azure Park . . ." She wriggled with delight. "By the way, what an adorable idea. Each of the children paint their faces on canvases. Picasso was never so inspired. Anyway . . ." She frowned. "Where was I?"

"My hopper," I said.

"Right. There I was, idly spending an hour with my granddaughter, when I spied that man with the mustache once again lurking. By the Art Institute booth."

I stiffened. "Christopher George?"

"Mm-hm. Watching Naomi circumspectly. He gave me the creeps, but he didn't do a thing. After a long moment, he turned heel and left."

My aunt prodded Gran. "See to those customers, Gracie." To me she said, "Jenna, wipe that concerned look off your face and relax your forehead. Naomi is —"

"This look is because you said you needed to speak to me and —"

"Oh, dear, you thought I had some personal news to convey?" She kissed my cheek. "I'm as healthy as an ox. Never you fret." She rubbed her phoenix amulet. "I'll live to one hundred."

She knew I did worry, having lost my

mother to cancer.

Leaving her to take over the register and Gran to handle the sale of salt shakers, I carried a few copies of *Fire & Wine: 75 Smoke-Infused Recipes from the Grill with Perfect Wine Pairings* to the display table. Summer was coming up and this book would entice men and women shoppers alike. I couldn't wait to try the maple chipotle cedar-grilled salmon. One reviewer had enjoyed the cookbook so much she'd begged the author to write another one with two hundred and ninety additional recipes to make a full year of deliciousness.

"What's going through your mind?" Bailey asked, standing a copy of the cookbook on the table, pages spread open.

"I suggested Cinnamon question Christopher George again."

"Funny you should mention him. I've been wondering whether he might have made contact with Quade, separate from his connection with Naomi. Perhaps he introduced himself as an art collector purely wanting to chat with an up-and-coming artist, but upon discovering a virtual gold mine in forgeries, he decided to horn in on Quade's operation."

"Wow, that had not crossed my mind."

CHAPTER 13

Rhett had taken the night off so the two of us could enjoy Watercolors and Wine on the Pier, an event that would feature art exhibits and demonstration tents, *plein air* painting, and lots of wine venues. Because the air was cool, I'd dressed in a warm navy blue sweater and jeans, and though I *preferred* to wear sandals whenever I could, my toes couldn't handle the chill, so I'd donned my favorite tennis shoes. They didn't match my cross-body purse, but I wasn't a fashion horse. I didn't care.

With my hand looped around the crook of Rhett's elbow, we sauntered beneath the arch of pastel balloons separating the parking lot from the Pier and instantly started admiring the variety of ocean-themed watercolors displayed along the boardwalk. Most of the vendor sites were protected by blue-striped awnings; a few were not. Down the center of the boardwalk stood an array of café-style tables and chairs. Many were filled with patrons, but there were a smattering of free seats.

At the Baldini Vineyards site, Rhett bought a hearty zinfandel for himself and a pinot noir for me, each poured into a memento wineglass, and then the two of us continued to walk and enjoy the art. We would sit when we purchased an appetizer-style dinner.

At one artist's display, Rhett whispered in my ear, "Your work is eons better than his."

"I don't do watercolors. I'm an acrylics and oils girl."

"Even so."

"With watercolors, unlike acrylics and oils, you can't cover up your mistakes. What he does is harder, in my humble opinion."

"Okay, don't accept my compliment," he teased.

"Keep them coming, pal. I love them."

We walked farther and stopped outside a demo tent to observe two high school–aged kids taking a lesson on how to create a unique effect using salt on top of watercolors. It glistened.

"There are so many techniques," Rhett whispered.

"That's what makes art so special. Like books, movies, and music, art features a variety of genres and styles."

He kissed my cheek. "Hey, there's Jake and Z.Z. exiting Mum's the Word. Let's say hello."

Mum's was a very popular diner. Its meat loaf was renowned, and their grilled cheese choices delicious.

We strolled to them and commented on the lovely evening. Z.Z. was as bundled up as I was. Jake, on the other hand, was in a button-down shirt, sleeves rolled up. Having spent most of his early years living hand to mouth and sleeping on the sand, he had become inured to cooler temperatures.

"Did you partake of the Make Your Own Art pizza?" Rhett asked, pointing to the sign in Mum's window.

"We did," Jake said. "I made pepperoni on pepperoni. It made quite a statement."

Z.Z. elbowed him. We all laughed.

"How do you think the festival is going?" I asked.

Z.Z. beamed. "Better than I expected. Other than, you know . . ."

"Quade," I murmured.

Sadness and concern filled her gaze. "Another murder. It's horrific."

"Is Chief Pritchett close to finding the killer?" Jake asked.

"You know Cinnamon," Z.Z. said. "She

keeps her discoveries close to the vest."

I didn't offer my thoughts on who'd done it. "At least Keller is in the clear, thanks to your son, Z.Z."

"Egan." She sighed. "I had no idea he was feeling pent up enough to sleep on the beach. We've chatted, but we have more to talk about, I'm sure. Motherhood isn't easy. Especially being a single mother."

I thought of Naomi, a single mother struggling to keep her daughter as well as her own secret identity safe. Was she at risk? Would Christopher George harm her or haul her into court?

"Egan's here somewhere." Z.Z. pivoted. "There he —" She stopped short.

I peered in the same direction she was staring and saw Egan at the far end of the pier accepting a paper bag from a man in a raggedy shirt and torn jeans, a backpack slung over one arm. In return, Egan gave the man money. I stroked Rhett's arm and hitched my chin toward Egan. I could tell by Rhett's frown that he had seen the shady exchange and was as concerned as I was. I turned back to Z.Z., but she and Jake had slipped away.

"I hope he's not disappointing his mother," Rhett said.

"I think her abrupt departure says it all."

"Jenna!" a woman yelled.

I turned to see Destiny, in her safari-style wine tour garb, leading a group of two elderly couples along the boardwalk.

"Want to join us?" Her polished wine tour guide voice was filled with confidence. "We're chatting up all the small-batch wineries on the Pier." She winked. "I happen to know many of them well, so they're letting us in on their secrets."

"What do you think, Rhett?" I asked. "Shall we?"

He whispered in my ear, "Can we leave whenever we want?"

I chuckled, then said to Destiny, "Sure, we'll tag along for a bit. Did my wedding planner contact you?"

"No."

"She will."

I looped my hand around Rhett's elbow and we mingled with the group.

"In California, wine styles are as diverse as terroir," Destiny said, continuing whatever spiel she'd been uttering before inviting us to the party. "Ranging from delicious sparkling wines to world-class pinot noirs to inky Syrahs and intense cabs. At Vast Horizons" — she gestured to a vintner's setup, protected by a blue-striped awning — "which is one of my favorite small-batch wineries, they do everything biodynamically."

She greeted the bearded server, who was handsome enough to make the "50 Most Handsome Men" list in *People* magazine.

The server grinned. "Nice necklace, Des."

Destiny caressed the rose-colored hand-blown glass pendant. "You like it? I bought it from the woman who runs Beaders of Paradise. It's filled with a love potion. Want me to get your girlfriend one?"

"Don't have a girlfriend."

"Really?" she flirted, batting her eyelashes.

"I have three," he said.

"You're a tease." Destiny giggled.

If only she'd had this kind of confidence with Quade the other night, I mused.

"All right, I'll get you three, *if* you'll offer a healthy pour of your chard to each of my friends." She said over her shoulder, "This chardonnay is the best in all of California, in my humble opinion."

The server filled Rhett's and my memento glasses and four more wineglasses nearly to the brim.

Destiny lifted ours and handed them to Rhett and me. "He's the actual vintner," she whispered. "We're old friends." To the others she said, "Pony up to the bar."

The couples did as told and started chatting with the server.

I took a sip of the wine. "Yum. Oaky, with notes of nuts and melons."

"What do you think, Rhett?" Destiny asked.

He tasted it. "It'd go well with crispy-skinned salmon."

"*Mmm,* sounds delish. I love a man who can pair wines with food."

Rhett rolled his eyes.

"Now, Jenna, why will your wedding planner be calling me?"

"Our wedding venue canceled. The fire in Napa . . ." I paused. "It's a long story. We'd still like to get married —"

"In this century," Rhett joshed.

I elbowed him. "This year. We were thinking a vineyard might be nice."

"Quade and I —" Destiny hesitated. Her eyes moistened.

I said gently, "I know you two dated. My aunt told me."

"We didn't merely date. We'd gotten to the point where we were talking about a vineyard wedding. We both agreed that it would be one of the most romantic things ever. Picture a beautiful white arch and the aroma of grapes maturing on the vine." Destiny painted the image in the air. "I'll be on the lookout for you. By the way, I heard the police think your friend Naomi Genet might be the killer. Why would they think that? Did they find some piece of evidence linking her to the crime?"

"She's not a suspect," I said, not responding to the question about the evidence. "They've released her. They don't know who did it."

"But my fiancée is trying to beat them to the answer," Rhett quipped.

"I am not." I swatted his arm.

"You have in the past," Destiny said. "You're getting quite the reputation. Do you have any clues?"

I flashed on the forgeries and Christopher George's interaction with Quade, and the black book filled with codes, but said, "None." It wasn't a lie. I had none that would jell.

Destiny said, "If I hear anything, I'll be sure to contact you."

"Contact the police," I said. "They'll solve this."

After the next small-batch stop, Rhett said, "I'm starved."

I begged off continuing with Destiny and her group. She totally understood but made us promise that the two of us would take one of her all-day wine tasting excursions soon.

Then we moseyed to a vendor that was selling gourmet crackers, a selection of cheeses, and a flute of crudités with spicy chipotle dipping sauce, and purchased enough for a light dinner.

"Will this be enough for you?" Rhett asked after he set his food and wine on a café table and pulled out my chair.

I sat. "Yes. Ample. My appetite isn't very big tonight, though this mini spread looks amazing." I couldn't wait to try the dipping sauce.

"Are you worried about something?" He took a sip of wine.

"Other than the fact that another murder occurred in our fair town? And Naomi's husband is stalking her? And Yardley had a panic attack? And Quade was a forger? And it's possible Cinnamon is pregnant again?"

Rhett clasped my free hand. "Is that what you're edgy about? Cinnamon?"

"No. Sort of. If she is and she didn't tell me —"

"Everyone's allowed a secret here and there."

"Like Sienna?"

Rhett released my hand and paired a wedge of brie cheese with a cracker. "What secret might she be hiding?"

I told him about Gran's revelation.

"Isn't Sienna in her forties?" He slipped the appetizer into his mouth.

"Honestly? As if a woman in her forties is over the hill? Women *do* get pregnant later in life."

Rhett swallowed and battled a smirky grin. "I apologize. I'm a dinosaur. So what secret might she be hiding? You know she was first on the scene at the cabana, so that's old news."

That pulled me up short. Because of Yardley's call to me, I'd put her at the crime scene first, but Sienna admitted that she'd gone into the cabana before then and, believing Quade to be asleep, washed the dishes. Had she made up that excuse on the spot? Would a murderer wash dishes? For all I knew, Quade could have washed the dishes himself, except his townhome made it clear that he didn't do dishes. Apparently it was beneath him. I flashed on the impassioned private conversation Quade had had with Sienna at the workshop as well as the one at the opening night event. Had their set-tos been about her being pregnant?

Rhett twirled a finger in front of my face. "What's cycling through that overly active brain of yours?"

"I was wondering if Quade got Sienna pregnant and she killed him to . . ." I shook my head. "No, that doesn't make sense. She wouldn't kill the father of her baby, unless —"

"Unless he'd forced himself on her."

"Right, but stabbing . . ." I shuddered. "It isn't usually a woman's MO."

"She was certainly strong enough." Rhett swirled the wine in his glass. "I saw her riding her horse in the forest the other day when I was walking Rook, and something startled the horse. The brute reared up, but she controlled it. No problem."

"If Quade was poisoned first, then strength might not have been required to kill him." I dipped a stalk of celery in the sauce and bit into it, relishing the combination of flavors.

"What other motive might Sienna have had?" Rhett asked.

"What if Quade made promises to her that he refused to keep, like marrying her and supporting the baby?"

"Sienna has plenty of money." Rhett leaned back in his chair, one hand holding the base of his wineglass.

"True. According to my aunt, Sienna has an interesting history. Her father was in the navy and the family relocated a lot. You'd think a navy brat would hate to travel," I went on, "but apparently Sienna loved it so much that in college she pursued a degree in hospitality with dreams of running a European villa."

"A villa?"

"Yep. But when her mother got sick, she settled in Crystal Cove to be with her during her final days. When her mother died, that was when she learned that her maternal grandmother had been an heiress" — I raised a finger — "a fact her mother had kept from her, to keep her normal." I leaned forward, folding my arms on the table. "Sienna inherited everything and with her newfound wealth bought the inn."

"Stuff of legends." Rhett raised his wineglass in a toast.

"Funny how vague Quade's history was, but I'd figured that was by design." I took another bite of celery. "That he'd made it up to give himself a mystical allure. When I found out that he was the son of a scam artist and Yardley —"

"Wait, what? You've been holding out on me."

"You've been working late hours." I filled him in about Yardley being Quade's birth mother.

Talking of Yardley made me once again think about the dishes in the sink. Did Sienna wash them for all negligent guests?

That was way beyond the call of duty for an establishment owner, in my book. Could one of the staff disprove her cover story? I said, "I wonder if Cinnamon questioned the employees at the inn."

"I'm sure she has. As you said to Jake, if she is one thing, she's thorough." Rhett and Cinnamon had been involved years ago. When she'd investigated the arson at the Grotto, that had put a damper on things. She'd suspected Rhett. When he was proven innocent, they'd become friends again, but by then, I was in the picture.

"True. But what if Sienna isn't on Cinnamon's radar because she can't come up with a motive for her?"

My cell phone buzzed against my hip. I pulled it from my purse and scanned the readout. My aunt was texting to ask if I'd checked in on Yardley. I hadn't and felt guilty. I apologized to Rhett and dialed Yardley's number. She answered, sounding tired but clearheaded.

"I'm home. Naomi left."

"You shouldn't be alone."

"I'm fine. Really. No more panic attacks. No more sobbing mess. I'm facing reality, all blinders off. Don't worry. My husband will be catching a plane tomorrow. He hates to leave a conference early, but for me, anything." She chuckled. "He says I'm a drama queen."

"He doesn't."

"He means it in an endearing way. Thanks for calling, but" — she yawned — "I'm going to go to sleep now."

"I'll stop by in the morning."

"That would be lovely."

I ended the call and gazed at Rhett. "I need to touch base with Cinnamon."

"Why?"

"Because of something Yardley said. She was a sobbing mess at the crime scene."

"So?"

"Sienna was as cool as a cucumber."

"Keeping one's cool under pressure" — Rhett jabbed the table with a fingertip — "doesn't make one a killer. Sienna runs a large business, after all. There must be plenty of fires to put out."

"Even so . . ." I dialed the precinct. Cinnamon was not in. As I rang her cell phone, I mulled over what I was going to say. "Hey, it's me, Jenna. I know you don't appreciate my two cents, but if Sienna Brown isn't on your radar, she should be. Gracie Goldsmith believes she saw Sienna going into a doctor's office and —"

I stabbed End without leaving a message

and revisited my earlier thought. Would Sienna have killed the father of her child?

Chapter 14

Tigger and Rook were all over us the moment we arrived home. You would have thought we hadn't seen them in months. It took an hour to calm them down before we were able to climb into bed. As I was falling asleep, I thought how lucky I was to have Rhett sharing the same house with me now. We would say *I do* someplace in a matter of months. If only I knew what that someplace would be. *Soon,* I told myself as I drifted off. *Soon.*

I awoke before sunrise. Something had startled me. And then I realized it was Rook shoving his face into mine. His breath was raunchy enough to wilt the staunchest of roses. "Got to go?" I whispered. He snorted. I peeked over my shoulder. Rhett was sound asleep. "Okay, boy, follow me."

I tiptoed out of the room to the kitchen and opened the door. "Have fun." He tore to the far corner of the yard, where he did his business and hurtled back to me, ready for a frolic and food. I was tired, but I couldn't say no to the big galoot. For three minutes, we played crouch and pant — his favorite people-acting-like-dog game — and then I made his meal. Tigger scampered to us and mewed.

"Yes, it's your turn." Obviously the two had worked out a pecking order, and Tigger didn't seem upset by it. He didn't want Rook to ride roughshod over him.

By the time I'd done my ablutions, dressed in an aqua checkered blouse and jeans, I headed to the kitchen to make breakfast. Within moments, Rhett walked through the doorway, hair scruffy, T-shirt untucked over pajama bottoms, bare feet. "Rook?" he asked.

"Fed and happy. Coffee's ready."

"You're a saint." He poured himself a healthy-sized cup and kissed me tenderly on the neck. If I didn't have work and a hundred other things to do, I would have led him by the hand to the bedroom, but I couldn't.

"Sit," I ordered. "I'm making bacon and scrambled eggs."

"A woman after my own heart."

A half hour later, Rhett shuffled back to bed, and I climbed into the VW with Tigger and sped to work.

Bailey had arrived before me with Brianna and had settled her into her floor seat. "Help! I've got to come up with a birthday party theme for you-know-who," she announced, pointing clandestinely to Brianna, as if the girl even knew what a party was. "I was thinking Disney something. Not a princess, though. I don't want to get her into that rigamarole."

"But Elena of Avalor is a wonderful princess and a terrific role model." I'd stumbled upon the animated TV show when I was sick one Saturday morning. "She's a vivacious Latina who saved her magical kingdom from an evil sorceress."

"Ooh, Tito would love the Latina aspect." Bailey clapped. "Yes! An Elena party. With guitars and mariachis and sass!"

I set Tigger on his kitty condo, slipped into the storage room to stow my things, and as usual stuffed my cell phone into one of my pockets. I hated to admit it, but I couldn't stand to be without it. It had worked like a lifeline in one dire instance. Ever since, when away from my house, I always had it with me. I returned to the sales floor and spotted Tigger beside the baby, drinking in her scent.

Laughing I said, "What is it with cats and

babies?"

Bailey snorted. "They love the smell of poop."

I wrinkled my nose. "Katie's Art of Plating demonstration is this afternoon. Is she —"

"Ready? Yep! She came in to give me an update about ten minutes ago. And a muffin." She indicated a plate on the counter. "Chocolate mint. Truly divine."

"Leave me one."

"You snooze, you lose."

"Show some self-control," I chided and then toured the shop, tweaking book spines and displays. My cell phone jangled in my pocket. I checked the readout — a reminder to touch base with Yardley — and said to Bailey, "I've got to make a call. You okay for a sec?"

"We don't open for ten minutes. Go on. But make it snappy," she kidded.

I settled at the children's table to tickle Brianna's chin while I waited for Yardley to answer. The baby giggled and cooed her appreciation. When I stopped, she reached her arms out for Tigger, who scampered to her and obliged her with a nuzzle.

"Hello, Jenna," Yardley answered, sounding lethargic. "I was just thinking about you."

"I'd love to come visit you this morning, if you're up for it." I didn't add that I was worried about her.

"That would be lovely. I'm here." She ended the call abruptly.

I kissed Brianna on the cheek and moved to the sales counter.

"Your forehead is pinched," Bailey said.

"I spoke with Yardley. She sounds lackluster. I'd like to visit her when there's a lull."

"Go now. Gran texted that she's on her way in. With all that's going on at Azure Park this morning, we shouldn't have a crowd until the afternoon."

"Tigger . . ." I began.

"Will be fine. Brianna thinks he's her baby brother." Bailey shooed me. "Say hi for me."

Yardley lived behind the Art Institute in a small cottage adorned with myriad azaleas. I trod up the cobblestone path to the front door and knocked. She answered the door dressed in a hand-painted cherry-blossom kimono robe, her tawny hair swept into a floral claw, wisps dangling about her face. "Come in. I look a mess," she said. "I was doing some reorganization of our website on the computer."

"You look amazing, considering."

I stepped into the foyer, admiring the framed pen-and-ink artwork on the walls, while inhaling the scent of lavender. Reeds disseminating the aroma jutted from clear bottles on the side table. The faint sound of gong-meditation-style music came from down the hall.

"When I'm not chatting with anyone, I put on that tape," Yardley said. "The gongs calm me. Come this way." She led me to a simple kitchen done in white with black trim. All the appliances were black. The black-speckled granite counter was two-tiered. On the top level stood a huge spray of irises in a ceramic vase. "From Wayne," she said. "He knows how much I love them. He was sorry he couldn't catch the first plane out. He'll be here this afternoon."

I'd met him a few times and, on each occasion, he had clearly doted on his wife.

"How's honey-infused peppermint tea?" she asked. "I made a pot five minutes ago."

"Terrific."

She set a tray with a pretty china teapot, two matching cups, a swarm-glass honey jar, napkins, and spoons, and said, "Let's sit on the patio." With her head, she motioned to the area beyond the kitchen, which boasted more azaleas. "Catch the door?"

I did and settled at the cedar table. She set down the tray and poured us each a cup of tea.

"What a lovely place this is," I said.

"It was one of the perks of buying the institute. Wayne and I didn't need much house, and this place was ideal, given its natural setting."

I sipped my tea and hummed my approval. "This is delicious."

"Teas are very important in our household. Like potions, they can affect emotions. Though peppermint tea is a misnomer. It's actually made with real peppermint leaves. I grow them."

A pot filled with herbs stood to the right of the kitchen door.

"Peppermint is good for stress and anxiety. I probably should have had some yesterday." She lifted her cup, inhaled the aroma, and replaced it. "Naomi said —" She blew air between her lips. "That girl. She sure could use a tea that would boost her confidence. She seems so frazzled and unsure lately. Maybe I've demanded too much of her. Teaching classes. Running the booth at the festival. Helping with the competition selections. And to be dodging her estranged husband to boot? Poor thing."

"I feel protective of her, too. I've heard red clover tea enhances serotonin, and serotonin affects not simply concentration but increases confidence in social gatherings and the like."

"Aren't you a font of information."

"Or . . ." My mouth quirked into a smile as I pictured Pepper entering the shop with the pushcart of pendants. "Or Naomi could buy one of the potion pendants Pepper Pritchett is selling."

"Pepper makes potions now?"

"No. Her friend is a crafter. She couldn't attend the festival. The woman has filled the necklaces with potions to address all sorts of emotions. Pepper says they're *magical.*" I mimed quotation marks.

"Magical," Yardley echoed, her eyes glistening with amusement.

I added a swizzle of honey to my tea. "Also, I've heard there are perfumes to heighten confidence. Destiny Dacourt . . . you know her, don't you? She has a business named Tripping with Destiny."

"Of course I know her. Wayne and I have taken her tour. We found all sorts of small-batch wineries we didn't know existed around here, thanks to Destiny. Nouveau was our favorite."

"Well, she bought a perfume at the festival that's supposed to help with confidence. She could clue in Naomi as to which perfume it is."

"Great idea." Yardley rose. "I'm going to

grab a few cookies for us."

"Not on my account."

"I need a little sugar." She returned in moments with a plate filled with thin sugar cookies. "One won't hurt you."

I chose a cookie and bit into it. "Lovely flavor. Cream of tartar?" I asked.

"Good palate." She downed a cookie and blotted her mouth. "You know, Quade dated Destiny for a nanosecond."

"So my aunt told me."

"He was never very good in the relationship department, he admitted to me. He was fickle. Like his father, I suppose. A rolling stone." She set another cookie on her saucer. "What I found fascinating, however, was that all the women he dated in Crystal Cove had the same first initial. Delia, Deborah, Dina, and Destiny."

"Were they all amicable breakups?"

"He said they were."

"Where do they live?" I asked, wondering if Quade had broken more hearts than Destiny's, and if any had it in for him.

"As far as I know, Delia is married and residing in San Francisco. Deborah is in a gay relationship in Sacramento. And Dina relocated to Los Angeles to pursue an acting career."

"Leaving Destiny to hope he would take

more of an interest in her."

"Yes, but that wasn't to be and Destiny knew it." Yardley tucked a loose hair behind her ears. "He'd fallen for Naomi, and nothing anyone could say was going to change his mind. She was the one woman who'd truly captured his heart. Artists," she said. "They're a unique breed."

"He didn't mind that she had a child?"

"Quade loved children. Loved them! He told me that when he had his own, he would be a better father than what he'd had." She lowered her gaze. "His birth father, not his adoptive father. That man is salt of the earth, even though Quade and he didn't see eye to eye." She sat taller. "But Naomi wasn't into Quade. Not an iota."

I could confirm that. "Was Sienna?"

Yardley blinked. "Sienna Brown? Into my son? Whatever gave you that idea?"

"It's only a thought." I didn't want to give voice to my notions about Sienna being first on the scene. "How well do you know her?"

"We've interacted in order to stage the workshop and the opening night event at the inn, but that's about all. Sienna. She's older than me." Yardley pondered the notion. "No, I can't see it."

I polished off my cookie. "I saw Quade and her argue once or twice."

"What about?"

"I didn't hear, but Sienna was quite upset."

Yardley rolled her eyes. "Probably about his housekeeping ability or lack thereof."

"Why did she give him the cabana while his place was being fumigated? You told me she liked supporting artists, but that was a pretty expensive gift."

"I believe he gave her a painting in exchange."

A painting? Interesting. "Yardley, I'm sorry, but I have to ask. I heard you were the one who tipped off the police about Keller Landry stealing Quade's painting. Which he didn't. He was framed. Did Quade put it there? To prank Keller? Did he tell you to alert the police?"

"No." She blinked rapidly.

"How did you know it was there?"

"I received an anonymous t-text message," she stammered. "I thought the police should know."

Anonymous. Not from Quade. From a burner phone?

Yardley's eyes grew misty. She swiped her forefinger beneath each eye.

"Are you okay?" I asked.

"I'm . . . I'm sad that I'm not going to get to know him better. All those wasted years.

And Wayne was so looking forward to meeting him. Now" — she brandished a hand — "that possibility is gone."

On the way back to the Cookbook Nook, I decided to swing by Home Sweet Home and pick up the orange plush kitten I'd ordered. Brianna had a cat at home named Hershey, who when first adopted had been a bully cat but now was a pussycat. However, she didn't have any cats among her plush toys. I knew because I'd stealthily scoped them out on my last visit to Bailey's house.

I parked in a spot across the street and jaywalked past a pair of female festivalgoers carrying items that they had purchased at one of the venues.

One hoisted her four-pack of wine bottles and said, "When we get back to the B and B, we are opening one of these and toasting your official divorce. You are well rid of him."

"Amen," the divorcée said.

I stepped into Home Sweet Home and paused, drinking in the colorful, festive array of items. It was a yummy store offering potpourri and candles, handmade crafts, linens, baby gifts, and collectibles. Willie Nelson singing "Always on My Mind" played softly through speakers. The aroma of hot apple cider hung in the air as it did all year. Flora adored cider and sold bags of her never-fail cinnamon spice mix.

Per usual, customers were gathered near the year-round Christmas tree to find Crystal Cove–themed ornaments. For this week alone, Flora had allocated a third of the tree for festival artists so they could sell their ornaments on consignment. A few of the handblown glass ones caught my eye, but not willing to be diverted, I made a beeline for Flora, who was helping a guest near the rear of the store.

She held up a finger, the universal sign for *Just a sec.*

While waiting, I spied Pepper chatting up Sienna near the baby section. Both wore cardigans over sheath dresses. Each was holding up a layette of infant T-shirts, onesies, and more. Pepper's was pink and Sienna's aqua green. I sidled behind a customer and peeked around her. Sienna's shopping basket, which was slung over one arm, was filled with more aqua green baby items. I pondered the implication but told myself to cool my jets. She could be buying things for a sister or a friend. Shopping for baby clothes was not exclusively a mother's ritual. And Pepper, who did not have a shopping basket, was probably browsing in the hope that Cinnamon was, indeed, pregnant.

"Here you go." Flora offered me a gift bag with a bright yellow bow and pale yellow tissue paper poking from the top. "There's a gift tag attached to the handle, unless you want to purchase a larger card."

"This is fine. Thanks." I hitched my chin toward the far end of the shop. "Sienna looks like she's enjoying herself."

Flora sniffed. "She's been in nearly every day for the past two weeks and hasn't bought a thing."

"Her basket looks full."

"She fills it every time," Flora said. "And then she abandons it."

Because she wasn't sure she was pregnant? Or was she contemplating some other option?

"She looks good," I said. "Her skin looks healthy."

"Do you think she's" — Flora toyed with her thick braid — "you know, with child? Ooh, I'll find out."

"If you do, share the news with me."

CHAPTER 15

When I strolled into the shop midmorning, Bailey and the baby were nowhere to be seen and my aunt was sitting at the vintage table with, of all people, Bucky Winston. Two tarot cards were turned faceup. Gran was at the counter, finalizing a sale. A pair of women were scouting out the *Fire & Wine* cookbook on the display table.

Tigger romped to me, mewed, and nuzzled my ankle.

"Not for you," I said, taking the gift bag and my purse to the storage room. I returned and approached Gran, who was depositing the sales receipt in the drawer beneath the register. "Where are Bailey and Brianna?" I asked.

"Katie needed some help preparing the demonstration. Two of her staff are out sick today. So Bailey offered and Lola took the baby." Gran retied the Gucci scarf she'd donned over her expensive-looking bouclé sweater. "Between you and me, I think Katie could use some girl time. To get some things off her chest."

"Good idea," I said. "I'll suggest it. By the way, guess who I saw browsing baby items at Home Sweet Home?"

"I'm breathless with anticipation."

I flicked her arm, knowing she was teasing me. "Sienna."

"I was right?"

"I'm not sure. Flora says she browses but doesn't buy."

"Interesting." Gran hummed.

Deputy Marlon Appleby strode into the shop and stopped short. He wasn't in uniform. He was carrying a single rose, as he often did, for my aunt. They had a date for lunch.

I clasped his elbow, drawing him to the cookware wall filled with aprons and other kitchen gadgets. "For me?" I asked coquettishly.

He grinned, his moose-shaped jaw stretching with good humor. "You know it's not. What's your aunt doing?"

"What does it look like she's doing?"

"A reading for Bucky?" His eyes widened. "Cinnamon won't like —"

At that moment, Cinnamon breezed into the shop, uniform crisp, her broad hat firmly planted on her head. She drew to a halt. "What's going on?"

Bucky sat taller. "What are you doing here, honey?"

"The better question is what are you doing here?"

Appleby and I sidled over to them. A third tarot card was turned over. The Ace of Cups. It was a pretty card, with a giant hand holding a gold cup from which water overflowed into a sea below, signifying the stirring up of emotions and excitement, as in bringing a baby into the world. The other two were the Empress, the ultimate mothering card, and the Three of Cups, which signified creation. Cinnamon had never had her fortune told, so she didn't know the significance of the cards, but my aunt had clearly told Bucky. His eyes were glistening with joyful tears.

He leaped to his feet and embraced his wife.

Cinnamon broke free. On duty, she remained professional. "Why did you feel you needed your fortune told?" she asked him, her tone tight with restraint.

"I had the day free. I thought it would be fun."

Liar, liar. He'd come seeking answers. Seeking *hope.*

"And did you have fun?" Cinnamon said, eyeing the cards, trying to make heads or tails of them.

"I did. Can we —"

"Not now. I'm here on business. Deputy," Cinnamon said, addressing Appleby, "I know you're off duty, but we need to talk."

"About the new guy?" Bucky asked.

"What new guy?" I glanced between them.

"Fuller."

"He's not the new guy yet," Cinnamon said.

"He's been helping you do research, you said." Bucky elbowed his wife.

Cinnamon backed away. "Not exactly true. I've given him a few tests and —"

"I'm not sure I like him," Bucky added.

Cinnamon sniggered. "Because he's handsome?"

"Bah!" Bucky's neck flushed.

I felt like I was viewing a contentious tennis match. "Why do you need a new guy?" I cut in.

"Because Deputy Appleby wants to retire." Cinnamon gestured to Appleby.

"You what?" my aunt cried, rising to her feet unsteadily.

The deputy clasped her shoulders. "I was going to talk with you about it. At lunch."

"But why?" My aunt was nowhere near

ready to retire herself. She enjoyed work and she loved to tell fortunes. She told me once that she'd probably work until the day she died.

"I think I want to spend more time with my kids and grandkids." Appleby's daughter had a nine-month-old, and his son and daughter-in-law had recently had a boy.

"They're infants," Aunt Vera said, as if that made all the sense in the world.

Appleby's mouth quirked up. "I haven't completely made up my mind. Don't worry. I will not be asking you to give up what you love." He said to Cinnamon, "Give me a sec." He drew my aunt to the breezeway for a chat.

"I'll catch you later." Bucky pecked Cinnamon on the cheek and left.

Cinnamon stood speechless then faced me. "You phoned me yesterday but you didn't leave a message."

"I . . ." *Tread lightly, Jenna.* "Are you pregnant?"

"What? No. What gave you that idea?" She skimmed a hand along her abdomen.

"Your mother thinks you are, and Bucky's tarot reading —"

"Is that what those cards meant?" Cinnamon whipped off her hat and ran the fingers of one hand through her hair. "They're wrong, and my mother is loony."

"Speaking of your mother," I said, seizing the perfect segue, "I saw her at Home Sweet Home talking with Sienna Brown, who was shopping for baby clothes."

"So?"

"Is Sienna on your radar for the murder of Quade?"

"No. Why should she be?"

I launched into my explanation. Gran seeing Sienna enter an obgyn's office. Sienna wearing larger clothes. Sienna and Quade arguing sotto voce. Sienna acting cool at the crime scene, calmly offering how she went into the cabana, not realizing he was dead. "Honestly?" I added.

"What's your point?" Cinnamon asked.

"What if she's pregnant? What if Quade was the father of the child?"

Cinnamon frowned. "I'm sorry, but I find it hard to believe she would kill the baby's father."

Exactly what I'd thought, but I didn't want to rule it out. "What if he forced himself on her? Retribution for being violated can be a strong motive for murder."

"That's a lot of what-ifs, but" — she touched my arm — "I appreciate your theories and I will follow up."

I couldn't believe how valued her words

made me feel.

"Now," she continued, "I thought you might have been calling me about Christopher George."

"Did you touch base with him?"

"No, but we will because we found correspondence between him and Quade on Quade's computer, linking them prior to this week, meaning Christopher George lied about not knowing Quade."

I whistled.

"In addition, Fuller —"

"The new guy," I inserted.

She held up a hand to slow me down. "Fuller said any emails exchanged were erased from George's cloud. We're bringing him in for further questioning."

"Fuller isn't an employee, yet he was looking at Quade's computer?"

"Like I said, I was giving him a few challenges to see what he could handle."

Deputy Appleby joined Cinnamon and me while my aunt, her face splotchy from crying, retreated into the storage room, probably to freshen up.

"By the way, Marlon, while you were out, Fuller broke part of the code." Cinnamon pulled a black journal from her pocket with *Quade* gold-stamped on the cover.

"That's it? The black book?" I asked

eagerly. Studying the code must have been one of Fuller's challenges.

"Yes. It turns out it's a ledger. Quade kept sales of his art. The customers' names were cryptic, but Fuller was able to decipher many. The artworks were notable because of the titles. We've followed up with the buyers and they've confirmed the entries. All are legit. All paid cash, it turns out, given the comparative deposits into Quade's bank account. But there are a few things Fuller couldn't figure out."

"Like what?" Appleby asked.

She handed him the book. He opened the pages, flipping through.

"None were about the forgeries?" I asked.

Cinnamon said, "No."

"What's got you stumped?" I tried to peer past Appleby's massive arm to peek into the ledger.

"The letters *STB* followed by the letters *HM*," Cinnamon replied.

"Sienna Theresa Brown," I murmured.

Cinnamon eagle-eyed me. "Are you sure?"

"Theresa was her grandmother's name. Her grandmother is the reason she's so wealthy. I won't bore you with details, but that has to be her. Yardley Alks believed Quade had given Sienna a piece of art in exchange for room nights at the inn."

Cinnamon said, "The others pertained to artwork titles. I suppose *HM* could stand for a piece of art or the style of art."

"True." Appleby's gaze swung from Cinnamon to me. "But the titles are each followed by the type. *AA* is acrylic art. *MA* is metallic art. *MM i*s mixed media. Is there a style that would correlate to *HM*?"

Cinnamon shrugged, clueless. So did I.

As they departed though, an idea formed in my mind. Could it be that simple? Had Quade recorded everything he'd earned? What if *HM* stood for *hush money* to keep a secret? Like the fact that Sienna Theresa Brown was pregnant?

Chapter 16

After Cinnamon left and Appleby escorted my aunt to lunch, Gran and I wheeled the bookcases to the sides of the shop and set out twenty chairs facing the register. Then we roamed the store making sure all the cookbooks we'd ordered for the afternoon event were neat and organized. Around half past one, I went to the café to check on Katie and Bailey, who had yet to return. The plating demonstration would start in thirty minutes. I needed them both.

"Are you doing okay, ladies?" I asked as I entered the kitchen.

"Yep!" Katie pushed her mobile cooking cart toward me. "Bailey was a big help." She yelled over her shoulder, "Reynaldo, I'll be next door if you need me. Bailey, grab my toque and apron."

Reynaldo, the head chef and quite a good-looking man, waved a hand fitted with a kitchen mitt. "Fear not. We will batten down the hatches and have smooth sailing."

As Katie flew through the breezeway with Bailey and me following, she said, "I adore that man. He has such a great attitude. Nothing ever ruffles him. Nothing. I could learn a thing or two from him."

"Good to hear," I said. "Listen, I've put out a bunch of plating cookbooks. *Grand Finales: The Art of the Plated Dessert.*"

"Isn't that a bit old?" Katie asked.

"I know it's not current, but some cookbooks are timeless, and this one is a visually stunning book. Exquisite desserts prepared by fifty of the nation's top pastry chefs."

To Bailey, Katie said, "The book was coauthored by Tish Boyle, who also coauthored *Payard Desserts* with the legendary pastry chef François Payard."

"I love that cookbook," Bailey said.

"I've placed that one out, too." I strolled through the archway into the shop and pointed to the display table. "I've also put a stack of *Plating for Gold* on the sales counter." The full name was *Plating for Gold: A Decade of Dessert Recipes from the World and National Pastry Team Championships* — a mouthful, but then many cookbook titles were long. The championships were considered the Olympics of the pastry arts. Katie had never entered, though I'd encouraged her to do so. She claimed she was a better savory chef than a dessert chef, but today, she was going to prove herself wrong. I'd seen her decorate desserts with flair.

"Your guests should enjoy the selection." I hurried ahead of her to the decorative cookware area. "In addition, I purchased a number of plating tool kits." I lifted one and held the leather case open. "They aren't too expensive. Good enough for a beginner. So throw these into your spiel."

"Will do."

"Also, I've been thinking I'd like you to put a cookbook together."

"Who has the time?"

"We'll all pitch in." I swiped the air as I said the title, "*The Nook Café's Best Recipes: So Far.*"

"OMG," she croaked. "I love that."

"We'll split the proceeds fifty-fifty. I'll make sure we find a good publisher."

"I'm in. But now, off to create art! *C'est voilà!*" She wheeled her cart into place and removed items from the cupboards beneath the cart's counter.

Bailey handed her the toque and apron.

Katie centered the hat on her head, tucked her curls behind her ears, donned the apron, tying the strings at the front, and said, "Bailey, sit in the back row. Tell me if you can see the mirror."

Bailey obeyed and shouted, "*Oui,* chef!"

"C'est bon!" Katie threw her arms wide. "That's all the French I know other than cooking terms."

As I tweaked displays, making sure our recent customers hadn't messed with my organization, I said, "Katie, Bailey, what do you think about a girls' night out tomorrow at Palette?" Palette was a fun paint and sip studio, where they served wine and encouraged guests to awaken their inner artists by painting along with a teacher.

"Won't the place be booked during the festival?" Bailey asked.

"I'm sure Orah can squeeze the three of us in." The owner loved coming into the Cookbook Nook. "She owes me." I'd found her a rare cookbook that a vendor on eBay had for sale. It had been the first cookbook she'd ever owned as a girl. She'd lost it when her family had moved houses. Memories anchored by a physical item, as I well knew, were invaluable.

"You're on," Katie said.

A half hour later, after the chatty Pacific Grove Foodies settled into their seats — they took so long mingling that they had to sit in the last two rows — I signaled Katie to start her presentation. I moved to the rear of the room and remained standing, arms folded.

As she explained what the audience could expect, I picked up the scent of tar, which made my nose twitch. I swiveled my head and spotted a youngish woman in the last row, two seats from where I was standing, dusting off her shoulder. Her cheeks were flushed with embarrassment.

The elderly woman sitting next to her leaned in and whispered, "I can help with that, dear."

The youngish woman startled. "Are you talking to me?"

"I have dandruff, too," the elderly woman continued, missing the younger's shocked expression. "But I've tamed it with Tara's Tar shampoo." She indicated the dandruff-free shoulders of her purple dress. "The stuff stinks, but it works."

No kidding. Hadn't the woman thought about using a cream rinse to dampen the stench? I inched away.

"Welcome, everyone!" Katie announced. After a brief introduction covering herself, the shop, and the café, she launched into detailing a few of the tools she would use, including an offset spatula, drawing decorating spoon, saucier spoon, and slotted spoon. "FYI, we happen to have a few of these plating kits for sale."

Bless her heart. She was a master saleswoman.

"Now, today, I'm going to demonstrate how to decorate simple, ordinary flan." She had made six flans for the occasion.

"For the first, I'll show you how a single line can make a statement." Using a pastry brush, she dipped it into a strawberry sauce and then swiped the brush lengthwise on an empty plate. "This style takes full advantage of the white space." She tilted the plate, just so. "Notice the sauce is not a solid line. Texture is important." She slid a flan on top of the sauce. The audience could see every move she made in the cart's slanted overhead mirror. "Simple but elegant. Of course, you could use two lines, making them parallel or crisscrossing. It's up to you. And now . . ." She held up a small pink vial. "For my secret potion." She turned the vial upside down and shook it. Out came red crystals. "Sugar!" She chortled.

The attendees applauded.

"Moving on." Katie's voice lilted with enthusiasm. "Arcs, or swooshes, as some of us call them, create a nice movement to a plate. The half-moon push is one of my favorites. You start with this." She held up a silver biscuit cutting ring. "Set it on the plate and with a squeeze bottle filled with your desired sauce" — she held up a bottle that reminded me of one you'd find in a diner for catsup, except this one was filled with blueberry sauce — "you add a thin stream on the inside of your cutter. Then, with a spoon, swipe around the inside. Remove the mold, and voilà, a lovely arc shape."

An audience member *ooh*ed.

"Place the dessert of choice inside the arc." She did so. "If you like, you could add a line to the plate. Arcs and lines do well together." Using a drizzle spoon with a tapered tip, she trickled some of the red sauce alongside the flan. "Use your imagination."

Over the course of the next half hour, she showed how to turn simple dots into swishes and how to create elegant triangles and circles and more. I was impressed and couldn't wait to try some of her techniques at home. Rhett, of course, knew how to do all of these things. I would love to surprise him.

"I've one more technique to show you," Katie said, nearing the end of her presentation. "Tweezer food. Heard of it?"

Heads wagged.

"Although the term *tweezer food* is sometimes used to describe fussy dishes with way too many bells and whistles, using tweezers can elevate your plating skill. This won't be fussy." She wrinkled her nose in mock horror. "Let me show you." She pulled a plate of chocolate shavings from the refrigerator beneath the cart's counter. "Chocolate and flan are a great match." Carefully, using her oversized tweezers, which she informed the audience were also called tongs, she set shaving after shaving on top of the flan. Then, using a decorating spoon, she drizzled droplets of strawberry sauce around the flan.

A few more in the crowd *ooh*ed.

"That's it, folks. That's all I've got to share, but I know the shop has set out lots of cookbooks helping you with these artistic tips." She made a grand sweeping gesture with one hand. "Any questions?"

She responded to a few and then ended the event.

Enthusiastically, the attendees sprang to their feet and roamed the shop gathering cookbooks and more. For over an hour, Gran, Bailey, and I were busy ringing up sales.

As the shop began to clear, I caught sight of the elderly woman in the purple dress chatting with Gran. She was going on and on about how wonderful Katie was and how adorable our shop was. Gran's nose was twitching as mine had, and a notion niggled at the back of my brain. At the soiree on Monday night, I'd seen Christopher George brushing off his shoulders as the youngish woman had. He'd made the same gesture when spying on Naomi the day Cinnamon took her to the precinct. Did he have dandruff? Did he use a special shampoo to treat his ailment? Was it possible that I'd detected the scent of his shampoo at the crime scene?

Bailey sidled up to me. "What's caught your attention?"

I explained.

"Let's check it out."

I frowned. "How?"

"We'll go to the Crystal Cove Inn. A double sawbuck might loosen a housekeeper's tongue."

"As in a twenty-dollar bill? Who's been binge-watching reruns of *The Sopranos*?" I joked.

She raised a hand. "C'mon. You've picked up the scent of what might solve this murder."

I groaned at her pun.

Bailey slung her arm through mine. "Ve-era!" she sang.

My aunt had returned to the shop in the middle of Katie's presentation. I hadn't had time to ask her how it had gone with Deputy Appleby at lunch. She didn't look forlorn, which was a good sign.

"Jenna and I are going to grab a coffee," Bailey said.

"Why are you lying?" I whispered.

"You don't want her to worry, do you? Besides, it's not a lie if we go to Latte Luck first."

I faltered, but I didn't resist. Bailey could be a force.

Minutes later, we purchased two lattes to go at the café, and then drove to the inn. Leaving our lattes in the car, I led the way to the concierge desk, my insides jittery from nerves, not from caffeine. Ginny with the perky smile was on duty.

"Hi, Ginny," I said. "We're looking for a guest. Christopher George."

"I know who he is this time." She beamed, pleased with herself. "But you missed him. He went to Azure Park."

"He's staying in the main building, isn't he?" I asked cagily.

"Oh, no, ma'am. He's secured one of the cabanas. Only the best for him." She propped her elbows on her podium to lean closer. "At least, that's what he likes to say."

She winked.

"Only the best," I echoed. "I'm going to show my friend the grounds, if that's all right."

"Be my guest."

As I led Bailey through the foyer and out the double doors to the grassy expanse, she said, "I was here the other night."

"I know, silly, but I want to go to the cabanas."

We strode down the walkway, past the wing of rooms, and turned left toward the cabanas.

"Jenna, look!" Bailey rasped. "Just as I'd hoped. A housekeeper. C'mon."

The forty-something woman, dressed in a green uniform of buttoned jacket, trousers, and sneakers, her hair tied in a bandana, was stocking a cart parked outside cabana three. The door to the unit was ajar.

"Good day, Lucia," Bailey said to the housekeeper, reading the woman's name tag. "Could you help us?"

"What do you need?" the housekeeper asked in a slight Eastern European accent.

"Mr. George's room. He forgot to give me the unit number."

"Two doors down. Seven."

"Thank you."

"But he's not there."

"Oh, no, I missed him?" Bailey gasped dramatically, utilizing the acting lessons she'd taken in college. "He was supposed to give me a bottle of the shampoo he uses. He said he had two. Would you mind . . ."

"I cannot."

Bailey had stowed the twenty-dollar bill in her pocket. She fetched it and pressed it to her chest. "Please. I have terrible dandruff." She brushed her shoulders. "He vowed it would solve the problem."

The housekeeper glanced right and left before snatching the bill from Bailey. She let us in to Christopher George's room. "One minute. No more."

"No more. Thank you!"

Bailey entered first. I followed.

"Nice digs," she said, gazing at the expansive room.

I whispered, "Unless you die in one."

She blanched.

"Sorry," I said. "No need for gallows humor."

The layout was similar to the cabana Quade had stayed in. The living room was well-appointed. There was an adjoining kitchen area and a door to the right, leading to what I presumed was the bedroom. Decorative pillows lay on the floor. There was a used coffee cup by the Keurig machine. The housekeeper hadn't yet attended to the room.

Bailey went into the bathroom first. I trailed her, knowing what we were doing was illegal and if caught, Cinnamon would slam us both in jail — simply to prove a point — but I needed answers. For Naomi's sake. I inhaled, catching the scent of tar, and peered into the shower. No shampoo bottle.

"Not in here," I said.

"Not on the shelf under the sink or in his toiletry or shaving kit." Bailey swiveled, looking for other places it could be.

"What kind of cologne does he use?" I asked.

"Molton something. Never heard of it."

"Molton Brown Russian Leather?"

"Mm-hm."

"David used that for a while. It sort of smells like rare books and horses."

That could have been the scent I'd picked up in Quade's cabana, I supposed. I caught sight of the garbage can. Grabbing a tissue from a box on the counter, I gingerly pawed through the garbage, finding wads of paper, an abandoned crossword puzzle, and more. I scored when I discovered an empty bottle of Tara's Tar shampoo at the bottom. "Gotcha!" I took a picture of it with my camera and pocketed the tissue. "Let's go."

At the door, I halted as another thought occurred to me. Would Christopher George have had the opportunity to poison Quade earlier that day? Perhaps during a meeting about the forgeries? "Bailey, quick, look for a vial of arsenic."

"No!" She beckoned with her hand. "Let's go."

"Please."

"What are you expecting to find? A bottle marked with crossbones? C'mon, Jenna. We came, we found, we conquered. We leave. Now."

She was right. I peeked out the door. The housekeeper named Lucia was nowhere in sight.

As we were heading along the walkway to the lobby, I saw a man striding toward us. Not just any man. Christopher George. *Heck, no! What happened to going to Azure Park?* My heart hammered the inside of my chest.

I said to Bailey, whose eyes were as wide as saucers, "Act cool." I forced a phony smile. "Mr. George."

"Miss Hart," he said. "What a surprise. And —" He gestured to Bailey.

"Bailey. Bird. Martinez." Her voice was thin and breathy. She fidgeted with the lace yoke of her sweater.

"Christopher George," he said in response. "What are you two doing here?"

I said, "We came to see Sienna Brown."

He hooked his thumb over his shoulder. "She's at the front desk. I just saw her. Why did you think she'd be out here?"

"A housekeeper told us."

"Mm-hm." His eyes narrowed and his mustache twitched with suspicion. "By the way, did you sic the police on me a second time, Jenna? I know you're close to Naomi. I've seen you chatting with her. Often." His steely gaze drilled into me. "At the park, at your shop, and on other occasions."

The hair at the base of my neck stood on end. How long had he been spying on Naomi? *How long?* I'd felt eyes on me at other times but didn't want to acknowledge the sensation.

"I'd like you to back off," he said, his voice crisp.

"Back off?" I asked innocently.

"She doesn't need you as a friend."

"I told you —"

"Naomi is my wife. I will choose her friends."

Bailey inhaled sharply. She'd dated a man way back when who'd been just as overbearing.

I stared down Christopher George. "Sir, forgive me, but I have it on good authority that Naomi doesn't want you as a husband. Does she need to file for a restraining order? If I were you, I'd keep my distance."

"Do not tell me what to do."

"No, sir, I wouldn't dare. But the court will."

Bailey edged closer to me. I could feel her fear, but I didn't dare glance in her direction. This was between Christopher George and me. Plus, I worried that if I made eye contact with her, she might blab about our foray into his cabana.

Christopher harrumphed and lifted his chin. "By the way, as for murdering that guy Quade . . . I didn't do it. I have a rock-solid alibi."

"Oh, yeah? What is it?"

"I was in my room here at the inn."

"Did you order room service?"

"No."

"Any witnesses?"

"No. I was watching CNN. Want me to tell you what they were discussing?" He smirked. "Or is it enough that I've already told the police?"

Chapter 17

To play out our lie of seeking Sienna, we stopped at the concierge's desk and asked about her, but as it turned out, she was making rounds of the inn. I said I'd touch base with her another time, and we left.

On the drive back to work, Bailey apologized repeatedly for coercing me to go to the inn. I told her I was glad we'd gleaned a clue I could share with Cinnamon — I'd have to figure how, of course, without incriminating the two of us — and I assured her I was fine with what had gone down.

However, when we walked into the shop, I felt my energy take a dive, and Bailey sensed it.

"Tea!" she said, taking my empty latte cup from me. "Coming right up." She disappeared into the stockroom.

My aunt approached. "Where have you been? You drove off. You don't need a car to go to Latte Luck."

I confessed everything.

She clasped my arm. "Jenna, dear, please don't pursue this. Let Cinnamon do her job."

"Uh-huh," I said dully, worried that I might have made things worse for Naomi.

"Call Cinnamon. Tell her what you found."

My stomach clenched.

"Tell her as much as you can." She winked and stroked her phoenix amulet, encouraging me to follow her suggestion.

"What happened between you and Deputy Appleby?" I asked, stalling.

"That'll keep. Go." She gave me a gentle shove.

I dialed Cinnamon and left a cryptic message, mentioning the tar shampoo angle without saying I'd found a discarded bottle of the shampoo in Christopher George's trash. Then I took the tea that Bailey brought me and sat at the vintage table. As I fiddled with the jigsaw puzzle, sipping tea and fitting pieces of the cheeseboard into position, I thought about Naomi's estranged husband. Would watching TV hold up as an alibi?

A few minutes later, my aunt sat down at the table. "So . . ." she began, "Marlon does want to retire but not quite yet. Perhaps in two or three years, when the babies are older and might actually remember him."

"Did you convince him of that?"

"No, he came upon the notion by himself." She put a few of the wineglass pieces together. "Actually, he was miffed. He thought Cinnamon was pressuring him by bringing that new guy in for an interview. He went back after lunch to have a chat with her."

"Do you think she did it on purpose, to push his buttons? To force him to decide?"

My aunt grinned. "I do, indeed. She is one smart cookie."

The afternoon sped by with customers coming and going in a steady stream. The most popular cookbook was *The Modern Art Cookbook,* which explored an array of artworks of food and eating, opening a window into the lives of artists like Matisse, Hockney, and Picasso in the kitchen. I'd set aside a copy for myself.

By five thirty, after I put in an order for two dozen more of that particular cookbook, I prompted my aunt, Bailey, and Gran to finish up. We would close exactly at six so those of us attending specialty events could go home and freshen up.

Tigger, looking as exhausted as I felt, was more than happy to settle in the house, and

Rook was ecstatic to a point of collision that the cat had come home, skidding into the furniture as well as me. Rhett had texted me that he'd visited the dog around two, but even so, Rook acted as if he'd believed we'd abandoned him for good.

I fed them both, took a shower, ending with a cold blast of water to wake me up, and then fixed my hair and makeup, slipped into my favorite black sheath and its jacket, added my mother's heart-shaped locket and a pair of sexy sandals, and headed out. I couldn't wait to see what Rhett had prepared at Intime for the Art of French Food event.

Buena Vista Boulevard was bustling with good vibrations. Locals and tourists had crowded outside all the restaurants that were offering art festival prix fixe dinners. The strands of lights that the town had strung across the street from building to building cast a lovely glow. Numerous caricature artists had set up easels and chairs along the sidewalk. People were lined up for those opportunities, too.

I entered Intime feeling light on my feet and totally in love with my community and Rhett, not necessarily in that order. Bailey and her mother, who had both dressed in jewel-necked silk rompers, were standing with my father, waiting to be seated.

"There she is, Cary," Lola exclaimed and rushed to give me a hug. "Don't you look fabulous."

"As do you and your daughter."

"Can you believe it? We need to talk about wardrobe selections in the future so we don't match." She released me and grabbed my hand to lead me to my father and Bailey. "Rhett said it'll be a minute. Look at the place. Brimming over with positivity." Lowering her voice, she said, "You'd never know there had been a murder in town days ago."

I glimpsed Bailey. Had she mentioned to her mother and my father about our afternoon adventure? Should I prepare myself for one of Dad's stern lectures?

"Lola, thank you, by the way, for doing all you did for Keller. Katie is so relieved that he's off the hook."

She smirked. "As if Keller would hurt a fly. However, I have to say that the evidence did not look good for a while. Be thankful Z.Z.'s son came forward."

"I am." An image of Egan on the Pier Thursday night flashed in my mind. I hoped he wouldn't break his mother's heart.

"Jenna," Dad said, kissing my cheek. "How's business?"

"Super. The festival has to be one of the best attended events Crystal Cove has ever had."

"I'd say. Sienna Brown was telling me that the inn has sold out completely."

"Sienna?" I asked, a tremor in my tone. "Why were you chatting with her?"

"She walked in right before us with a friend."

I scanned the restaurant and saw Sienna sitting at a table near the window. Like all the tables, hers was draped with a white tablecloth and set with a single white rose in a crystal vase and a small candle. Her dinner companion was about the same age, same build, with similar taste. They were admiring each other's bracelets.

"Aren't the aromas heavenly, Jenna?" Bailey asked.

"Divine."

As Rhett's parents had for their restaurant in Napa Valley, he had chosen to make Intime resemble a classic French bistro, paneled with deep mahogany and mirrors hanging on all the walls to catch the reflection of the light from the candelabra-style chandeliers. The strains of an instrumental version of "La Vie en Rose" played softly through speakers. The scent of onions and melted cheese and fresh-baked bread stirred my senses. I was hungry!

Rhett, looking dapper in tan jacket and ecru shirt over chocolate brown slacks, strode from the kitchen to where we were standing and kissed my check. "Hello, beautiful." His warm hand at the base of my spine sent a tingle of delight down to my toes.

"Great turnout," I said.

"Wait until you see the *carte de jour.*"

He grabbed specialty prix fixe menus and guided us to our table. "Here we are." He seated me first. Lola sat opposite me, and Bailey and Dad flanked me. Handing us the elegantly printed menus, he said, "You have choices for each course. I'll send our finest server over to take your beverage order. Enjoy the evening."

I loved how he spoke formally but warmly to his guests. He was in his element and it showed in his sparkling eyes.

Our server arrived in less than a minute. My father asked her about a few of the chardonnays on the list. She said her favorite label was the Soberanes from the Santa Lucia Highlands. Its wine exhibited bright ripe fruits along with a rich, crisp finish. Dad ordered a bottle and four glasses.

As I perused the menu, a woman's laugh cut through the hushed tones. I swiveled to look for the source. Sienna's friend was clasping a hand to her chest, roaring with clear abandon. She stopped abruptly as if realizing how loud she'd been and stifled an impish grin, then she leaned forward to inspect Sienna's glimmering pendant.

"That Sienna," Lola said. "She's interesting, don't you think?"

I turned back. "How so?"

"She has such a rich history. Moving around the country as a navy brat, becoming a fine horsewoman and one of the top fencers in the country until she fizzled under the pressure."

She was a fencer? How fascinating. That meant she knew how to wield a sharp weapon.

The server returned with our wine and uncorked it using a classic sommelier-style corkscrew. She poured a taste for my father, who deferred to Lola. She took a sip and approved.

While the server poured, Lola continued, "And to top it off, Sienna never realized she was as wealthy as all get-out. Her mother, rest her soul, was superior at keeping a secret."

Is Sienna as good? I wondered.

"Bon appetit," the server said and left.

We raised our glasses and toasted the festival.

"You know, Sienna is a regular at the Pelican Brief," Lola said.

My father brushed the back of her hand with a fingertip. "Isn't everyone?"

"Oh, you." She knew he was teasing her. "She loves our honeyed fish fry."

"So do I." Dad grinned. "I'm starting to like Sienna more and more."

"She and her friend seem enamored with each other's jewelry," Bailey noted.

"Probably because it's something new." Lola sipped her wine. "Each week for the past few weeks, Sienna seems to have been wearing a new piece. A bracelet. A ring. Earrings. If I didn't know better, I'd think she was robbing the jewelry store."

I gawked at her.

"Joking," she added. "Though each thing she's worn has been something I've seen in the window at Sterling's."

Across the street from Fisherman's Village was Artiste Arcade, a collection of high-end stores including Adorn Yourself, my favorite accessory shop, and Sterling's, once known as Sterling Sylvia's until Sylvia was forced to sell. The arcade featured a brick archway adorned with purple morning glory vines.

"Well" — my father took a sip of wine —

"I'm sure Sienna can afford whatever they sell. Not to worry. Now, what are you all having?"

"I'm torn between the French onion tart and the asparagus Gruyere tart," I said.

Bailey raised a hand. "I'm going for the chicken Provençal and crème brûlée for dessert. You might have to wheel me home."

"Boeuf bourguignon for me." Dad set his menu aside.

Lola didn't answer. She was staring in Sienna's direction.

"What's wrong, Lola?" I asked.

"Why does she need so much jewelry?"

Dad frowned at her. "Because she's a woman."

Lola batted his arm. "Be serious. She's not dating anyone. When she goes out, she's with a girlfriend."

"It's possible she prefers women," Dad suggested.

"No, she's been married and has had beaus."

"Mom, girlfriends covet what other girlfriends have," Bailey said. "It's one-upmanship."

"True. I'm being inane." Lola returned to studying the menu. "Profiteroles with chocolate sauce."

"Anything else?" My father eyed her wryly.

"Whatever you're having."

She gazed at him with such love that my heart swelled. I couldn't believe how lucky my father was to have married her.

We ordered and chatted about the festival. When our appetizers came, we grew quiet. After downing the asparagus Gruyere tart in a matter of bites and relishing every mouthful, I needed to go to the ladies' room.

Upon entering, I saw Sienna standing at the mirror applying lipstick.

"Hello, Jenna," she said. "You stopped in to see me earlier?"

Apparently, the concierge delivered the message. "Yes." How could I ask her about her relationship with Quade? I drew alongside her at the mirror and pulled my lipstick from my purse. "It was nothing important. A few weeks ago, you'd mentioned that you'd like to find a cookbook for Hawaiian food. You want to throw a luau at the inn."

"Good memory."

"I may have landed on the perfect one." I really had done the research but had forgotten to follow up with her. I dabbed lipstick on my lower lip and pressed my lips together. "Come in and I'll show you some preview pages. Let's see if you'd like me to order it."

She looked at me askance. "You drove up to the inn to tell me that? You could have phoned."

"I also wanted to show Bailey the grounds. She didn't tour them the other night. You've really done marvelous things with the gardens."

"They are spectacular, aren't they?" She leaned forward to get a closer look at her face. "I found a great landscaper."

"You look lovely, by the way," I said. "Nice necklace."

She stood taller and pinched it between two fingers. "This old thing? It's been in the family for years."

"Your friend was paying particular interest to it."

Sienna smiled but the smile didn't reach her eyes. "Were you spying on us?"

"Don't be silly. Your friend's laugh" — I put my lipstick back in my purse — "is quite distinctive."

"Aha. Yes, it is." Sienna relaxed and offered a wink. "She's as blind as a bat, though. She's seen me wear this dozens of times."

"How are you holding up? Are ghoulish customers still on the hunt for a room at the inn?"

She tilted her head. "I'm not following."

"The other night at the Wearable Art event you said —"

"Oh, yes, I remember now." She tapped her temple as the memory formed. "Yes, we have a steady stream of customers. I don't think there's one free room except —" She gripped the edge of the counter to steady herself. "Except, of course, the cabana."

"The police haven't released it?" I hadn't noticed crime scene tape across cabana five's door earlier.

"They have, but I don't feel it's right to . . ." She twirled her tube of lipstick. "You know."

"I was wondering . . ." I pulled a comb from my purse, stalling.

"About?"

"About you and Quade."

"What about us?"

"You were arguing that night."

"No, we weren't."

"Well, then, let's call it a heated conversation. Was it about his black book? His ledger?"

Her gaze narrowed.

"Did he threaten to reveal something about you if you didn't pay him hush money?" I continued, knowing I was overstepping and unable to help myself. I blamed the wine.

"Honestly, Jenna!" Her gaze turned steely. She dropped her lipstick into her silver clutch lying on the counter and folded her arms across her chest, which, given her stance, did make it look like she was with child. "My dealings with Quade don't concern you in the least. Keller is exonerated, so why you would persist in a quasi-investigation —"

"Naomi Genet!" I blurted, my insides aching with the need to know the truth.

"What about her?"

"I want this to be over for her sake."

"She wasn't in love with him," Sienna hissed. "She's not brokenhearted that he's dead. I certainly never saw any interest on her part."

So, she had been paying attention.

"No, you're right," I conceded. "But I want to learn the truth because her fate seems to be linked to his."

Sienna clucked her tongue. "Ridiculous. No one's fate is linked to anyone else's. Ever. We each stand alone. For eternity. Now, I'll take my leave." She tucked her clutch under her arm and turned on her heel.

Pausing at the door, she glowered at me over her shoulder. "For your information, I have met with the police. I am not a suspect in Quade's murder. They have determined that he was asleep or passed out when I went into the cabana. The ME has determined he was killed between ten and eleven, for which I have a verifiable alibi. I was in my residential unit at the inn within minutes after I'd finished doing my rounds, approximately ten p.m., and did not emerge until later, after you arrived. I ordered chamomile tea from room service. They can corroborate my whereabouts. Ask Chief Pritchett if you need confirmation. I know you two are close."

Chapter 18

During the rest of dinner, I glimpsed over my shoulder at Sienna. She didn't seem bothered by my intrusion in the least. In fact, she continued to entertain her friend with stories that made the woman laugh riotously. I noticed Rhett standing near the hostess desk, staring in their direction once or twice, probably wishing he could shush them.

I'd expected to hear an earful about their behavior when he arrived home at three a.m., but I didn't. He was elated by the turnout, ecstatic about the kudos he'd received from patrons, and thrilled that my father had thoroughly enjoyed himself. He and Dad got along rather well, but he knew my father could be a food critic. We snuggled for about ten minutes, and then both fell asleep.

The next morning, Bailey romped into the store pushing the stroller, the flaps of her aqua striped cardigan wafting. "The DIY Craft Fair and Small-Batch Wines event takes place on Buena Vista Boulevard to-day." She went into the storage room. "We should get a lot of foot traffic from it." She returned to the shop, set Brianna in her owl-themed floor seat, made sure Tigger didn't scuttle into the girl's lap, and then joined me at the sales counter. "Festival planners must have worked well into the wee hours erecting all the blue-and-white awnings. The street has been closed off and it's trans-formed with colorful banners, venues, and carts."

I'd seen as much on my way in. Small-batch wineries were stationed at the south end of the boulevard, near Fisherman's Vil-lage, and the craft booths, demo booths, and foodie carts were positioned between stores to the north, none blocking entrances to any of the regular shops. Loads of people were already wandering the area.

"I saw a bouncy house with slides by the dolphins," Bailey went on. "How I would love to do that! I adore bouncy houses. But it's for kiddies."

At the crossroad, where Buena Vista Boulevard met Seaview, the road that wound up the mountain and ultimately turned into an egress out of town, stood a statue of a pair of dancing dolphins. It was a popular tourist spot for photographs.

"And get this," Bailey continued, "the bouncy house is in the shape of a giant octopus."

"How cool!"

She added, "When we have our break later, why don't you, Brianna, and I take a stroll and drink it all in?"

"Sounds perfect."

We had not planned any events for Saturday morning because we didn't want to draw attention away from the festival happenings on the boulevard. To support today's theme, I had stocked a number of DIY books, not cookbooks, like *Martha Stewart's Encyclopedia of Crafts: An A-to-Z Guide with Detailed Instructions and Endless Inspiration* and *The Complete Candle Making Recipes for Beginners to the Expert.* I didn't want to compete with whatever DIY manuals Pepper was selling at Beaders of Paradise, but having a few selections to accompany a cookbook purchase would be nice for our customers. Many hostesses enjoyed making place mats or candles for their special dinners.

An hour before noon, when the crowd left to venture onto Buena Vista Boulevard in search of lunch or a snack, I grabbed my ultralight down jacket, threw it on over my crew-neck sweater, and told my aunt that Bailey, Brianna, and I would be back soon.

"No shenanigans," she warned.

"We're simply in search of a good time." I gave her a hug, scrubbed Tigger under the chin, and we left.

I couldn't believe the number of people milling about. Azure Park had been crowded the other day, but the festival throng had doubled since then. The boulevard was shoulder-to-shoulder people. A stream of folks was heading toward the south, where the small-batch wines were the focus. Bailey and I had agreed that we would abstain today; we needed to keep our wits about us.

"I'm loving the art-themed music," Bailey said as she checked on Brianna's blanket and hat to make sure she was warm.

"It's colorful."

Through speakers that were located every forty to fifty yards, a new rock song rang out. The first song we'd heard, "Vincent" by Don McLean, was melodic and mournful. The next, "Andy Warhol" by David Bowie, was rousing the crowd.

We passed a variety of artisans, including basket weavers, wind chime makers, and copper foil designers.

At Repurposed Bicycle, the artist had used

bicycle parts to make some amazingly different art. The bike chain bookends caught my eye. They were so unique. The modestly priced bottle openers made with chains and cogs were a big seller, too.

"Isn't it amazing what's considered art?" Bailey asked.

"I'm astounded."

We stopped at a small booth named Open Your Imagination, where a woman from Carmel-by-the-Sea was showing how to install a fairy garden of succulents in a wide-mouthed pot. Bailey picked up one of the fairy figurines that were for sale and held it in front of Brianna's face. "Isn't she pretty? Look at her blue wings." Brianna reached for the fairy. Bailey said, "No, baby girl. Not a chance. When you're older." She said to me, "I can't wait to teach her how to plant and dream."

"You're a good mom." I shivered. The sun was out but the temperature was only in the fifties. "Hey, I'm hungry and cold. How about a cup of lentil and chicken soup?"

"Sounds great."

I purchased two to-go cups from Soup's On, a regular festival vendor, and we continued walking.

At the furniture maker venue named Minimalist, a long-haired man was showing onlookers how to turn old scrolled legs of a desk into feet for a chair.

At Get It Off Your Chest, a pair of female artists were demonstrating how to paint an ordinary three-drawer dresser after it had been stripped of its veneer and repainted white. Currently, they were painting branches of cherry blossom trees on the front, turning the dresser into something gorgeous.

"Jenna!" a woman warbled.

Faith Fairchild, wearing wildly colorful leggings and a neon green top, was standing alongside Candy Kane, who was manning a pushcart similar to Pepper's that featured her jewelry: Kane's Korals.

I moseyed to them. "Pretty," I said, admiring Candy's work. Earrings hung on decorative gold trees. Necklaces and bracelets were displayed on a T-type stand. I was particularly fond of a silver and coral rope-style bracelet. "Do you carve and polish the coral yourself?"

"Mm-hm." She was a shy woman with a wispy voice. During our workshops she hadn't said more than ten words. I couldn't imagine her killing a flea, let alone Quade.

"Isn't she fabulous?" Faith lifted a pair of hand-carved earrings that resembled leaves and held them up to her ears. "Bailey, these would look gorgeous on you."

Bailey never could resist earrings or an artful sales pitch. She bought the pair, and I reflected that if Faith didn't make it as an artist, she might mull over going back to being an artists representative.

"Good choice," Faith said, adding, "Flora wants to talk to you, Jenna. If you have a moment."

"What about?"

"I don't have a clue." She plucked her spiky, lime-green-tinted hair. "As if she tells me anything."

Candy slipped Bailey's purchase into a coral-colored mesh bag and handed it to her. Bailey tucked her purchase into the pouch on Brianna's stroller and we moved on.

"Hey, is that the pet store the other artist in the competition owns?" Bailey asked. "Jaime something?"

Next to Nuts and Bolts, the hardware shop my father bought after he retired from the FBI, was a new shop I hadn't been aware of until now, Exotic Pets. The window was covered with Save the Rainforest stickers and peace signs and exceptional pictures of lizards, geckos, and iguanas in their habitats, which made me smile. My aunt was right. Jaime Gutierrez, like Candy

Kane, wouldn't hurt a soul. He was all about preserving life.

As we strolled on, I questioned the way my mind worked, reading murderous intentions into everyone's behavior when there were none. But someone had murdered Quade. How was Cinnamon fairing with her investigation?

I spotted Flora standing in front of her shop beside a kiosk-style cart filled with homemade candles. Before opening Home Sweet Home, she had started out selling candles.

Nudging Bailey in that direction, I strolled to Flora and lifted a tall candle. Decorated with red-white-and-green-striped wax ribbons, it screamed Christmas. "This is amazing, Flora."

"Check out this one," Bailey said, lifting a candle, similar in style, done in black, green, turquoise, and red. "Exquisite."

"I take special orders," Flora said, her voice burbling with enthusiasm. "A person can choose the colors to go with their décor."

"Smart," I said. "Hey, your sister said you wanted to see me."

"Yes." Flora lowered her voice. "I saw you last night at Intime."

"I didn't see you there."

"I was with my brother, toward the front, to the right. It was a lovely menu. Rhett outdid himself."

"Thank you. He'd be pleased to hear that."

"I mention it because I saw you follow Sienna into the ladies' room."

"I didn't follow her. She was there when I entered."

"Oh, my mistake," Flora said quickly. "When she came rushing out, I thought you'd embarrassed her by asking about her necklace."

"Why would she have been embarrassed?" Bailey asked, intrigued.

Flora leaned in. "I'm pretty sure she stole it."

"Flora," I said in the same tone my aunt would use when reprimanding anyone for spreading rumors.

"It's the truth. She's got sticky fingers."

"C'mon." I *tsk*ed.

"She's stolen from my shop. Little things, knickknacks, nothing she needs. Of course, whenever I press her, she takes umbrage. You know how it is."

Actually, I didn't. I'd never caught anyone swiping something from the Cookbook Nook. Was I too naïve for words?

"My mother thought Sienna had bought

the jewelry at Sterling's," Bailey said.

"Oh, it came from Sterling's all right," Flora said, "but I don't think she bought it."

This was a serious accusation. Was Sienna a thief? Had Quade known? Was that what they'd argued about? Had he threatened to tell the police about her proclivity? Yardley thought he might have given Sienna a piece of art in exchange for the room, but what if he hadn't given her anything? What if Sienna had paid him hush money as well as free room nights at the inn to buy his silence? Perhaps her being pregnant — if she was pregnant — had nothing to do with him.

I said, "Flora, if —" My cell phone buzzed in my jacket pocket. I pulled it free and checked the readout. Yardley had texted: *Naomi was attacked. She's at Mercy. Please come.*

I typed: *On my way.*

"We've got to run," I said.

"What's wrong?" Flora looked as panicked as I felt.

"Naomi. She's in the hospital."

"Oh, no."

Bailey and I hurried back to the shop. I told my aunt what had happened and then I hopped into the VW and sped to Mercy

Urgent Care.

As it had been the other day, the emergency area was buzzing with activity. I searched for Yardley among the crowd but didn't see her. My cell phone buzzed again. Yardley had texted *Room 101.*

I walked-ran down the corridor to the room and rapped on the partially closed door. "It's me, Jenna."

"Come in," Yardley said.

Naomi, dressed in the standard blue hospital gown, eyes closed, was lying in bed, her arms and bandaged hands above the sheet and cotton blanket.

Yardley was standing on the far side of the hospital bed. Her husband Wayne stood with his arm around her. Yardley was as white as her sweater and ready to crack. Wayne, tan and clad in a Wild Blue Yonder T-shirt that clung to his muscular chest, reminded me of an intrepid adventurer, able to handle any stressful situation.

"You know Wayne," Yardley whispered.

I nodded hello.

Yardley beckoned me to the bedside. "Naomi is lucid but drifting in and out."

On the hospital bed table was a plastic cup with straw and a clear packet holding what I assumed were Naomi's personal items: a wallet, cell phone, and pink potion necklace like the ones Pepper had been selling. Pink for confidence, I recalled. Yardley must have told her about it or gifted it to her.

I stared at Naomi's face, inspecting the square-shaped bruise on her cheek that had been salved with ointment, and my insides flinched ever so slightly. "Ow," I whispered.

"She was struck this morning outside her house," Yardley continued. "She —"

Naomi opened her eyes. "Hi, Jenna." Her voice was thin and weak.

"What happened?" I asked.

"Someone knocked," she said with effort. "Before dawn. I peered out the peephole. It was too dark to see anyone. I heard footsteps. Thinking the intruder was headed to my daughter's window, I grabbed the baseball bat I keep by the door. The next thing I knew, I was on the ground."

"Given the buckle imprint on her cheek," Yardley said, "the doctor thinks she was hit with some kind of purse or backpack. She wasn't robbed or . . ." Yardley didn't finish, but I knew what she meant. *Raped.*

Naomi licked her lips. "Water."

Yardley offered her the plastic cup fitted with a straw. Naomi took a long pull of liquid and handed it back.

"Was it Christopher?" I asked.

Naomi murmured, "I don't know. The footsteps . . . were heavy."

"Did you see anything?" I asked. "Smell anything?"

"Nothing. When my head cleared, I heard Nina crying. Inside. I couldn't" — she bit back tears — "get to her. My arms ached and my hands . . ."

I glanced at her bandaged hands.

"She couldn't even crawl," Yardley finished. "Luckily, she had her cell phone on her. She dialed 911 and the EMTs contacted me."

I petted Naomi's shoulder.

"She's going to be fine," Yardley said. "Nothing broken."

"And I'll be at the poster competition tomorrow when the winner's announced," Naomi promised.

"We'll see." Fondly, Yardley brushed a strand of hair off Naomi's face. "We'll see."

"Where is Nina?" I asked.

"With my friend," Naomi rasped.

"The one with the daughter the same age?"

"Yes."

"The EMTs brought Nina along," Yardley said, "but I didn't think this was the proper place for a child."

"You're too good to me." Naomi cleared

her throat.

Yardley handed her the water cup again.

For a moment, I pondered whether Naomi had faked the incident for sympathy and to take suspicion off herself regarding Quade. Keeping her identity a secret was a strong motive for murder, and her alibi for the night of the murder — being home with her daughter, a three-year-old who wouldn't be able to corroborate her story — was weak. But looking at the injury on her face and the bandages on her arms and hands, I couldn't imagine her doing such a thing to herself.

We chatted for a while about the festival and such, and then her eyelids fluttered and she drifted to sleep. I had to get back to work but told Yardley to call me if there was any change. She looped her arm around her husband's back and promised she would.

On the way down the hall, I was surprised to see a nurse wheeling Destiny on a gurney. I hurried to them and drew alongside. Destiny's forehead, like Naomi's cheek, had a square bruise on it. Her left eye was turning purple. There were also scratches, unbandaged, on her arms. I said to the nurse, "I know her. Are you taking her to a room?"

"We're full up with festivalgoers. I have to position her outside one that's being cleaned."

When they pulled to a stop, I said, "Destiny?"

She squinted, not recognizing me.

"It's Jenna Hart. What happened?"

"Someone rang my doorbell around seven. I think it was then. I'm not sure of the time. I didn't see anyone but heard . . . footsteps." The words came out slowly and slurred. The emergency team must have given her medicine for the pain. "I took a candlestick. My mother's. Big. Heavy." Her cadence was stilted. "The moment I stepped outside, someone whacked me. Hard. Something swung into my face. I bumped into the wall and —"

"Ma'am," the nurse said, "she needs her rest."

"Yes, but another woman was attacked the same way. Naomi Genet, room one-oh-one. If it was the same assailant, shouldn't we alert the police?"

The nurse hesitated.

"Destiny. Were you robbed?" I asked.

"No."

"Do you know if it was a man or woman?"

"I think it was a man."

It sounded like Destiny had been assaulted by the same person who'd attacked Naomi.

"When I came to, I heard my dog barking like crazy. I had to get to him. I crawled inside." Her hands were scraped. "He licked me, so I knew he wasn't hurt. Then I phoned 911."

I addressed the nurse. "Will she be okay?"

"She didn't suffer a concussion."

"I'll be at the finals for the wine tasting," Destiny rasped. "Tell Hannah."

"I'll do better than that. I'll text her right now." I did and then I dialed the precinct and asked for Cinnamon, only to be told she was at the hospital.

"Jenna!" a woman called.

I knew the voice and turned. Cinnamon was striding toward me. Appleby followed.

"What are you doing here?" she asked as she took note of Destiny.

"Naomi Genet was attacked. I came to see her and subsequently learned Destiny Dacourt had been assaulted, too. In the same way. Struck with a heavy object that probably has a square-shaped buckle. Neither was robbed or . . ."

"Which room is Miss Genet in?" Cinnamon asked.

"One-oh-one, but she's asleep."

Cinnamon said to Appleby, "This week keeps getting better. First the murder, then the hit-and-run and the bar fight, and now this?" She told him to go to Naomi's room.

As he walked away, a theory came to me. "I asked Naomi if she thought Christopher George did this. She wasn't sure."

"Why would he attack her?"

"Because she left him."

"Why would he harm Miss Dacourt?"

"So it wouldn't look like Naomi was his primary victim. She's been present at many of the functions this week. You talked to him again. Did you find out when he first met Quade? What their relationship was?"

"Jenna, I got your message about the tar shampoo. Let me do my job."

"He claims he has a rock-solid alibi for the night Quade was murdered."

Her eyes glinted with annoyance. "You asked him —"

"He said he was in his room. No room service. No witnesses. Watching CNN. Sounds weak to me. You should find out his alibi for this morning. To rule him out. Or here's another thought." I raised a finger as a second idea came to me. "What if Sienna Brown hurt Naomi, knowing Quade liked her, and hurt Destiny because she'd dated him at one time? A woman scorned. Plus . . ." I said what Flora Fairchild had shared about Sienna and added my two cents about the initials *HM* in Quade's ledger standing for hush money. "Except Sienna swears she has a verifiable alibi, too. She was in her residential unit at the inn and ordered chamomile tea."

"Actually . . ." Cinnamon paused.

"What?" I hung on her unspoken thought.

"Actually, her alibi is in doubt. The tea was left outside the room. The hospitality person did not see her." Cinnamon smiled tightly. "Thank you, Jenna. You can go now."

At least this time she hadn't ordered me to leave before hearing me out.

Chapter 19

On my way to my VW, I dialed Hannah. She was horrified to read my text about Destiny and said she would drop everything and visit her at Mercy Urgent Care. I told her not to worry. Destiny was clearheaded and a fighter.

Despite my assurances to Bailey and my aunt that I was unshaken by the latest turn of events, for the remainder of the afternoon I slogged through chores, selling books and reviewing preorders, trying not to dwell on the fact that not only was a murderer still on the loose but now someone was attacking women. I tried to seek comfort knowing that Cinnamon and her people would catch the culprit or culprits, but when?

Around three p.m., when Katie brought chocolate mousse mini cupcakes out as a treat — I ate two! — I found a second wind and sat at the register to create a suspect list. I wrote the names of those I deemed the likeliest suspects at the top of the list.

Christopher George. Motive: jealousy and/or financial gain, but I really couldn't see him risking his entire empire to take over a forgery gig. On the other hand, he was obviously besotted with Naomi. Did he really have a solid alibi? Cinnamon didn't refute it.

The scent of tar or cologne or whatever I'd detected at the crime scene continued to plague me.

Sienna Brown. Motive: to hide the secret about her thievery and/or her pregnancy. The first seemed the more likely of the two. Was that why she was so cagey at Intime? Also, she was a skilled fencer. She knew how to wield a sharp weapon.

Naomi Genet. Motive: to keep her whereabouts secret. But would she really risk going to jail and losing her daughter? Wouldn't it have been likelier that she would pack up and run? She'd reinvented herself once. She could do it again.

Who else? I tapped my pen on the pad of paper. Destiny? Quade had rebuffed her, but I imagined she would have wanted him alive so she could continue to try to win his heart. Yardley? No, she was Quade's mother and was clearly heartbroken. Z.Z.'s son Egan? Had he lied about sleeping on the beach and seeing Keller? What would his motive for murder have been? And then it came to me.

I revised what I'd written for Christopher George and applied it to Egan.

Egan Zeller. Motive: desire to be artists representative. Had he secretly become Quade's representative and brokered a deal, only to find out the art was a forgery, which infuriated him, knowing something like that could ruin his entire career? Or perhaps the driving need to get out from under his mother's wing by owning and selling the forgeries had propelled him to commit murder.

At a quarter past four, I realized I was flagging, my brain was mush, and I needed to go home if I was going to regroup for the girls' night out evening at Palette. Bailey asked if she could leave early, too. My aunt and Gran were more than happy to man the fort.

To my shock, when I got home I found Rook curled on the floor in the kitchen, reeking and covered with dirt. I groaned. "What have you been doing, young man?"

I set Tigger on the floor. Wanting nothing to do with the smelly dog, he bounded onto his kitty condo.

"Did you go out the doggie door and find

a skunk in the backyard, big guy?" How I hoped Rook hadn't overpowered the critter and brought it inside. I did a quick search of the house and, finding nothing, returned to the kitchen. Rook, still curled up, raised his head, his eyes pitiful. "I know you're sorry, fella. It's okay. But you're getting a shower." I pointed. Rook didn't budge. He'd never been bathed at this house. "Ahem. I'm the boss today. Let's go. On your feet."

He blinked.

"Fine." I attached a leash to his collar, grabbed the dog shampoo from under the sink — Rhett had thought to include all of Rook's items when he'd brought some of his clothes and toiletries earlier this week — and led the dog to the master bathroom. I turned on the shower to warm it up, then grabbed the anti-seborrheic shampoo and, stripping down to my bra and underwear, stepped into the shower, pulling Rook with me.

Tigger leaped onto the bathroom counter and scrutinized us from afar.

Planning ahead for exactly this purpose, we had installed a sprayer showerhead in addition to the overhead one. I soaked Rook, then turned off the water, poured a big dollop of his shampoo into my hand,

and rubbed it all over his fur. The tarlike aroma invaded my nose and I was reminded of the scent of Christopher George's shampoo. Both scents smelled like the odor I'd detected at the crime scene. I was sure of it.

I shook free of the memory and sprayed the dog with water until all the shampoo was gone. "Stay," I ordered and got out of the shower, closing the door.

He shimmied as much water as he could from his body. Droplets pelleted the shower's walls and glass door.

I fetched two towels for the brute from the cabinet — Rhett had also brought the dog's towels — and slipped back into the shower. I rubbed him down, inhaling as I did to make sure I'd gotten rid of the stinky odor. When he was good as new, I kissed his nose, unhooked the leash, and opened the shower door. "You're free!"

He jumped out as if escaping jail.

I mopped up the hair he'd shed, took my own shower, and then dressed for Palette.

Bailey and Katie had arrived before me. Bailey had dressed in a multicolored short-sleeved shirt and capris. Katie had donned an ancient college T-shirt over jeans. I'd thrown on a blouse I'd purchased at Anthropologie with a paint-splatter design. If I accidentally got paint on it, as I had the first time I'd gone to Palette, who would know?

In rhythm to the Michael Bublé song being piped through the speakers, I cha-cha'd to where they were selecting aprons.

"Brianna is wonderful," Bailey said, mid-conversation. "And Min-yi?"

"Eleanor is babysitting her tonight. How she adores her granddaughter." Katie beamed.

"Sorry I'm late," I cut in. "Talking babies?"

"Of course," Bailey said. "But we'll put that on pause. Why are you late?"

"When I got home, the dog —" I explained Rook's adventure and subsequent bath. "I'll get us each a glass of wine. What do you prefer?"

"Red," they both said.

"On it."

Palette was a colorful but narrow space with four rows of tables set with canvases on tabletop easels, brushes, palette knives, paint, and palettes. Aprons and cubbies for personal items were on the right side of the room. At the back was the food and wine counter. The place offered a few gourmet appetizers plus finger-food snacks, like nachos and popcorn. I purchased three glasses of Hurricane Vineyard pinot noir —

Hannah had made an exclusive deal with Palette as well as a few other locations in town — and three cheese plates with rosemary sea salt crackers and gherkins. After grabbing a few napkins, I carried the treats to my pals, who'd taken three spots in the row closest to the door.

A few newcomers entered and a breeze followed them in. I shivered.

"When everyone's here," Katie said, "it'll get warmer."

"Hope so."

"Hello, artists!" Orah, the owner and instructor, a thirty-something woman with startling blue eyes and wavy red hair, hailed us from the small stage on the side of the room where a canvas was set on an easel. "I'm Orah, spelled O-R-A-H. It means light. Yes, my mother was living in a commune when I was born. Where else would I get such a ridiculous name?"

The class of twenty laughed.

"I'll be your instructor for the evening." Orah was wearing a mauve peasant dress and long feathery earrings. "Today, we're going to tackle flowers. How many of you are artists?"

A few raised their hands.

Katie nudged my elbow. "Arm up."

"No. She knows." I wriggled away, doing

my best to stay perky even though thoughts of Naomi and Destiny being attacked and Cinnamon mentioning all the other crimes that had occurred in our fair town was running roughshod through my brain.

"That's okay," Orah said. "We're here to have fun. If it's your first time or your tenth time, this is all about trying something new and encouraging the inner artist in you to rise to the occasion. Are you ready?" She raised a paintbrush and a glass of wine. *"Salud!"*

Katie, Bailey, and I toasted.

"I needed this," Katie said.

For the next ten minutes, Orah gave her spiel, showing us a painting named *Perfect Posy* by Varaluz that we were going to try to copy or not copy, depending on our artistic talents. The painting was simple in structure, with vibrantly colored large and small flowers on a grayish background. Orah started by showing us how to cover the canvas in white and grays to create the background. "Layering," she said, "is key."

As the three of us followed her guidance, dipping our brushes in paint and swiping the brushes across our canvases, Bailey said to me, "How's Naomi?"

"I'm sure she's fine, but her face . . ."

"What happened to Naomi?" Katie's eyes

widened.

I explained. "Destiny was attacked, too. She has the same square-shaped welt on her face. I hope Cinnamon can match the bruise to a buckle."

"You said the doctor thought it might have been made by a purse," Bailey sipped her wine.

"Or a backpack."

"What about a shaving kit?" she asked. "Christopher George's had two buckles on it."

"Good thought."

"How do you know that?" Katie glanced between us.

"You don't want to know," I whispered conspiratorially, "or we'll have to —" I stopped short, the words catching in my throat.

"Christopher George is your main suspect?" Katie asked, missing my faux pas. She took a palette knife as Orah had demonstrated and scraped her paint to create the texturing for the background.

"Yes." I told them about the scent I'd detected when bathing Rook. "It smelled just like Tara's Tar shampoo, the odor I'm sure I detected at the crime scene. Then there's Sienna Brown," I continued. "She entered the crime scene. She washed dishes.

She might be pregnant with Quade's child. Plus, she might have paid him hush money to keep the fact that she's a petty thief quiet."

"No way. She's a thief?" Katie gaped. "How'd you figure that out?"

"Flora."

"Those Fairchild sisters sure do glean a lot of gossip."

I proceeded to tell them how Cinnamon hinted that Sienna's alibi was in question.

"Guilty," Bailey whispered.

"All right, everyone, listen up." Orah explained how we should create the stems of the flowers. "Dripping is a technique. Gravity won't cause the paint to run downward, but if you add a dab of water, like so" — she demonstrated on her canvas — "this is what happens. For these stems, we'll start the drips in the middle and upper third of the canvas."

We each tried to follow her instructions. My drips came out pretty good. Katie muttered that hers looked like a five-year-old had done them.

"Do you still suspect Naomi?" Bailey asked.

I mentally reviewed the suspect-motive list I'd created. Because Naomi was a mother, a *doting* mother, I couldn't see her as a killer. "I don't think so."

Katie tucked a stray curly hair behind her ear. "Keller's been driving me crazy wondering when Cinnamon will solve this case. He feels like she'll change her mind and charge him."

"She won't. Promise. But, you know, there's something else that has been bugging me." I told them about going to the pier for Watercolors and Wine the other night and seeing Egan Zeller giving money to that guy. "What if he and Quade had some kind of arrangement?"

Bailey scoffed. "Okay, now you're being ridiculous. Z.Z.'s son?"

"Out of the blue, he gave an alibi for Keller. What if he was lying to create an alibi for himself?"

Katie gripped my arm. "No! *Shh!* If he lied, then Keller won't have a witness putting him on the beach that night. Please, don't tell Cinnamon this theory. Please."

"Do you think Egan is dealing drugs?" Bailey asked. "Did Quade use drugs?"

Katie moaned. "Stop."

"Egan said he wanted to become an artists representative," I replied. "What if he had an agreement to represent Quade but came to realize Quade was dealing in forgeries? What if he'd already brokered a deal for one and worried that the deal could blow his entire future to smithereens?"

Bailey said, "That doesn't explain the exchange of money with the guy on the Pier."

"Stop!" Katie barked and covered her mouth, surprised at her outburst.

Orah swooped up behind us and peeked over our shoulders. "Okay, ladies, I see you've got the backgrounds down and a couple of stems. Want to add a few more?"

I winked at her. "Don't rush us. Brilliance takes inspiration."

Orah giggled. "Good point, Jenna. Have a fun time. If you need help, let me know." She sauntered to her canvas on the stage and resumed the lesson, this time showing how to form the underpinnings of the flower petals.

"What about Destiny?" Bailey asked, moving on. "She dated Quade a while back. She was hounding him at the soiree the night he was killed."

"I don't think she was hounding him," I said. "She was trying to build up confidence to ask him out."

"And he rebuffed her. A woman scorned . . ." she said, echoing my words to Cinnamon about Sienna.

CHAPTER 20

I woke to the sound of church bells, Rook's nose next to my face, and Tigger digging into the comforter by my feet. I rolled over to give Rhett a hug and was alarmed not to see him in bed. "Where is he, boy?" I asked Rook.

The dog yawned.

I slipped out of bed, threw on my silk robe, and padded to the kitchen. "Rhett!" I yelled.

He didn't answer. He wasn't in the yard. I opened the front door and peered at the beach. I didn't see him taking a walk. Panicking ever so slightly, I checked my cell phone.

He'd sent a text message: *Kitchen fire. Out. Safe. But have to deal with insurance adjuster.*

I responded: *Why didn't you call me?*

He replied: *Didn't want to wake you.*

Me: *What was the issue?*

Him: *Grease in the vent. Typical. Not a big*

deal. Love you.

I replied in kind and made a pot of coffee, extra-strong. While it brewed, I gazed at the painting of flowers that I'd done at Palette. I'd set it on the red Ching two-door cabinet that held my art supplies. It was nice but not my best work. I wasn't sure if I'd keep working on it or simply paint over it and start fresh. Inspiration wasn't grabbing me, certainly not when I had to get to the shop. I'd agreed to open and tend the register by myself for the first two hours.

After feeding the pets, drinking a cup of coffee, and downing a power shake made with bananas, strawberries, Greek yogurt, and protein powder, I tossed on a floral shift, ecru bolero cardigan, an imperial jaspar goddess bracelet that my aunt had given me to inspire serenity and strength, my jade-colored cross-body purse, and sassy sandals — I wanted to look my best at the finals presentation this afternoon. Then I switched on music for Rook, told him to be a good boy and avoid skunks, and drove with Tigger to work.

As I was distributing cash into the slots of the register, my cell phone rang. Not Rhett. It was Harmony Bold, the wedding planner.

"I'm so sorry," she said without preamble. "I did not see your text about touching base with Destiny Dacourt regarding vineyard locations. I'm not sure how it escaped me."

"It's okay. I've lost texts, too. It's amazing these newfangled contraptions work at all. I saw her the other night and mentioned you'd be in touch."

Harmony chuckled. "You know, Destiny and I worked together before. She helped me land CC Vineyard for the Naylors. What an extravaganza that was!" The Naylors were one of the founding families of Crystal Cove in the 1850s. The town wasn't officially established until the 1880s. Last December, their daughter had married the son of one of the other founding families. Talk of the upcoming nuptials had dominated the *Crystal Cove Courier*'s front page for weeks. "At the time, CC Vineyard was booked for two solid years, but miraculously a window of opportunity opened."

"If Destiny can pull those kinds of strings, then she's got superpowers."

"I'll call her this afternoon, or at the latest tomorrow. And I've got four sites, not two, for you and Rhett to see next weekend."

"Perfect."

A few minutes shy of eleven a.m., Gran scuttled in with her three adorable granddaughters. She always took Sundays off. Tigger scurried to greet them. All of them were dressed up. Gran, as she often did, was wearing a classic silk blouse and linen trousers. The girls were in party dresses. The youngest kept swishing the skirt of her dress to and fro. Tigger thought it was a game and pranced around her ankles.

"Is everything okay, Jenna?" Gran asked.

"Super. We've already had a dozen-plus customers, thanks to the festival traffic."

"Wonderful."

"I can't wait to see the poster art finals," the eldest granddaughter said.

Gran squeezed the girl fondly. "She's a budding artist. You should see her pen-and-ink drawings."

"That's how I started," I said. I had loved to sketch, and my mother had encouraged it, claiming sketching helped an artist learn perspective. "Bring your work in someday," I added. "I'd love to see it."

"Um, okay," she said shyly.

"We're going next door for tea before we head to Azure Park," Gran said.

I leaned down to meet the three girls, eye to eye. "Do you like chocolate?"

They all nodded.

"Then make sure Chef Katie brings you her famous chocolate scones, and if your grandma will allow it, a double-chocolate hot chocolate with chocolate-dusted whipped cream."

The youngest hopped from one foot to the other in anticipation. "Let's go, Gran."

And off they went.

Aunt Vera swept in, the train of her royal blue caftan wafting in her wake.

"Aren't you dressed up," I said. "What's the occasion?"

"I thought I should dress for dinner in case we had a barrage of customers this afternoon."

Our family ate dinner together on Sundays whenever we could. The number of attendees varied. Tonight's dinner would be at my father's house. I couldn't wait until Rhett and I hosted our first one. We agreed it would be after we'd taken our vows.

"You look pretty," she said, assessing my outfit. "Perfect for this afternoon's ceremony."

"Thanks."

"I think Lola and your father will attend. I'm sorry I can't be there."

I clasped her arm. "Knowing you're there in spirit is enough for me. Trust me, I know I won't win, but I'd like to place."

"Sweetheart, you made the finals. You've already placed." She offered a supportive smile.

For the next hour, we attended to business. Twice, customers requested to see Chef Katie to ask her a question about plating. She was more than happy to oblige. During a lull, I went to the kitchen and inquired whether she'd like to give some group lessons. It would be a way for her to boost her income. She said she'd consider it, but with Min-yi, she might not have time.

At noon, I said to my aunt, "I'm off."

"Too-ra-loo!" she trilled.

I strolled to Azure Park, drinking in the sunshine but aware that a bank of storm clouds loomed on the horizon. Tomorrow could get quite wet.

When I arrived at the venue, I couldn't believe the throngs passing beneath the arch of crisscrossed silver bars and ribbons. Moving slowly so I didn't bump into anyone, I listened to the cheery chatter. One woman had found the perfect gift for her daughter-in-law. Another had learned how to refurbish her old bedroom furniture. A mother with a six- or seven-year-old child asked what the child's favorite thing was so far. The answer: making origami.

"Jenna," Cinnamon said, drawing me to a halt in front of Holy Guacamole. She and Bucky each held a taco and a memento drink glass. Not wine. Cinnamon was in her uniform. So was Bucky. Neither would drink while on duty.

"Lunch break?" I asked.

"Catching a quick hour together. This week, it's been hard to find time."

"Tell me about it." I wondered if Rhett had gone home to sleep yet.

"Then it's back to the precinct. I've got a load of paperwork to finish. Hey, I viewed your artwork again." Cinnamon hooked her thumb toward the south end of the park. "It's quite good. Your father boasts about your talent, and I happen to agree."

I swelled with pride. "Thank you. A compliment from you means a lot." I didn't know why I craved her approval, but I did. I supposed it was because over the past few years we'd become friends; not to mention, my father had mentored her during her acting-out phase in high school — her father was out of the picture by then — which sort of made her family.

"Good luck," she said. "Hope you win."

"I won't, but it's nice to be included in the finals. By the way, did you find whoever attacked Naomi and Destiny?"

"Not so far."

"And how's the other —" I clipped off the rest of my thought.

Cinnamon grimaced. A deep crease formed between her eyebrows. "The other investigation going?" she finished for me.

"I didn't —"

She held up a hand. "Jenna, Jenna, Jenna, when will you understand that I want you to butt out?"

"Never," I said with a sly smile.

"That's the way." Bucky gave me a thumbs-up. "Don't let her bully you."

Cinnamon blew a raspberry and guided her beloved away.

Pressing on, I passed many well-wishers before arriving at the Art Institute booth. Yardley was supervising while three judges, two elderly men and a middle-aged woman, each pinned with an official ribbon, examined the art. Yardley, though petite, appeared commanding in her tailored knee-length white dress, hands folded in front of her and shoulders squared.

The female judge, who sported thick-rimmed glasses, was standing with her nose inches from my painting. The thin red-headed man was using a photograph loupe to examine the finer points of Keller's work. The other man, the chief judge I presumed, given his age and officious bearing, was talking on his cell phone. He ended the call, snapped his fingers, and signaled to the others that it was time to make a determination. Quickly, the three of them huddled beyond the easels.

Someone tapped me on the shoulder. I turned and smiled when I saw Naomi, pretty in pink — well, almost pretty. She'd done what she could to cover her bruise with makeup, but the square imprint was still evident.

I clasped her elbow. "How are you feeling? Should you be up and about?" I searched for Christopher George in the crowd but didn't see him.

"I wouldn't have missed this for the world. Chief Pritchett was just here. I don't think she likes me very much."

"Why do you say that?"

"She kept staring at me and whispering to her husband."

"She was probably as concerned as I am that you're not in the hospital."

"I heard Destiny was hurt, too. She was released before I was. Did she describe" — Naomi worked her lip between her teeth — "who attacked her? Could it have been the same person?"

"Destiny was as clueless as you, though she was pretty positive it was a man."

"Christopher," Naomi said under her breath. "He —"

"Ladies and gentlemen, may I have your attention!" Z.Z. Zeller announced through a microphone from the main stage. "Welcome to the final day of Crystal Cove's fabulous Fifth Annual Art and Wine Festival."

Applause rang out from the crowd.

"I'd like to direct your attention to the South Stage at the other end of the park. The judges are making their final decisions regarding the poster art competition, and in less than three minutes they will present their awards."

Wayne, the model of ease and grace in white shirt and gray linen pants, was chatting with Yardley and Sienna near the stage. Sienna, in contrast, looked like the wind had blown her to the event, her hair askew, the folds of her billowy floral dress twisted. Her tote, a heavy leather style, seemed to be the single thing anchoring her to the ground. Nearby, my father, Lola, and Bailey were huddled together with Katie, who had taken off work for two hours, her daughter Min-yi, and Keller. Katie gazed lovingly at her husband. He fidgeted from foot to foot. His mother Eleanor, standing on his right and clad in her Taste of Heaven uniform, put a firm hand on his shoulder to calm him.

My cell phone buzzed in my purse. I pulled it out. Rhett had texted: *I'm parking.*

Overslept alarm. Am I too late?

I typed back: *Moments to go.*

He responded: *I'll make it.*

"And after that," Z.Z. continued, "we'll announce the wine tasting awards on the East Stage." She gestured to the other temporary stage. I couldn't see through the crowd, but I imagined Hannah, her husband Alan Baldini, and Destiny — if she'd been released from Mercy — and others were convening nearby.

The judges climbed the steps to the temporary stage. A banner was slung across the front hyping the *5th Annual Art and Wine Festival Poster Competition Finals.* A draped table holding three colored glass, swirl-style trophies stood beside the microphone.

The officious judge stepped up to the microphone and tested it. It crackled, signaling that it was on. "Ladies and gentlemen," he said in a distinctly British accent, "it is my proud pleasure to introduce you to the finalists in the Poster Art Competition. Naomi Genet, winner of last year's competition, would you please join us on stage? Give her a big hand, folks."

Naomi grabbed hold of my arm. "I can't. Not looking like this."

"You look lovely," I said, "and from a distance, no one will be able to see your bruise. Go! You deserve the recognition."

Courageously, she climbed the stairs to the stage.

"Next, Yardley Alks," the head judge continued. "Owner of the Art Institute. She has been instrumental in seeing that all of our artists —" He balked and turned to Yardley standing beside the stairs. "Forgive me, folks. My sincere apologies. Would you please join me for a moment of silence to honor one of the artists, Quade, who met with an untimely death this week?"

In an instant the mass of people near the stage quieted. The judge allowed the silence for about thirty seconds and resumed.

"Where was I? Oh, yes, Yardley Alks has been instrumental for this program. She oversaw it last year and then again this year. Thank you for all your hard work."

The audience applauded, and Yardley climbed up the stairs and stood next to Naomi.

"I think we can all agree that the works this year were marvelous," he said. "Over two hundred participants . . ." He droned on about the requirements to enter and the subsequent use of the winning work. He raved about Naomi's art, which had been featured on this year's poster. Finally, he said, "And now, without much ado" — he picked up a trophy from the table — "third place goes to . . ." He consulted a card. "To Faith Fairchild."

Faith whooped and hugged Flora. Both had worn flowery prints but they couldn't have appeared more different. Faith's dress fit her like a glove. Flora's sparkled with beading. Flora bussed her sister's cheek, and Faith trotted up the steps to the stage.

"Thank you, thank you," she gushed into the microphone, even though the judge hadn't ceded it to her. "I am beyond words."

"Second place," the judge said, regaining command, "goes to Keller Landry."

Katie whistled using two fingers. Eleanor threw her arms around Keller. Then Katie crouched beside their daughter and helped her clap her hands for Daddy. Taking the steps two at a time, Keller made the stage in three strides. He stood beside Faith, beaming. No speech. He didn't even attempt it.

"And the first-place prize goes to . . ." The judge turned pale. Mustering courage, he forced a smile and announced, "Quade." He regarded his fellow judges. "Of course, these are unusual circumstances. We will have to figure out how to award the prize posthumously."

Rhett flew to my side, skidding on his

heels. "I'm sorry I'm late, but I heard everything, and I'm sorry you didn't win, but in my eyes —"

I threw my arms around his neck and kissed him heartily. "You are all the prize I need."

"Does anyone know how to contact his family?" the judge asked, rotating his head right and left.

Fighting tears of grief, Yardley raised her hand. Wayne made a move toward the stage. Yardley waved him off. "May I, sir?" she asked the judge, gesturing to the microphone. He nodded for her to take the lead. "Ladies and gentlemen —" Her voice cracked. She raised her chin. "I know that Quade would have been so proud to have won this prestigious award, and I will do all I can to make sure that his art and his memory are respected and treasured going forward."

The head judge resumed his place behind the microphone. "Thank you all for joining us in this celebration. Look for next year's flyers to feature Quade's unique and fabulous work. If you'll now focus on the vintners' competition results on the East Stage."

A photographer jogged onto the South Stage and shouted for the winners to convene. Covertly, Naomi skirted the group and fled down the stairs.

As if he'd been hiding, lying in wait, Christopher George emerged through a break in the crowd and gripped her elbow. He pulled her behind the easels.

"Rhett!" I hurried after them, wishing Cinnamon hadn't gone back to the precinct.

Rhett kept pace. "I'm with you."

"All I want to do is talk," Christopher rasped.

"Let me go," Naomi cried.

Rhett and I rounded the easels.

"Your face," Christopher said, reaching out to touch.

Naomi recoiled and wrenched free. She dashed off.

"What happened?" Her husband pursued her.

"I was attacked."

"By whom?"

"I don't know. You? It had to be you."

"Me? Never!"

"Where were you at dawn yesterday?" she demanded.

"I had a Zoom call breakfast. Three of my board members can vouch for my whereabouts. C'mon, sweetheart. I want you back, Nancy."

"The name is Naomi."

"Whatever you call yourself, you're still

my wife. I want to woo you, but you won't give me the time of day."

"Woo me?" She whirled around. "What are you talking about, *woo* me? You've been stalking me."

"C'mon, Nancy, I want answers. Is Nina my daughter? Tell me." Christopher grabbed her arms and shook her. Naomi's head lolled right and left.

"Christopher, don't!" I yelled.

"Tell me," he repeated.

Naomi glared at him. "No!"

Christopher raised his hand as if preparing to slap her.

Rhett and I both yelled, "Christopher, stop!"

We needn't have. Naomi gripped his wrist and twisted it. Hard.

He yelped, pulled free, and clasped his nearly offending hand with the other. "I'm sorry, sweetheart. I only meant to scare you. I'd never hit you."

Rhett ran at Christopher, shoved him away from Naomi, and held him at bay. Christopher threw up both hands, agreeing to the distance.

"He killed him," Naomi sobbed. "He killed Quade."

"No, I didn't," Christopher protested.

"Christopher," I said, trying to divert his

attention. "You have a flimsy alibi for the night Quade was murdered. You say you were in your room at the inn with no room service, no witnesses, watching CNN."

"I was."

"Being able to recount the coverage is weak. You could have watched a recap. It would have been easy for you to sneak out."

"I didn't —"

"Did you kill him because you thought Naomi was in love with him? Or because you thought he was the girl's father? Or did you kill him because he fooled you with his forgeries?" I pressed.

He gawked. "What forgeries?"

"I was in Quade's place. I saw the David Smith forgeries. I told the police about them. You and Quade communicated via email."

"Not about any forgeries."

"The police have a paper trail," I lied, not willing to reveal I knew they'd been erased from his cloud.

"I . . . I wrote him about Nancy. I'd seen him pursuing her. I . . ." He jammed his lips together.

Naomi's gaze tracked from me to Christopher and back again. "You did do it, didn't you? You were jealous and you killed him."

"No. I do have an alibi. But not the one I told the police." Christopher glanced helplessly in Naomi's direction and then to Rhett and me. "I lied because I followed Nancy home that night."

"Naomi," she muttered.

"I didn't tell the police," he went on, "because I didn't want it getting back to . . . *Naomi* . . . that I went there."

Naomi thrust out a hand. "Told you. Stalking."

"No. I wanted to approach you. I wanted to knock on the door" — he splayed his hands — "and ask you to start over. To go on a date. But then the door opened and I froze. And you sneaked out."

Naomi's eyes squinted with confusion. "I didn't sneak out. What are you accusing me of?"

"You went around the side of the house, and you didn't come back."

"What time was this?" she demanded, fisting her hands on her hips.

"At a quarter to ten."

The ME had fixed the time of Quade's death between ten and eleven.

"For Pete's sake, Chris." She threw up both hands. "I went out back to have a cigarette. I don't smoke in the house. Not around Nina."

Christopher gazed at me. "I didn't tell the police because I was afraid you were the killer."

"Me?" Naomi clapped a hand to her chest.

"That guy Quade kept pursuing you. He threatened you last week."

She groaned. "You really have been spying on me. How long have you been in town?"

"Did you kill him?" Christopher asked.

"Get real!" she cried. "No, I didn't kill him. I had a cigarette, and I slipped into the house through the back door."

"Why didn't you go out through the back door?" I asked.

"I keep the cigarettes in my purse, which was on the table by the front door."

Christopher said, "You didn't turn off the lights."

Naomi glowered. "If you'd been paying attention, you'd have realized that I never do. I sleep with the lights on. Because . . ." She gasped for breath. "Because of you!" She folded her arms protectively over her chest and stamped her foot.

"Both of you need to tell Chief Pritchett," I said.

"Yes, fine," Naomi said testily, and zeroed in on her husband. "Listen to my words, Christopher George. Leave me alone. I am never coming back. Ever. Goodbye." She marched through the break between two booths, leaving Christopher with me and Rhett.

Christopher hung his head. "I'll contact the police," he whispered.

As he left, I eyed Rhett. "What do you think?"

"They sort of corroborated each other's alibis."

"Except I've never seen Naomi smoke."

Chapter 21

Bailey raced up to us. My father and Lola trailed her. "What was that all about?" She gestured to Christopher's retreating figure.

I explained.

When I finished, Rhett kissed my cheek and apologized because he had to leave for work. I whispered in his ear, "Thanks for being here."

"I wouldn't have missed it. You are fearless, I'll give you that."

I texted Cinnamon and told her to expect a visit from Naomi Genet as well as Christopher George. She texted back, *Why?*

I responded: *I'll let them tell you.*

"I think you need to have a glass of wine," Bailey said, looping her hand around my elbow. "This way to the finals. Afterward, we'll grab a taste of something. There's a venue featuring all the finalists' wines right next door."

Dad and Lola begged off. She, like Rhett,

had to go to work, and Dad had agreed to meet a builder at the hardware store.

"I'm so proud of you," he whispered in my ear before leaving. "Your mother would be, too."

"Thanks, Dad."

The East Stage had been set like the South Stage, with a banner strung across the front hyping the finals, although its table held three silver grape-cluster trophies. A female judge in a sleek blue dress approached the microphone. "Ladies and gentlemen, may I have your attention, please?"

Hannah, in typical black, stood to the right of the stairs with six other vintners. Her husband Alan Baldini, gawky and unmuscular, was standing, hands in jeans pockets, about three feet away. Even in profile, I could tell he was beaming. Near Alan, Destiny was chatting with a leggy blonde, seemingly about their matching pink-and-black halter dresses. They had to be chilly and mutually miffed at whomever had sold them the distinctive dresses. Destiny's face looked pretty good, considering. Like Naomi, she'd done the best she could to cover her bruise with makeup.

The judge explained the rules of the competition and the backgrounds of the finalists. Hannah's vineyard was the largest local winery. Two of the finalists were the small-batch wineries Nouveau and Vast Horizon. The other three were well-known vintners from Napa, Sonoma, and Mendocino.

"Go, Hannah!" Bailey shouted.

I elbowed her to hush. She chuckled. Alan wheeled around and, seeing us, waved. I waved back.

The presentations began. The judge asked the finalists to join her on stage. Hannah's winery won third place, Nouveau won second, and the Napa Valley vintner won first place.

As Hannah was cheered by the others, I heard a woman call my name.

"Jenna, there you are." Yardley and her husband Wayne drew near. Her face was tearstained, her lower lip quivering as she tried to maintain a positive façade. "I was hoping to see you before I headed back to the institute. I got waylaid after the presentations. There was so much to explain to the judges about my relationship to Quade."

"Congratulations on his behalf." I hesitated. "I know my words sound hollow, but knowing his art will live on through the festival should give you a smidgen of solace."

"Sadly," she said, "due to the issue with the forgeries and his impending dubious reputation, I've told the judging panel to withdraw his entry. Keller will be declared the official winner."

Wayne slung a supportive arm around his wife.

"By the way, Jenna," Yardley went on, "you did such a lovely job with your art. I hope you're very proud."

"I am."

"Don't let it go to your head," Bailey joshed.

"One other thing," Yardley added. "Sienna —"

Wayne shook his head, cautioning her.

"But I have to tell Jenna, sweetheart," Yardley protested. "She's been so close to this investigation."

"Go on then." Wayne motioned for her to continue.

"You won't believe what Sienna told me minutes ago," Yardley said.

"That she killed Quade?" I asked.

"What? Heavens, no." Yardley batted the air. "She said an employee at the inn, a housekeeper who was home sick for five days, told Sienna less than an hour ago that she saw Destiny outside Quade's cabana on Sunday morning. The woman had been so sick, she hadn't heard the news. She hadn't realized a murder had occurred."

"Sunday means nothing as far as the murder is concerned, time-wise," I murmured as I caught sight of Destiny hugging Hannah.

Yardley continued. "I don't know Destiny well, and I can't imagine she's guilty of murder, but Sienna said there would have been no reason for her to have been at the inn. No wine tours were scheduled. Why was she there?"

"She was in love with Quade."

"Ahh." Sadness mixed with regret flashed in Yardley's eyes. "Loving without being loved in return is a bitter pill to swallow."

"Tell me about it," Bailey groused.

Yardley clasped her husband's elbow. "It took me five years to win Wayne's heart. I shed a lot of tears in those sixty months." She turned her attention to me. "Thank you for all your support."

"My pleasure." I smiled. "Come by the shop soon. We'll go to the Nook for tea."

"I'd like that."

As Wayne guided Yardley away, I thought about Destiny. Why had she gone to the inn? Why linger outside Quade's room? Had she really wanted to talk to him or to plan his murder?

"What're you thinking?" Bailey asked.

"I was —"

"Hi, Jenna." Hannah, holding her husband's elbow, strolled toward us with her third-place trophy in hand.

"Congrats!" I cried.

"Yes, way to go!" Bailey hooted.

Hannah broke free of Alan and I hugged her.

"I can't believe it," she gushed. "I was certain the Sonoma vintner would beat me. I knew the first two entries were better. The pinot from Nouveau is something special. The winemaker has an exquisite sense of timing for harvesting and providing the exact amount of water for each crop. I'm jealous."

Alan caressed her arm. "Don't be jealous. Be inspired."

Hannah smiled adoringly at him. " 'Be inspired.' I love that."

"Hey, Hannah," I said, "I have a question. About Destiny. Sienna Brown said one of the inn's housekeepers saw her loitering outside Quade's cabana on Sunday morning."

Bailey's eyes widened. "Do you think she was staking out the place?"

Hannah scoffed. "To plan a murder? No way. She was in love with him. Not to mention, the housekeeper has to be wrong. Destiny was home all day Sunday. I happen to know because I was in touch with her. Via text messages."

Alan bobbed his head. "Constantly."

"She could text from anywhere," I said patiently.

Hannah rolled her eyes and tucked the trophy under one arm so she could gesture with the other. "I know that, but there were a few texts she didn't respond to. In the hills where she lives, cell reception can be bad, and driving to town can make it even worse. So, desperate to know if she was in the vicinity because I needed her to pick up a few items for Monday evening's soiree, I pinged her cell phone. The locator showed she was at home. Plus, she was posting online on Facebook at the time."

Facebook posts could be scheduled, I theorized and quickly chided myself. Why was I doing my best to come up with an answer to convict Destiny of all people?

"How about following the event Tuesday night? Do you know where she went after you two packed up?"

"Home. To do PR. She never stops. You and I both know how that goes." Hannah squeezed my arm. "Hey, Alan and a few of our friends and I are going out to celebrate.

Do you two want to join us?"

"Can't," I said. "Work and then family dinner."

"Your loss," Alan kidded. "I'm paying."

As they walked away in a loving embrace, Bailey pointed at my face. "What's going on in that brain of yours?"

"Even if Hannah's wrong and Destiny had been seen . . . it wouldn't make her guilty. Like I said, she was in love with Quade. Hanging around the cabana, hoping to catch a conversation with him would be logical."

"Do you think Sienna is kicking up dirt to throw suspicion from herself?"

"Good thought." I texted Cinnamon a recap.

Cinnamon responded in less than ten seconds. *Jenna, what did I tell you?*

I texted: *Butt out. Got it. But I can't help it if people talk to me.*

She wrote back: *Yes you can. Put your fingers in your ears.* She added a few sassy emojis.

It was my turn to blow a raspberry.

By the time I got back to the shop — I'd decided to pass on wine tasting with Bailey — I was starving, so I breezed into the café to beg Katie to make me one of her renowned grilled cheese and spicy tomato sandwiches. Simply thinking about the serrano pepper sauce she added made me salivate. However, I drew up short when I spotted Z.Z., Egan, and Jake at the first table beyond the hostess's station. Z.Z. was doing the talking. Jake was chowing down on a fish burger. Egan was digging in a backpack that he'd set on his lap.

Seeing the backpack, I flashed on my conversation with Bailey and Katie at Palette about Egan and the guy on the Pier, and felt my cheeks warm, embarrassed by the trajectory my curious mind had followed that night.

He caught sight of me and frowned. "What?" he said aloud.

Z.Z. and Jake stopped what they were doing and glanced in my direction.

I peeked over my shoulder, wondering if Egan was addressing someone behind me. No one was there. I turned back and put a hand to my chest. "Are you talking to me?"

He beckoned me with a terse gesture.

I skirted the hostess's station and proceeded to the table. "Is something wrong with your meal?"

Egan said, "You were staring at me."

"No, I —"

"Yeah, you were. Like you didn't trust me.

What's up?"

"I wasn't —" I halted. *Admit it, Jenna, you were gawking at him.* "Okay, I was staring because I was wondering —"

"What you were doing on the Pier the other night?" Z.Z. demanded, as if reading my thoughts. She'd probably been dying to ask him the question throughout their meal. "On the night of Watercolors and Wine?"

Egan fixed me with a withering look. "Was that what you were going to ask, Jenna?"

"Give me the backpack." Z.Z. held out her hand.

"No, Mom," Egan snarled and slung the backpack on the arm of his chair.

"That man," Z.Z. said, "in the raggedy clothes. He handed you something. You gave him money."

Egan heaved a sigh. "Yeah, we made an exchange."

"Of what?"

"He's homeless. I've been paying him to use his tent to sleep on the beach."

Z.Z. gasped. "You're sleeping in a homeless man's tent?"

"Don't worry. It's clean. The guy is a germaphobe."

"Oh, please."

"It's true. On the Pier, he was giving me disinfectant wipes to make sure I cleaned things down before returning the tent. Did you think I was buying drugs?" He huffed. "You know me better than that. At least, I thought you did." He jabbed his chest with a finger. "Nothing bad goes into this body."

"What were you digging around in your backpack for just now?" she demanded.

He lifted the pack and handed it to her. "Here. Be my guest. I was looking for my bottle of organic no-salt substitute. Seeing as Dad died of a heart attack, I figured I should cut back on my salt, starting like yesterday."

Jake guffawed. Z.Z. gave him the stink eye.

"C'mon, Zeez," Jake chided. "I spent many nights on the beach when I first arrived in Crystal Cove. You know my story. It's not a big deal. It didn't ruin me for life. Plus, it gave me a great appreciation for the finer things."

Egan turned his gaze on me again. "What did you think went down, Jenna?"

"Like your mother, I was wondering if you were dealing drugs."

"No fricking way."

"And I was wondering," I continued, "if you lied about seeing Keller to give yourself an alibi."

"Why would I need an alibi?"

I held out a hand. "Did you have any dealings with Quade? Artistic dealings?"

"Quade?" He arched an eyebrow.

"The artist who died," Z.Z. inserted.

"I know who he was, Mom," her son snapped. "No, I never had *artistic* dealings with him. Why would I?"

"Because you want to become an artists representative," I said.

Egan placed his hands palms-down on the table. "Look, I haven't approached any artists. I'm learning the ropes. I'd be a fool to take on clients before I was ready to direct their careers."

Jake tattooed the table. "That's my boy. You've been listening." He folded his hands and gazed lovingly at Z.Z. "Hon, I've been mentoring Egan on the side. I can assure you, he's a good kid. He has promise."

"Also, Mom, FYI," Egan said, "I've been thinking it would be more lucrative for me to go into something more stable, like managing all these festivals that come to town. What do you think?"

Z.Z. said, her voice thick with emotion, "I think I could find a position for you."

"Egan," I said, "I'm sorry for misjudging."

"S'all right," he slurred. "And, for the record, I did see Keller. That's no lie."

Chapter 22

I scored the grilled cheese from Katie and was walking through the breezeway to the shop when I saw Sienna inside Beaders of Paradise near the window. She was hunched over a tray of beads, pawing through them. Clandestinely, she slipped her hand into her heavy leather tote bag. Was she stealing merchandise or was I reading into her movements? Given what Flora had revealed, I decided to find out. *To protect Pepper's business interests,* I told myself.

I set my to-go box on the snack table in the breezeway and made a U-turn. I exited through the café and breezed into the craft shop. Customers were browsing the racks filled with colorful twine, wire, and string while others were sorting through the spools of thread.

Pepper, glowing with energy, her skin tone as rosy as the rose-colored beaded sweater she had on, was at the counter ringing up a customer. "Hello, Jenna," she said. "Be right with you."

Sienna cut a look in my direction. She straightened and smiled at me, but the corners of her mouth twitched nervously. She held her tote tightly against her chest as if she was afraid I'd rip it from her.

I walked to her. "They're pretty beads, aren't they? Are you a crafter?"

"My niece is. Her birthday is coming up. I was contemplating what to get her."

Quick response. Maybe she was being truthful.

"How did you like the art competition and wine tasting results?" I asked.

"Nice." She passed a hand over her hair. "Although I thought your work was better than Faith's as well as Flora's."

"That's nice of you to say."

"Hers was much too pastel-y for my tastes."

"Speaking of Flora . . ." I let the name hang.

"What about her?" Sienna's innocent tone sounded forced.

"She told me that you —"

Sienna held up a hand. "Don't go on, Jenna. I know what she says about me. And . . ." She glanced at Pepper and then back at me and hiccupped out a sigh. "It's true. I'm a kleptomaniac. I can't help myself. It's funny, you know." She let out a regretful laugh, clearly not believing any of this was funny. "I fear it's a syndrome for the bored well-to-do."

"Did Quade know this about you?"

"Why are you bringing him up again?"

"Because, as I said at Intime the other night, you were mentioned in his black book. In fact, he put the initials *HM* next to your initials, *STB. HM,*" I repeated. "It means hush money, doesn't it?"

Sienna's broad shoulders shuddered. She teetered and settled into a ladderback chair positioned to the right of the beads. "Oh, Jenna. I can't believe he's dead. Yes, I went there that night to talk to him because he was dunning me for money. The door was open" — she fanned the air — "and I saw him there, asleep. I didn't want to talk to him when he was . . ." Her eyelids fluttered. "When he was nude and most likely drunk. It would have made me so uncomfortable, and he wouldn't have covered up. He had no shame." Her chin began to quiver. She pressed her lips together, as if working hard to gain control of her emotions. "I saw the dishes on the counter, as I told you — there was one clean wineglass but the rest were dirty and disgusting. So I decided to do a nice deed. I'd wash up and chat with him in the morning. But then —"

"Hold on. There was a clean wineglass?"

"Yes."

"You didn't mention that before."

"I didn't think it was important. It was one of the handblown ones Hannah sells."

"Can you describe it?"

"It had beautiful green-and-gold wavelike swirls."

Was I right? Had Quade drunk something that was laced with arsenic? "Was the glass drying upside down, as if it had been washed?"

She nodded.

Aha! It had been among the other cleaned dishes. That was why I hadn't noticed it.

"Sienna, did you smell —"

"Jenna." Pepper approached. "May I help you?"

"Um, no, I saw Sienna through the window and wanted to . . ." I paused for a moment, trying to concoct a reply that wouldn't make Pepper want to linger. "I wanted to ask her whether the inn might be available for a wedding event."

"What a shame. I heard you lost your venue." Pepper *tsk*ed. She made a rolling motion with her hand. "Continue on. I have other customers." She shuffled away.

"Sienna, did you smell anything unusual in the cabana?" I asked.

"Like blood?" Her voice cracked. "No. I told you. I didn't realize he was dead."

"Anything at all?"

"Well, there were smells of oil and metal. He was working on a mixed-media piece. It was on the easel."

"Did you smell tar or a pungent men's cologne?" I asked.

"I don't think so." She started to rise from the chair but couldn't find her balance. She sat back down. "Listen, Jenna, the other night at Intime, you were right."

"About you paying Quade hush money?"

"You might as well know. I'm pregnant. With Quade's child. I was enamored with him. With his talent. When he showed me the slightest interest, I threw myself at him. I know I'm older than he was, but men being men . . ." She grunted. "He didn't say no. We met on and off for a month. I didn't know until two months later that I was with child. I'd taken all the precautions, and truly thought I was past child-bearing age, but . . ." She placed her palm on her abdomen. "I didn't think he would be a good father, so I never told him, but I didn't kill him."

"Your alibi. The police think it's weak . . .

Hold on. Then why were you paying him hush money?"

"My alibi is weak. It's bogus." Her face flushed pink. "Let me start at the beginning. The owner of Sterling's — Edith McNary — was staying at the inn for her niece's wedding party a month ago, and she left her keys in full view in her room. I took them, made a copy of the one for the jewelry store, and that night — the night Quade died — I slipped out of the inn, went down the hill, and stole a necklace. *The* necklace my friend was admiring at Intime." Sadness suffused her face. "As I said, I'm not proud of my affliction."

"You made a copy of Mrs. McNary's key?" I asked, wondering if Sienna would have been able to make copies of other keys, like Keller's garage key. She had access to all the rooms at the inn.

"Yes. And I knew the security code at Sterling's. Purposely, I'd visited the shop often when Edith was opening."

"The security cameras at Sterling's would have caught you on —"

"They were down that night. I knew they were. They'd been down for a week. Edith has complained more times than I can count about the faulty craftsmanship. But I swear, that's where I was."

Lowering my voice, I said, "You need help."

"I know."

"And you need to come clean with Chief Pritchett. Now."

Tears leaked from her eyes.

The afternoon passed without incident, but I couldn't get the chat with Sienna out of my mind. Did I believe her? Had she gone that night to steal the necklace? Had the security cameras truly been down at the same time the security cameras on her property were glitching? What were the odds? So many possibilities were in play. I hoped she would go to the precinct and confess everything. How would I know if she did? I didn't dare text Cinnamon for fear I'd incur her wrath for intruding. Again. Could I help it if people liked to open up to me?

At six, stewing over Sienna's confession, I finalized receipts, grabbed Tigger, and hurried home to change for the family dinner. After feeding Rook and the cat, I swung by the grocery store. I'd agreed to bring sourdough bread.

My father's place was a one-story Mediterranean set high in the hills with a beautiful view of the ocean. My mother had decorated it in ocean tones, but Lola had added her own touches, including dozens of framed pictures of Brianna. Proud grandma.

"Something smells great," Rhett said from the armchair near the fireplace.

"Sure does," I said. We'd arrived within minutes of each other. His second-in-command was overseeing Intime for the evening. "Aunt Vera's up first."

My aunt was making one of her favorite appetizers. The aroma of shrimp sautéed with lemon and herbs wafted into the living room. My mouth was watering already. For the entrée, Lola was cooking up fried fish tenders, a Pelican Brief specialty. Katie was putting together dessert, and I couldn't wait to taste it. She'd been practicing for the past few weeks to get this one right — individual chocolate coffee bombes with gold foil. It was a famous chef's recipe.

"Who's ready for more wine?" Bailey asked.

"I am." My father raised his glass.

Bailey crossed to him with a bottle and poured. "Here you go." With Tito out of town, and Brianna out with Tina for an extra-long walk on the Pier because Tina had missed seeing all the watercolors, my pal was flying solo.

"This is delicious," Dad said. "With bright

cherry notes and floral scents as well as a hint of citrus."

"Oho!" I teased. "Who's been memorizing what the vintners have been saying this week?" My father liked wine, but he preferred a good scotch.

"I might even detect the aroma of tobacco, or is it tar?" he jested.

I shuddered, flashing on the crime scene. On Quade. Dead. The image made my insides snarl. Needing fresh air, I rose and passed through the opening between the sliding glass doors to the balcony. Holding on to the railing, I inhaled deeply.

Rhett emerged from the living room and slung an arm around my back. "You okay?" He had donned a cable-knit sweater, which felt good against my bare arms. "Want your shawl?"

I'd worn a sleeveless aqua blue sheath and sandals because I'd been running hot all day, but the night had cooled substantially. I caressed his hand. "You're all I need."

"Did you wear that perfume for me?" he asked, nuzzling my neck.

"You know I did." I tilted my chin up for a kiss. He obliged.

"What's going on?" He turned me toward him.

"Why can't I leave well enough alone?"

He arched an eyebrow in a wickedly sexy way. "Are you talking about your insatiable curiosity? Your thirst to know the truth? Your desire to solve a crime before the police?"

"It's not a race," I argued.

"Oka-ay," he said, dragging out the word. "Your desire to solve a crime *just* in case they don't?" He cupped my elbow. "It's because you are who you are. You care about your friends. About Crystal Cove. You want life to go back to normal."

"Whatever that is," I grumbled.

"It's your former husband's fault," he said. "Leaving you with a mystery that haunted you for years."

"You're probably right."

"You crave answers. You yearn for balance. It's made you doggedly tenacious." He smoothed the side of my hair. "It's one of the main reasons I love you. And I know you still have your suspicions about Naomi. You'd like her to be innocent."

"I would, plus I'd love to put this behind us so I could focus on next week's Cinco de Mayo festival and our wedding plans and you. Not necessarily in that order."

"Let's trust that Cinnamon is putting in the work."

"She is." I wished I knew what else she might have discovered.

Katie waltzed onto the balcony with a glass of chardonnay in hand, her apron splattered with brown — chocolate, I figured — and chips of gold foil. It reminded me of one of Keller's mixed-media paintings. "Am I interrupting?"

"No, of course not." I swiveled.

"I'll be inside." Rhett hooked his thumb. "Your father and I need to finish a conversation about the best lures for deep sea fishing, the Green Machine or the cedar plug."

"Definitely the Green Machine." I winked. To Katie I said, "Keller couldn't make it?"

"No, he's helping his mother at Taste of Heaven. The Art of Dessert event is tonight. Lots of bakers are in attendance. I heard the customers are lined up nearly to the statue of the dolphins."

I whistled.

She worked her lip between her teeth. "Can we talk?"

"What's up?"

"It's Eleanor, actually. I'm not sure she likes me."

"What?" I squawked and instantly lowered my voice. Katie was serious. "Don't be silly. Number one, nobody doesn't like you, and number two, Keller's mother loves everyone."

"She doesn't hug me. Ever. Not only

when I'm a mess, like now, but ever!" Katie folded her arms.

"Have you asked her why? It's not like you're breakable."

"As if. She could barely break a toothpick."

"Maybe" — I clasped my friend's arm — "it's because you remind her of her younger sister. Eleanor lost her years ago."

Katie's mouth turned down. "I had no idea."

"Like you, Kitty had a headful of curls and a big belly laugh. Come to think of it, her name even sounds like yours."

"Keller never talks about her. In fact, I've never seen a picture."

I heaved a sigh. "My aunt said she was Eleanor's best friend and an excellent pastry chef. The two of them were like this." I crossed my fingers. "When she jumped —"

Katie gasped. "She committed suicide?"

"No, let me finish. Sheesh!" I released her arm. "When she jumped in front of a truck to save a child, it was one of the most heroic things she could have ever done. The child survived, but she didn't. With both of their parents dead, Eleanor had the hardest time forgiving Kitty for leaving her."

Katie pressed a hand to her chest. "I get it now. She doesn't want to get attached to me. That makes perfect sense. Thank you. I'll be patient."

She retreated into the house, and I turned back to drink in the lights of the town below as a new thought invaded my mind. Had Quade felt like Eleanor, not wanting to get attached to anyone because his mother had given him up for adoption? Did Naomi feel that way because she'd gone through a bad marriage? Did Sienna and so many others in our community remain single because it was easier than to risk falling in love and suffer the pain of rejection? It had taken me quite a while before I'd let myself trust that Rhett wouldn't up and leave me.

I drew in a deep breath and returned inside. The chopped shrimp on baguette toasts were nearly half eaten. "Hey, I want one!" I cried.

Rhett patted the couch. He'd saved a spot for me. I sat and descended upon the platter. Each bite was better than the one before. I loved shrimp *anything.*

The conversation revolved around the success of the festival and the happy faces of tourists and locals. Bailey had found a new wine to enjoy, and Katie said that even Keller was impressed by the scope of artistry — everything from mixed media, to woodcrafting, to ironworks, and miniatures.

When it was time to dine, Lola seated us at the table. At each place setting, she'd arranged a trinket in a gold box. For the women, the potion necklaces Pepper had been hawking for Purple Unicorn Crafts. For my father, Rhett, Keller, Tito, and Marlon — who was also a no-show; police business — she'd bought hand-painted enamel quartz tie clips.

"Mom, thanks," Bailey gushed. "I bought one of these for Tina the other day."

"Yours is for calm," she said.

Bailey gave her the stink eye. "Who says I'm not calm?"

Lola blew her a kiss. "Let's just say it takes two to raise Brianna. I know you can't wait for Tito to return."

"Wow," my father said. "I'll impress the ladies who visit the hardware shop when I wear this!"

Lola knuckled his shoulder. "There wasn't a lot of artsy jewelry that was suitable for you men."

Rhett appreciated his and said it would go nicely with his blue silk tie.

I lifted my necklace and stared at the sparkly crystals within.

"Yours, Jenna, is to stir your imagination," Lola said.

"Am I supposed to drink it?"

"Don't be silly. Its power emanates magically."

"Uh-huh."

A diabolical theory formed in my mind. I recalled Katie opening a teensy vial and dusting her dessert with *magical* sugar crystals. Was it possible that the killer had put arsenic in a necklace or some other small conveyance, merely enough to dose Quade's drink in passing without him knowing? Artisans throughout the festival had been selling such items, including Pepper. She'd said the young were snapping them up. Yardley had given one of Pepper's potion necklaces to Naomi. Destiny owned a few, too.

"Sweetheart?" Rhett said. "Are you okay?"

"She's probably thinking about murder," my father said wryly.

I stiffened.

He groaned. "Don't tell me you were."

Aunt Vera took the seat next to me. "Let us help you theorize."

Dad glowered at her. "If you want to help someone, Sis, help Cinnamon."

"But that's what Jenna is doing, Cary," my aunt retorted. "She's thinking outside the box."

"Cinnamon is perfectly capable of thinking outside the box."

"But Jenna has helped her in the past."
"Balderdash!"

CHAPTER 23

Grumbling, Dad pushed away from the table, grabbed his wineglass, and stomped out of the room. Lola dashed after him saying over her shoulder to the rest of us, "Dinner will be just a minute."

My aunt took a hunk of sourdough bread from the basket and pulled off part of the crust. "Talk to us, Jenna. Let us bat around your theories."

I mentioned my idea about the potion necklaces.

"Hold on," Katie said. "Both Naomi and Destiny were attacked and wound up at Mercy Urgent Care. I can't imagine either would have done that to themselves."

"What if Destiny hurt Naomi because Quade liked her?" I asked.

Bailey wagged her head. "I'm not buying it. Quade's dead. If she'd wanted Naomi out of the picture, she would have done it before."

"Unless she thought Naomi killed Quade," my aunt said. "And she wanted retribution."

I sipped my wine.

Rhett slung an arm over the back of his chair. "Why hurt herself?" he asked.

"To put the blame on Christopher George," I replied.

"Christopher." Bailey took a slice of bread and slathered it with clarified butter. "In his cabana we found —" She balked and quickly took a bite of the bread.

"You went into his room at the inn?" Rhett shot me a look.

"For one second."

"One?"

"Okay, more like a full minute. We were careful." I told him about the odors of the tar-scented shampoo and the leathery cologne, one of which I was certain I'd detected at the crime scene. "Bailey says his travel kit had buckles on it that could match the buckle print found on Naomi's and Destiny's faces."

Rhett worked his tongue inside his cheek. "As you said earlier at the park, his alibi about watching Naomi in her house is sketchy, but it corroborates hers."

I gazed at him as Naomi's name sizzled in my mind. Quade's text to Yardley had ended on the word *Naomi.* Had he meant to text more? That night she'd been wearing her mother's heart-shaped locket. Was it possible it had contained arsenic? If I recalled correctly, stained-glass artisans worked with arsenic. Cinnamon had said the initial *N* was on the scrap of paper found in Quade's cabana. On the other hand, she'd admitted that the *N* didn't match Naomi's handwriting. Had Christopher George lied about his whereabouts? Had he killed Quade and, furious with Naomi, framed her by tossing the wadded-up sketches on the floor and leaving a fragment of a note? Had Naomi's whole name been on the paper at one time? Had it been a note to entice Quade to imbibe the poison?

Drink me, read the note in *Alice in Wonderland.*

"What about Sienna?" Bailey asked me.

I trained my gaze on her. "She has a really quirky alibi. I saw her this afternoon at Beaders of Paradise, and . . ."

As I was filling them in on her alibi, I heard the front door open. A woman cried, "We're here!"

Tina, svelte even though she was clad in a puffy pink parka, jeans, and Uggs, carried Brianna bundled in a fleece blanket into the dining room. "Hope you don't mind us barging in. I guessed you were eating by now. I left the stroller on the porch. Somebody is excited to see you," she trilled as she handed Brianna to Bailey. "We had such a good —"

"Everyone, I apologize!" My father returned and stood behind me. He clasped my shoulders and squeezed gently. "Sorry for my outburst. I worry."

Lola blew me an air kiss — she could work miracles with my father in the same way my mother could — and strutted into the kitchen calling, "Dinner in a minute!"

"What did I miss?" Dad asked and resumed his seat.

"A recap of everyone's alibis," Rhett said.

Without waiting for an invitation, Tina plopped into the chair set for Marlon, whisked her long tresses over her shoulders, and folded her hands on the table. "May I listen in?"

"Sure. Join the fun." My father waggled his eyebrows comically at me.

"Sienna Brown," my aunt prompted. "You said she admitted to paying Quade hush money."

"What for?" Dad asked.

"She's a petty thief," Bailey said.

"A kleptomaniac, actually," I revised. "She claims she was swiping something from

Sterling's jewelry store that night."

"Kleptomania is one thing, but that's breaking and entering," my father said, always looking at crimes from the perspective of the law.

I nodded. "She's going to come clean."

"I thought she had another alibi for the evening," my aunt said.

"She did. Drinking tea in her residential unit at the inn, but Cinnamon told me there are holes in it."

"You spoke to Cinnamon about Sienna?" Dad asked.

"Briefly," I said. "She doesn't know about this part of the story."

"I saw Miss Brown near Sterling's the other night," Tina said.

"What?" I turned to face her.

"You're talking about Tuesday, right?" She squinched her pert nose. "When that artist Quade died?"

I bobbed my head.

"Yep," she continued. "I was on my way home from the Art of Baked Mac 'n Cheese at Mum's the Word. I went there after Bailey came home. And I was heading to my father's. It was around ten thirty. He lives in the hills south of the art school, not far from here. Anyway, as I was passing Artiste Arcade, I happened to see Sienna Brown ducking into the shadows."

"Sterling's is in the arcade," I said to the group.

"We know," Dad said tartly and rolled a hand, suggesting Tina continue.

"Thinking she was acting suspiciously, I took a picture with my phone. It turned out fuzzy, so I wasn't completely sure it was her, but then" — Tina pulled her bejeweled cell phone from the pocket of her parka and handed it to me — "I saw her a minute later, clear as day, even though it was night. On the boulevard. She must have ducked out the side entrance of the arcade."

I swiped through Tina's photo app until I saw the picture to which she was referring. It wasn't an ideal photo — a woman wearing a coat, shoulders hunched, blurred by shadows. A time stamp showed the photo had been taken at 10:32. That would not have given Sienna enough time either before or after to have killed Quade and make it to town to steal a necklace.

"So she wasn't lying. She was robbing Sterling's," I said.

"Or she was in the vicinity," my father countered.

"But nowhere near the inn," Bailey added. Brianna cooed her agreement.

My aunt said, "Hold on. Edith McNary is

a client." She fetched her cell phone from the satchel she'd set on the sideboard and dialed a number. "Hello, Edith? It's Vera. No, dear, nothing is wrong. Yes, I know I never call you this late, but I have a question to ask." My aunt *tsk*ed. "Do not fret about that. I know you'll visit when you have a spare moment. The tarot waits for you."

My father rolled his eyes.

"My question is this. Have you had a robbery recently? Anything missing from the shop?" Aunt Vera batted the air. "That many? Oh, my." She paused. "No, dear, don't cry. No, you're not slipping. You didn't misplace anything. I happen to know who broke into the shop, or rather, let herself in with your key." My aunt nodded. "Yes, you guessed it." She sniffed. "Don't blame yourself for having an extra glass of wine, Edith. Yes, Sienna will admit all to the police, and I'm sure she will make reparations." Aunt Vera listened. "Bless you. That's quite forgiving of you." She ended the call and gazed at the group. "Edith thought she'd misplaced over a dozen pieces. She has been forgetful of late. Her daughter has been ill."

"So that rules out Sienna," I said.

Silence settled over the table.

■ ■ ■ ■

Monday morning arrived too soon. I ran a quick mile before the thunderclouds overhead let loose with rain, then I fed the animals, showered, dressed in yellow to brighten my mood, kissed Rhett goodbye, and told him I loved him. He mumbled that he loved me, too. Rook, who had nestled onto the bed beside Rhett, lifted his head and yawned.

"Yeah, buddy," I whispered. "I'm tired, too. Be good."

With Tigger in tow, I drove to the Cookbook Nook. Despite the drizzle, people were disassembling the festival right and left. Vans and trucks loaded to the max were driving south as well as north. A few people lingered on Buena Vista Boulevard, but not many. It would be a slow day at the shop. I didn't mind. I needed a couple of hours to catch up, order cookbooks and paraphernalia, and plan for the next event. There were times I wished Z.Z. would let well enough alone and allow the town to have two to three weeks of total calm, but even I knew that wasn't wise. We were a tourist-driven town. It needed the influx of money to survive, and special events did lure tourists.

I set a rubber mat by the front door to prevent anyone slipping as they entered with wet shoes, then I tended to the register. Tigger scooted to the top of his kitty condo and peered down at me like a ravenous eagle.

"Cut it out," I told him. Like a goofball, he rolled onto his back and played with his tail.

My aunt entered and trilled, "Too-ra-loo."

Gran followed with her cheery, "Hello-o!"

Then Bailey swept in with Brianna, tucked beneath the stroller's rain guard. "Good weather for ducks," she chirped.

"We only get a few of these kinds of storms a year," I said.

"True. I won't grumble. What's on the agenda?" she asked as she transferred Brianna from the stroller into her owl floor seat.

"Replacing stock. Ordering cookbooks for Cinco de Mayo." We carried numerous Latin-themed cookbooks like *Salsas and Moles: Fresh and Authentic Recipes for Pico de Gallo, Mole Poblano, Chimichurri, Guacamole, and More,* but having some new ones on hand would be a good idea. "And creating a display window for the event, too."

An hour later, as I was kneeling at the front of the shop, removing art festival items from the display window and arranging a couple of colorful items I would use for the upcoming Cinco de Mayo festival, a woman said my name, followed by, "Oh, no! Oh, heck!"

Smack!

I turned toward the sound. Naomi was propped on her hands and knees on the rain mat, the hood of her loden green slicker flopped forward, hiding half her face. "Naomi! Are you okay?" I hurried to help.

"I didn't see the rubber mat," she said and groaned when she spied the contents of her crocheted purse scattered to one side — pens, paper, sketches, a pack of Marlboros, and cell phone.

Had she put the cigarettes in her purse for my benefit, to corroborate her alibi? I wondered, but recalled having seen a cellophane wrapper spill out of her purse with other items in the workshop room last Monday. Had the wrapper been the remains of a pack of cigarettes? Had she told the truth about being a smoker?

"Sorry." She pushed off her hood, shoved everything into the purse and scrambled to a stand, brushing raindrops off her slicker. "I wanted to talk to you if you had a free moment. About yesterday. At Azure Park. With Christopher."

Bailey and my aunt watched as I guided Naomi into the breezeway. Katie had set out a three-tiered serving dish filled with mini lemon-coconut muffins. I gestured for Naomi to take one.

"Not hungry." She finger-combed her brown hair forward over her shoulders. "When I told Christopher I'd gone around the back for a smoke, you seemed shocked," she said. "I've been hiding my habit. I wish I was a stronger person and could quit. My mother was a smoker, and she . . ." Her voice trailed off.

She'd died of lung cancer, I recalled.

"Ever since I ran away from Christopher, I've been edgy. Smoking calms me." Naomi's mouth twitched with sadness. "I wasn't lying. I did go around back for a smoke that night. I went out the front because that's where my purse was, but I went inside through the rear door. And" — she fiddled with a toggle on the slicker — "if I'm being honest, I saw Christopher out there. Hanging by a lamppost. It's why I didn't go back inside through the front and why I didn't switch off the lights. I was afraid. I probably shouldn't be. He says he loves me."

"He hurt you."

"Once. Only once. Which was why I took

self-defense classes."

"That explains how you were able to grab his wrist midair."

"My instructor said I was a natural. Look out, *Karate Kid.*" She chopped the air with glee, a smile brightening her face. "I'm going to call Christopher. I'm going to let him see Nina."

"Are you sure? He might have been involved with Quade and the forgeries."

"I can't believe he would do that and risk ruining his lifelong reputation." She shook her head. "I had a Zoom meeting with my therapist last night. She's in favor of me owning up to the truth." She snuffled. "But I hate the name Nancy George, so I'm never going to own up to *that.*"

"Naomi, may I ask you something? It's quite sensitive."

She lowered her chin and gazed at me from beneath her long lashes, looking like a child ready for a scolding. "Sure."

"Quade wrote Yardley a text right before he died. At the end of the text, he wrote your name. No message. No instructions."

"Um, okay."

"Is it possible Christopher stole into the room, poured a glass of wine, and left Quade a note that the wine was from you? Maybe it said something like *Congratula-*

tions, love NG."

She blinked rapidly. "Why would he do that?"

"To lure Quade into drinking something laced with poison."

She tilted her head, confused. "I thought Quade was stabbed with Keller's tool."

"He was poisoned first. With arsenic. I think it was in something he drank." I didn't think Cinnamon would mind me revealing this clue. "I believe the killer — possibly Christopher — came back and tore up the note, leaving the scrap of paper on the floor with your initial on it."

Naomi's eyes sparked with anger. "Do you suspect me of colluding with him?"

"What? No. Of course not."

"I use arsenic in stained-glass preparation."

"I'm aware of that."

"You're staring at my locket." She clasped the necklace, her voice crackling with indignation. "Do you think I keep a trace of arsenic in it? Do you think I gave the locket to Christopher to use?"

"No, I don't. I really don't." I held out both hands, palms up, to reassure her. "But I wouldn't put it past him to have slipped into your house or your art room and stolen arsenic. You said you work out of your house. Do you keep arsenic on the premises?"

"In a locked cabinet."

That gave me pause. Whoever had killed Quade was adept with opening padlocks. He had broken into Keller's garage and possibly into Naomi's cabinets.

"Is Christopher handy with tools?" I asked.

"As handy as anyone who fixes TV boxes and computers, I suppose. Why?"

I explained about the padlocks.

"How would he have gotten into Quade's cabana or the communal room?" Naomi asked.

"Maybe he stole a key off a housekeeper." Or he'd paid an employee to look the other way, as Bailey had.

In my mind, I replayed the scenario of Quade finding a note beside a glass of wine. Imagining Naomi was softening to the idea of dating him again, he toasted her and drank. Soon after, he started to weaken. He didn't put two and two together. He texted Yardley to say he wasn't feeling well and had wanted her to tell Naomi thank you for the congratulations, or whatever else might have been on the note, but the poison made him too sick to finish.

I said, "The arsenic was probably added

to a drink poured into one of the glasses Hannah sold. Did you buy one from her?"

"No. I don't have funds for frivolous gifts." She wrapped her arms around herself. "Jenna, you're wrong. It couldn't have been Christopher who did this. He's controlling, but he's not a monster. And I saw him. Outside my house! Not to mention why would he have poisoned Quade and then left the glass there?"

"To frame you."

Naomi drummed her fingers on her arms. "Call Hannah. There were a lot of people at the party that night, including all the other artists. She must have records of who bought what."

Why hadn't I thought of that?

CHAPTER 24

Naomi left, looking slightly more confident than when she'd entered.

Seconds later, as I made a beeline for the display window, Bailey, my aunt, and Gran circled me. "What was that about?" they asked in unison.

I told them.

Gran snapped her fingers. "I knew that man was bad news."

"But Naomi corroborates his alibi," I said.

"True." She folded her arms. "What're you going to do?"

"Call Cinnamon," my aunt advised while rubbing her phoenix amulet. "Please, dear, be smart about this."

"Call Hannah," Bailey suggested. "Get the scoop first. The more ammunition you have for Cinnamon, the better."

I agreed with her and moved to the children's table. I sat on a stool, cell phone in hand. Tigger climbed into my lap, his heart chugging like crazy. Was he sensing my excitement? Was this case coming to a close? I dialed Hannah, but the call went to voicemail. I tried Hurricane Vineyards next and reached Hannah's assistant. She said Hannah was in the field, which often caused her cell phone to be out of range.

"Bailey," I said, "want to join me?"

"Sure."

I told my aunt and Gran that we would finish the display case when we returned. We hadn't had a single customer. Aunt Vera replied that she'd put together a list of books she wanted me to order.

And we were off, umbrellas in hand. On the way over, I whizzed past Destiny and her dog in her oversized Jeep, the ragtop in place to block the rain. She was parked outside Parker Printers.

"No wine tours today, I'll bet," Bailey quipped.

"She probably won't care, exhausted from this week's hullabaloo."

Halfway up Seaview Road, the rain let up and sunshine tried to peek through the clouds. It would fail. There was more rain in the forecast.

Rows upon rows of healthy-looking vines flanked either side of the winding driveway to Hurricane Vineyards. The main house, which was three stories and featured turrets and multiple chimneys, reminded me of a mini castle.

I parked in front of the house and, leaving the umbrella in the car, roamed to the right of the driveway to peer over the stone wall at the acres of vines. I saw someone in a broad-brimmed rain hat and black raincoat over jeans and boots moving between two rows.

A crow cawed and dive-bombed us. Bailey ducked. I snorted. The crow, which was conveniently named Crow, was Hannah's husband's pet. In addition to being a talented vintner, Alan was a falconer and practiced with the bird often. I was pretty sure it wasn't Alan in the vineyard. He was probably on the patio of his neighboring estate. That was where Crow liked to start and end his flights.

"You clown," I sniped at Crow as the cackling bird winged away. Then I cupped my hands around my mouth and yelled to the figure in the vineyard, "Hannah, is that you?"

Hannah turned and looked upward. "Jenna? Hi!"

"Can Bailey and I come down and chat?"

"Follow the steps but be careful. They're slippery."

There must have been a hundred steps to the third tier of grapes. I rued the idea of having to climb up them to return to the main house, but *c'est la vie.* I craved answers.

Hannah was tapping notes into an iPad. "I'm making a to-do list for my crew," she said as we drew near. "I want to grow the best crop we've ever had. Mother Nature deals her hand in the spring and how the cards play out makes all the difference for the finished wine. This is the most stressful time for all of us. Weather is such a factor."

Thanks to the rain, the grapes were free of dust and glistening with moisture. "The crop looks beautiful to me." I was a novice and knew nothing about how to grow grapes, other than what I'd learned from movies or cookbooks.

"We must keep up with the *drumbeat of the vintage,*" Hannah said. "That's what Bruce Cakebread calls the steady march of the seasons, the progression of the plants from buds to bloom to the onset of ripening — *veraison,*" she added in a French accent. Cakebread Cellars was a renowned vineyard in Napa Valley. "Forgive me," Hannah went on. "I'm waxing rhapsodic. I'm just so hopeful. Alan has been instrumental in helping me understand it all."

She and Alan were well matched. I was happy for her.

"Why are you here?" she asked, moving us beneath an awning that provided cover should the clouds open up again.

"I have a question for you."

"About wedding sites?" She winked. "A little birdie told me you are on the lookout."

"Not about wedding sites. About the handblown wineglasses you've been selling. Do you keep a record of who bought what?"

"Sure do," Hannah responded, looking between Bailey and me. "I have to in order to pay the proper proceeds to the artist. Why?"

"This is confidential," I said, "but a wineglass was found in Quade's cabana. After he was dead. Sienna Brown, who saw the glass —"

"Because she went into the room," Bailey said, cutting me off, eager to help me tell the story. "To do the dishes. Thinking Quade was asleep."

Hannah wrinkled her nose. "But he was dead?"

"Maybe not at that time," I said. "Anyway, Sienna told me the glass was beautiful with green-and-gold wavelike swirls. Did Quade buy it?"

"Hardly." Hannah scoffed. "He stayed

miles away from my tasting station. Probably because of Destiny."

Bailey said. "Do you know who bought it?"

"How about Christopher George?" I suggested.

Hannah said, "That name doesn't sound familiar."

"A hip-looking middle-aged man with a mustache."

Hannah strained to remember him. "No, sorry, but we served a lot of people that night and many customers paid cash. For my records, I wrote down the design name and the amount paid, and I added an initial to remind me of the purchaser."

"That makes sense."

She tapped a fingertip on her chin. "Flora and Faith Fairchild each bought one. I believe Flora chose a lavender one while Faith went for the bolder Aegean blue. Yardley Alks bought an aqua one. Naomi Genet wanted one, too."

"But she couldn't afford to buy it," I cut in.

"You're right. She had her eye on a red one, not a green one. Come with me to my office," Hannah said. "I'll give you a full account."

"I don't mean to keep you from your work."

"I need a break. Besides, it's getting ready to pour again. Some tea is in order."

Hannah took the steps two at a time while Bailey and I slogged up the last thirty heaving. We both worked out, but we did not do stairs. Perhaps we needed to change our regimens.

As predicted, rain started right as we entered the main house. A rumble of thunder rattled the sky.

"Phew! Just in the nick of time." Hannah shrugged off her raincoat and hat, hung them on a peg in the foyer, smoothed the front of her black turtleneck, and led us into the wood-paneled den that served as an office.

The room, like the rest of the house, was decorated in taupe and white. All of the furniture were quality antiques.

I scanned the myriad books on the floor-to-ceiling bookcases, which had been fitted with a rolling ladder. "Have you read all of these?"

"My father and mother did. They were avid readers." She rang a bell.

Within seconds, a slim young brunette in a tan dress, whom Hannah introduced as her assistant, came to take our order: three cups of Earl Grey tea and a plate of sugar cookies.

"Is Nana sleeping?" Hannah asked her assistant.

"Snoring like a champ."

Hannah suppressed a smile. She adored her grandmother, though the woman had the reputation of being a tyrant. As the assistant left, Hannah walked to a heavy oak filing cabinet by the picture window. She opened the second drawer from the bottom and pulled out a file. She placed it on the mahogany twin-pedestal partner's desk and turned to the first document. "Let's see . . ." She continued scanning pages and then stopped on one. With her finger, she guided her gaze through the sheet. "Here we are. Monday to Tuesday night. Workshop and opening of the festival events at Crystal Cove Inn." She mumbled a few *mm-hms* as she perused her notes and viewed the next page.

She paused on an entry and let out a breathy, "Huh."

"What?" I hurried to her to see what had caught her eye.

"The green-and-gold wave was sold by Destiny on Monday." Hannah tapped the notation. "To a customer with the initial *N.* Destiny personally purchased a green-and-gold one with a raindrop pattern on Tuesday. She wrote her entire name by that sale."

"She bought one?" I repeated. "Why?"

"Because they're pretty. She has quite a collection of glass bottles, vases, and such that she inherited. You bought a couple, too, Jenna. For your store display."

Bailey peeked over my shoulder. "Are you sure that's her writing?"

"Yep. Big and loopy." Hannah squinted to reread the sales memo, as if reading harder would tell her what had occurred.

But she needn't, as everything became evident to me.

Destiny. At one time, she and Quade had made plans to get married, but he'd made it clear that would never happen. He had fallen for Naomi. Monday night after the workshop, Destiny tried again to win his favor, but he rebuffed her. Therefore, deliberately with malice aforethought, she purchased a glass and wrote the letter *N* in Hannah's log, with the idea of killing Quade and framing Naomi.

I flashed on the multiple necklaces Destiny owned; she'd been wearing the ebony perfume bottle necklace the night Quade was killed. Years ago, I'd read a magazine article about arsenic at one time having been utilized for medicinal purposes, and though banned, traces of it would show up in vintage bottles in antiques shops.

"Destiny's mother," I whispered. She had owned an antiques shop.

"What a sad story that was," Hannah said, not on track with my theorizing.

"Sad how?"

"She died of a broken heart. About twenty years ago. Her husband and she had quite a to-do on their front porch, my nana said. He accused her of being off-kilter, always fussing with those antiques, not living in the real world. He said she was detrimental to their daughter and ordered her to leave and never come back. Chastened, she left. Two days later" — Hannah held her breath and let it out — "she fell down a steep incline."

"Oh, no!" Bailey cried.

Hannah said, "My grandmother said the police determined she'd misjudged the stability of the rocks."

Had she really, or had she committed suicide? Was Destiny off-kilter, too, but rather than take her own life after being rejected by Quade, she took his?

"Her father was devastated by the way things turned out," Hannah went on.

"Didn't you tell me he was a well-to-do builder?" I asked as another idea formed.

She nodded. "He'd started out as a tradesman. Tile, wood carving, cabinetry. He could do it all. He built the company into something grand."

The man had probably known how to open padlocks without a key. Had he taught Destiny tricks of the trade?

"Tea," Hannah's assistant announced. She set the tray down on the coffee table between the white brocade love seat and two armchairs. "Sugar and cream, if you want it. Need anything else, boss?"

"No, thank you. Bailey, Jenna." Hannah motioned for us to sit on the love seat. She took an armchair.

I perched on the edge of the love seat, my mind reeling with more theories.

Bailey sat beside me and offered me a cup of tea. I waved it off. "What are you thinking?"

"I was wondering about the incidents that landed Naomi and Destiny at Mercy Urgent Care Saturday morning."

"So awful," Hannah murmured as she stirred sugar into her tea.

"Destiny implied that a man had attacked her."

"Implied?" Bailey arched an eyebrow. "You don't believe her?"

"What if she was lying? About all of it?"

"No, no, I saw her face and eye!" Hannah

exclaimed, the spoon clacking on the china saucer.

"What if she hurt herself to make it seem that there were two victims?" I went on. "The buckle imprint on Naomi's cheek was deeper than the one on Destiny's forehead, which was smack in the middle, as if she'd whacked herself like this." I mimed holding my purse in both hands and slapping it against my face.

Hannah grimaced. "Why would she do that?"

"To make herself a victim and remove any notion that she might be a murderer."

"Were the police considering her?" Bailey asked.

I should have mentioned her to them after she'd readily offered up an alibi for the night of the murder, saying she'd been home doing PR. I should have questioned why she'd felt the need to share.

"What if Destiny, not someone with the initial *N*, bought the wineglass Monday?" I went on. "What if she filled it with wine laced with arsenic on Tuesday and set it in Quade's cabana with a note from Naomi?"

Hannah shook her head, not believing a word. Bailey, on the other hand, rolled her hand, encouraging me to continue.

I rose to my feet and walked to the desk

to have another look at the sales form Destiny had filled out. Would her cursive *N* match the one found on the scrap of paper the police had? "Wadded-up sketches of Naomi's daughter were on the floor of the cabana," I said. "I saw them spill out of Naomi's purse at our last workshop. Remember when Destiny ran away from the soiree, upset at being rejected by Quade? She fled to the communal room. It wasn't locked until after the event. She could have stolen them."

"No," Hannah said. "Destiny is kind and caring."

"What if she brought the sketches as props to make it seem like Quade had gotten angry after Naomi revealed Nina was not his daughter?"

"I can't believe it," Hannah went on. "I won't. Jenna, please don't bring this wild theory to the police's attention. It's outrageous."

I heard the roar of an engine and squeal of brakes and hurried to the window. A large Jeep, its ragtop in place, was doing a U-turn halfway down the hill. *What the heck?* "Hannah, is Destiny bringing a tour group today?"

"No, why?"

"You're kidding me!" Bailey dashed to my

side and peered out. “She’s here? How could she have guessed we’d visit Hannah to talk about the wineglass?”

Hannah joined us at the window. “That’s not Destiny. That’s Alan. He’s scoping out a new vineyard to purchase. In the rain, a four-wheel-drive vehicle is necessary.”

As the vehicle drove away, I flashed on Destiny and her dog in her Jeep outside Parker Printers, and another notion struck me. Did she wash her dog using the same shampoo that we used for Rook? Had she bathed the dog earlier that day and tracked in its hair, which left a trace of tar-scented fragrance in Quade’s cabana instead of a whiff of Destiny’s confidence perfume? Had the crime scene techs found any dog hair?

“Hannah, we have to go,” I said. “Not a word of our conversation to Destiny.”

“But —”

“Not a word. If she’s not guilty, great. But if she is . . .”

I didn’t wait for her promise. I rushed out the front door — the rain had stopped — and hopped into the VW. Bailey did the same. I switched on the car, flicked on the wipers to clear the windshield, plugged the USB cord into my cell phone — the phone was running low on juice — and ground the car into gear.

As I drove down the hill, with the intent of looping Cinnamon into the conversation, I sorted through my thoughts. The murder had been premeditated. No doubt about it. The killer had stolen Keller's personalized burin from the communal room. That hadn't been done on a whim. Did Destiny stab Quade in the heart because he'd broken hers?

Something puzzled me. Quade's stolen painting. Why hide it in Keller's garage? Why frame Keller? To drive home the ownership of the murder weapon?

No, I had the timeline screwed up. The art had gone missing first. Quade had needed to create an entirely new piece by Monday night. Had Destiny feared Keller would win the poster art competition and outshine the love of her life for years to come? Had she stolen Quade's original piece of art to force him to create something new?

A bolt of lightning flashed in the distance, way out in the ocean. A few seconds later, thunder rumbled overhead.

"Did you see that?" Bailey cried. "It's a good ten miles away, but the brunt of the storm is coming in this direction."

I didn't respond.

Bailey twisted in her seat to face me.

"What're you mulling over? Your eyes have that glazed thinking-hard look."

"If Destiny is the killer, she was running hot and cold." *She loves me, she loves me not.* "One minute she adored Quade, the next minute she despised him. What if she took Keller's burin with the idea of killing Keller to remove Quade's competition?"

"Wicked."

"But in the middle of the night, she realized her reasoning was faulty. Quade would never love her. She pondered suicide, but then, stronger than her mother, unwilling to die of heartbreak, she decided to turn the tables. She would poison the man who'd rejected her. Tuesday, after the evening's event began, she slipped into Quade's room and preset the wineglass with the note from Naomi while Quade was mingling with all of us."

"Except the poison didn't work."

"Right. When she went back to the room to retrieve the glass, sometime between ten and eleven, he was still alive." I thumped the steering wheel. "He stirred. Maybe he mumbled Naomi's name. Destiny went wild. She wanted him dead. She remembered she had Keller's burin and convinced herself she could do this. Quade was weak, nude, defenseless. She took the burin and stabbed him in the heart. Before she fled, she crumpled the art of Naomi's daughter and left a corner of the note that had enticed Quade to drink from the wineglass. To frame Naomi."

"Why not leave the whole note?"

"If she did, a handwriting expert would definitely be able to tell that Naomi hadn't written it."

"But the *N* was enough to prove that."

"Destiny didn't know that."

"We should call Cinnamon," Bailey said.

"You're right. Even if she doesn't want me to butt in, she'll want to hear —"

My cell phone pinged. I had a message. I pressed the Message icon on my console. Siri said in her British-accented voice, "You have one new message from wedding planner, Harmony Bold. Would you like me to read it?"

"Yes," I replied.

"Spoke with Destiny Dacourt. She's on board for helping you find a vineyard. If you meet at her office, she can show you a stack of brochures. Are you game?"

A black Mercedes sped up behind me and, despite the sharp turn ahead, cut around me and took the lead.

Bailey craned her neck and whistled. "Was

that —"

"Hannah!"

Chapter 25

"Where's she going in such a hurry?" Bailey asked.

"To Destiny's. To warn her. She's her friend. She doesn't believe Destiny is guilty."

I pressed the Voice icon on my steering wheel and said, "Siri, send a text message to Harmony Bold."

Siri asked, "What do you want the message to say?"

"Harmony," I dictated, "please call Destiny and ask if I can come over now. I'm eager to get this done."

Siri repeated the message and, with no changes, sent it.

In seconds, my cell phone pinged. I had received a reply from Harmony. Siri, reading the message, said, "Destiny said, 'Come on over!' "

Lightning flashed again. Thunder followed five seconds later.

"Slow down." Bailey bare-knuckled the

door handle as I took a turn too fast.

"Sorry." I righted the steering wheel while tapping the brakes. The VW's tires slewed slightly on the pavement. My pulse hiccupped. I pumped the brakes again and held firm to the steering wheel as I asked Siri to make a phone call. "Crystal Cove Precinct."

"About time," Bailey muttered.

The phone rang and then a woman said through the car's speaker, "Crystal Cove Precinct. How may I direct your call?"

"Chief Pritchett, please. It's Jenna Hart."

"One moment."

Cinnamon answered. "What now?"

"Was dog hair found in Quade's cabana?"

She clicked her tongue but didn't respond.

"Was the green-and-gold artisan wineglass checked for signs of arsenic?"

"What's going on?" Cinnamon asked, an edge to her voice.

"Did you know that Destiny Dacourt's mother was an antiques dealer and arsenic can be found in an antiques shop?"

"Jenna, I've begged you not to snoop."

"I did not snoop. BTW, I believe the handblown wineglass that was found in the cabana may have been purchased by Destiny Dacourt. I'm on my way to her place right now."

"Jenna, no!"

"Hannah Storm zoomed past me. I think she intends to warn Destiny. If I'm right and Hannah reveals anything to Destiny, Hannah could be in danger."

"Crap," Cinnamon said and ended the call.

"Jenna, what are you doing?" Bailey carped.

"If Hannah tells Destiny our theory, Destiny might hurt Hannah and bolt. She has nothing tying her to Crystal Cove. Her parents are dead. Quade is dead."

Minutes later, I reached Destiny's home, which also served as headquarters for Tripping with Destiny. I'd visited when I'd first moved to Crystal Cove and was handing out Cookbook Nook flyers to every business in town. Wine lovers, I'd imagined, liked cooking as much as the next person, and we stocked plenty of wine-themed cookbooks.

The car skidded as I turned right onto the gravel driveway.

"Hannah's here," Bailey whispered.

The Mercedes was parked next to Destiny's oversized Jeep. Hannah wasn't in her car. She had to be inside the house. The front door hung open.

I parked beside the Mercedes and climbed

out of the VW. Seconds later, Destiny's Labrador retriever bounded from the house. I bent to give his nose a rub and inhaled. Yep, he smelled like tar-scented shampoo.

"Pinot, sit!" Destiny exited the house while primping the collar of her khaki uniform. The dog obeyed. "Good timing, Jenna. I just arrived. Welcome." She smiled but the warmth didn't reach her eyes.

Bailey exited the car tentatively.

"We were nearby when I got a message from Harmony," I said. "You have some brochures to show me?"

"I do." Destiny fetched a hefty waxed-canvas knapsack from the rear seat of her Jeep and slung it over her shoulder. I noticed the square shape of the two buckles that fastened the knapsack's top. Was that what she'd used to whack Naomi and herself? She retrieved a box with a Parker Printers label on it and kicked the door closed with her foot. "That Harmony. She sure is on top of things. No moss grows under her feet. Let's get inside before the next storm hits us. Follow me. Hannah's here. How about we all have tea?"

"Sure."

Though the two-story home maintained the same white exterior and red-tiled roof so many establishments in town did, that was where the resemblance ended. It was shaded by gigantic oaks, and, by design, none of the surrounding bushes were groomed. Destiny had wanted a natural look. I recalled Z.Z. telling me once that if Destiny could have bucked city ordinances, she would have made the building look like an Italian farmhouse. One of the customers at the shop who had taken Destiny's all-day tour said that Destiny had set up a grape stomping vat made of oak slats in the backyard. I didn't know if she'd hosted a stomping party to date.

The interior of the home, which lacked a foyer, was an open floor plan that reminded me of the lobby of a romantic Italian hotel, complete with wood beams, heavy furniture covered with elegant brocades, multiple Persian rug runners, a burbling marble fountain, and numerous sculptures. There were nooks for reading, and art hung on all the walls. A winding staircase with a wrought-iron baluster resembling grape leaves led to the second floor.

As Destiny forcefully closed the door, Pinot tore through an archway into the kitchen beyond. Within seconds, I heard him lapping water.

"Hannah, look who's here!" Destiny crooned.

Hannah emerged from the kitchen and offered a weak smile. “Hey.”

“Hey, yourself,” I said, keeping my eye on Destiny.

She strode to the massive desk in the adjoining office and set down the Parker Printers box. Beyond the desk stood a hefty stack of moving boxes. To the right of the boxes I glimpsed a painting on an easel and stifled a gasp. It was a sixteen-by-twenty acrylic of what I could only describe as an angry ocean with lots of blue upon blue and swipes of black and gray — Naomi’s missing painting.

Loath to have Destiny catch me gawking, I strolled deeper into the grand room. Bailey followed.

Hannah approached. “The moment you left, Destiny phoned me and told me she was giving up the business and leaving town. The festival was a bust. She barely made a dime.”

“Given these surroundings, it doesn’t look like she needs to work at all.”

I paused beside one of the tables to study a statue. On my previous visit, I’d come and gone in less than two minutes. I hadn’t had a chance to explore. The statue was an abstract metal work with what I presumed was a torso and slender legs. Looking closer,

I saw the *DS* signature and inhaled sharply. Was it a David Smith forgery? Bailey peered where I was looking.

"Isn't it beautiful?" Destiny, carrying her knapsack over one shoulder, drew alongside us and touched the leg of the statue. "Quade gave it to me before . . ." Her eyes misted over. She swiped a tear as it dripped down her cheek. "Before we broke up."

"Destiny," I said, "I don't know how to tell you this, but it's a forgery."

"No." She blinked.

"Yes, Quade was copying Smith's work and selling it to unsuspecting buyers."

"No," she murmured. "He wouldn't. He wasn't like that. He . . ." She shook off the concern and turned to us, face composed. "Tea?"

Without waiting for an answer, she headed to the kitchen. We followed. Like the grand room, the kitchen was done in Italianate style — ecru cabinets trimmed with brown, golden speckled granite countertops, and Travertine tile floors lined with more Persian rug runners. Below the oversized center island were shelves filled with cookbooks and a honeycomb wine rack. An array of colored vases, bottles, and glasses stood in the bay window by the sink.

"How do you like your tea?" Destiny

asked. "Cream? Sugar?" She dumped her knapsack on the island between a knife block and a pile of magazines. "Pinot, pillow," she ordered.

The dog snuffled and nestled on a big tawny dog pillow near the rectangular farm-style kitchen table.

"Just sugar," I said. One of the buckles on the knapsack I'd spotted looked like it was bent. Might there be a smidge of Naomi's or Destiny's blood on it?

Deftly, Destiny set a tea kettle on the stove to boil and suggested we sit at the table. "I'll be right back."

I took a seat.

Bailey perched on the chair opposite me and leaned forward on both elbows. "She knows. We should leave."

"She doesn't know. Relax. Hannah, sit."

She sat beside Bailey and whispered, "Destiny didn't do it, Jenna."

"Did you ask her?"

"No, but —"

"How can she afford this place?" Bailey asked, perusing the kitchen.

"Her father passed away," I said. "I imagine she inherited everything. Hannah, didn't you say he was wealthy?"

"Well-to-do."

"Does it make sense that she wants to

leave town because she's not making enough on the tours?"

Destiny returned right as the tea kettle whistled. She placed a file folder marked with my name onto the table and tended to the tea. "Jenna, there are brochures for a number of vineyards I think you should consider. My favorite is the topmost, Vast Horizons."

"The small-batch winery we visited on the Pier the other night?"

"The same. It's so lovely. Top of the mountain."

I opened the folder and perused the first brochure, which featured the main house of Vast Horizons.

"Three hundred and sixty-degree views," Destiny added.

"Oh, no, isn't that where Cinnamon Pritchett and Bucky Winston got married?"

Destiny cocked her head. "I don't know, is it?"

"It was this grand estate with a barn at the top of the hill with pinholes in it to let the light through. It was magical. Not far from Monterey."

Hannah flicked her hand. "Vast Horizons is not at all the same. It's less than thirty minutes from here. It's a small vineyard, more like mine in scope. The views are of the ocean and the mountains, not unlike our view from the roof terrace."

Destiny gazed at me. "Hannah, didn't you show them the terrace when they were there earlier?"

"It was raining too hard, besides, the winery hasn't hosted a wedding in over ten years, so I don't think we could meet the timeline."

Destiny said, "I heard the three of you had a good chat."

Hannah remained stoic, her hands woven together. What had she told Destiny?

"Show me the next brochure," Bailey said.

I did. It featured a ranch-style main house with multiple images of grapes about to burst.

Destiny opened a cupboard and removed a colorful Raffaellesco teapot and four matching cups and saucers. "What did you all talk about, by the way?"

"We went there to discuss" — I gazed at Bailey, who mimed lifting a wineglass and then indicated her wedding ring — "purchasing a set of handblown wineglasses for an engagement gift for a friend. I'd hoped Hannah hadn't returned them all to the artisan." I pointed to the collection of glass items displayed in the bay window by the kitchen sink. "I see you have one."

Destiny stared at it and back at me.

I rose and crossed to the sink. "May I see it?"

"Sure." Destiny poured hot water from the kettle into the teapot.

I gripped the glass by the stem. "It's a lovely shade of green and gold. I like the raindrop design. Did the designer make others with this kind of pattern?"

"Not this pattern, but others in the same shades," Destiny said.

"Pretty." I set it back on the sill. "Did most people buy single glasses, Hannah?"

"Most did, but a few, like you, bought two or three."

Where in the heck was Cinnamon?

I said, "Some of the other glass pieces on your shelf look vintage, Destiny. Your mother was an antiques dealer, wasn't she?"

"She was."

"Did she give you that beautiful perfume bottle necklace you're wearing?"

"Good guess. Yes, on my tenth birthday." She set a trivet on a blue lacquered tray and set the teapot on top. "A year before she died."

"Hannah mentioned" — I acknowledged her with a nod — "that your mother perished in a horrible accident. I'm so sorry."

"My father drove her to it. He called her

crazy. In public. Told her she was no good for me." Destiny added the cups and saucers and a companion sugar bowl to the tray. "She wasn't" — she brought the tea service to the kitchen table — "crazy. She was a delicate, precious soul. She had a lot of ups and downs, but Dad grew tired of taking care of her. She left that day when he ordered her to. On foot. We found her days later in the woods. She'd slipped and fallen down a steep incline. At least that's the story my father told me. *Slipped and fallen,*" she repeated.

"You didn't believe him?"

She shrugged a shoulder. "He was the adult. I was a kid. What could I say? I remember him tucking me in that night, begging me not to grow up and be like her, ordering me to become strong and vital. So that's what I did." She raised her chin. "I became an all-around athlete. When I nearly made it to the pros as a beach volleyball player, he was ecstatic. But then I hurt myself — I took a spike to the head, suffering a mild concussion, and I shattered my ankle, making it impossible for me to play at the level I once had — and suddenly I was worthless in his eyes. Insignificant. Disgusting. He deserved . . ." Her voice trailed off.

Hannah sucked back a sob.

"What did he deserve?" I asked.

"Nothing," Destiny murmured.

Possibilities zinged through my mind. Had she killed him? To punish him for abusing her mother?

"How did he die?" I asked.

"Heart attack," Hannah said. "I told you, Jenna."

Bailey mouthed, *Where is Cinnamon?*

Beats me, I mouthed back.

Destiny filled the four cups with water, fetched a tea caddy stuffed with a variety of teas, and returned to the table. She took a seat at the head of the table.

Bailey looked green at the gills and didn't reach for a cup. Did she think Destiny might poison us? Hannah was scowling, probably wishing she could boot me out and protect her friend. I chose a Darjeeling tea bag, and after seeing Destiny lace her tea with sugar, followed suit.

Destiny sipped her tea but didn't set the cup back on the saucer. "Quade" — she gazed at the liquid — "loved tea."

Thankful for the lead-in, I said, "Why did you and he break up?"

"He didn't love me."

"He must have at one time. You'd talked about marriage."

"Talking about marriage is easy. Committing to marriage? That's the hard part." Destiny took another sip of tea.

Pinot rose from his bed and waddled to me. He pressed his chin between my legs. "Hey, boy." I rubbed his snout and inhaled. "Gee, he smells exactly like our dog. Do you use anti-seborrheic shampoo?"

Bailey kicked me under the table.

"Sure do," Destiny said. The dog returned to his pillow. "He gets itchy skin. What kind of dog do you have?"

"Also a lab. His name is Rook. And we have a cat."

"Tigger," Hannah said.

Destiny nodded. "I've seen him at the Cookbook Nook. He's a ginger, right, Jenna? I love his kitty condo."

"My father made that for him."

"Your father sounds nice. Lucky you." The corners of her mouth pulled into a frown.

"You know what's interesting?" I said, determined to keep getting answers while Cinnamon took her sweet time. "I smelled something like the dog's shampoo at the crime scene."

"Jenna!" Bailey rose to her feet, hands defiantly on her hips. "You know you're not supposed to share details like that."

I glimpsed her. Her green pallor was gone.

She wasn't upset with me. She was backing me up with attitude. *You rock, Bailey!*

"C'mon, girlfriend. It's Destiny!" I stabbed the table with my finger, playing along. "We can let her in on a few details. After all, she was attacked."

"Not by the killer," Bailey argued.

"We don't know that."

Keeping up the ruse, Bailey glowered at me and sat down, but she pushed her chair away from the table, giving herself room if she needed to rise quickly.

I said, "At first I presumed the scent had come from a cologne of some kind. Christopher George wears a leathery cologne."

"Who?" Destiny asked.

"Christopher Michael George, a self-help guru from Silicon Valley. Naomi's husband. Actually, estranged husband. She ran away from him a couple of years ago. He wasn't happy about that and tracked her down."

Hannah jumped on that. "Do the police consider him a suspect?"

Destiny leaned forward, intrigued. "Why would he have killed Quade?"

"Jealousy," I replied. "Seeing as Quade was interested in Naomi. Plus, he might have had his heart set on selling the David Smith forgeries," I improvised, having come to agree with Naomi that the notion of her husband killing for the forgeries and risking his reputation seemed far-fetched. "I thought George had deduced what Quade was doing and might have wanted to horn in on his operation, but it turns out George didn't kill him. He has a firm alibi for that night." I stirred another spoonful of sugar into my tea but didn't drink.

"For a brief time, the police thought George might have been the one to have attacked you and Naomi with something like a backpack" — I cut a look in the direction of her knapsack — "but that morning he was on a Zoom call with three board members." I peered at her forehead. "Your bruise is healing nicely, by the way."

Destiny folded her arms and lasered me with a look. "Why are you really here, Jenna?"

CHAPTER 26

Hannah opened her mouth to speak.

I held up a hand to stop her. "We're here to discuss wedding locations."

"Cut the crap!" Destiny snapped. "You've been glancing at my knapsack off and on. Why?"

Lightning flashed outside. The dog mewled. Bailey started to rise. I waved for her to sit. Thunder rumbled. The storm was close. At the same time, my cell phone buzzed in my pocket. Was Cinnamon texting that she was nearby?

"Well?" Destiny asked impatiently.

"Did you attack Naomi because Quade was in love with her?" I dared to ask.

Hannah moaned. "No, Jenna. Don't."

"Men can be such fools," Destiny rasped.

"Why did you steal her painting?" I asked.

Her mouth curled into a snarl. "I thought you'd noticed that on your way in. So, you know her work?"

"She described it to me. Why did you take it?"

"Originally? To throw darts at. But then it grew on me. It's good. She's talented. And pretty. And —" A tear slipped down Destiny's cheek. She swiped it away.

"What happened, Destiny? When did things go south between you and Quade?"

"Two years ago. One year ago. Six months ago." She flailed a hand. "We were on a crazy roller coaster. In and out of love, over and over. I went to talk to him Saturday morning, to celebrate his upcoming win, but when I saw his painting, I knew he'd lose. It was too pale, too *meh.* I suggested he start fresh. I gave him the idea to make it darker, moodier."

More like the painting she'd stolen from Naomi, I noted.

"He hated me offering an opinion, of course. 'Nobody will dictate what I should or shouldn't paint,' " Destiny said, mimicking Quade's haughty tone. "But I was certain his first painting would lose to Keller's."

As I'd imagined.

"You went back the next day, Sunday," I said. The inn's housekeeper had spotted her, despite Hannah's account of a ping locator placing Destiny at home all day.

"You stole it and planted it at Keller's, and then sent an anonymous text to Yardley Alks to get Keller in trouble."

"Keller," she scoffed. "He made Quade nervous. Made him question his talent. That was one of the reasons Quade fell for Naomi. She liked his work. She praised it. He believed she was his muse. What a crock!" She slapped the table. "How quickly he forgot that I'd been his muse once upon a time."

"On Monday night, at the wine tasting event after our workshop, when he brushed you off," I said, "you ran to the communal room. Was that when you stole Keller's burin?"

"His what?"

"The tool with the six-inch shaft and wooden handle."

Destiny shot to her feet. So did I. Hannah and Bailey gasped.

Stabbing a finger into her palm, Destiny said, "Yes, I took it. I wanted to convince Quade to kill Keller."

To convince Quade to do the deed? Whoa. I hadn't seen that coming.

"But that night, I went to the attic where I keep my mother's things — I was missing her something awful — and she told me Quade needed to die, or I'd never be able to move on with my life. She said he would never love me."

Her mother talks to her from beyond the grave? Holy moly!

Gently, I said, "That's when you came up with the idea of poisoning him."

"By adding arsenic to a glass of wine," Bailey added, matching my tone.

Hannah made a muffled sound. Her face pinched with sorrow.

"Your one challenge was how to get him to drink it," I said. "That's when you hit upon the plan to leave a note from Naomi."

Destiny didn't utter a sound.

"You left the note and wine in his room Tuesday while he was at the opening night soiree," I went on. "What I don't get is why you didn't poison him earlier and be done with it?"

She raised her chin. "I thought I'd give him one more chance. At the soiree. I reasoned I could always go back and remove the glass if he realized I was the love of his life, but then —"

"But then he denounced you in public, saying he'd never be into you. That reminded you of how your father had treated your mother."

Her shoulders began to shake. Her lower lip trembled.

"So you left the poison in place, but when you went back later to get the glass, you realized he was still alive."

"My father died from the arsenic!" she shrieked. "Why didn't Quade?"

Hannah keened. Bailey and I exchanged a look. Had Destiny just admitted to killing her father, too?

"He was a monster," she hissed. "He beat me whenever I didn't win. He . . . he was a frustrated athlete. He'd wanted to go pro. For football. But he wasn't good enough. Not *good* enough," she stressed. "Therefore, I had to be."

"Oh, Destiny," Hannah said. "How horrible."

"My teammates never saw where he hurt me. He was discreet. But when I shattered my ankle, and he rejected me" — she smacked one hand against the other — "that was the end. I'd had it."

"Didn't the police suspect you killed him?" I asked.

"No." Destiny scoffed. "They never deemed it a murder. I laced the coffee that he kept cold in the refrigerator. The cops never tested the container because Dad washed the container before he died. Arsenic doesn't work immediately like other poisons." Her cheek ticked with tension.

"When I went back to the cabana to get the wineglass — I was wearing gloves so I wouldn't leave fingerprints — Quade looked dead and very peaceful, so I bent to give him one last kiss goodbye, and he roused."

"Omigosh," Hannah whispered.

"He said he'd never love me. He said he would always love Naomi. That . . . That was when I lost it. I remembered I had Keller's tool in my purse. I pulled it out and jabbed it into Quade's chest. He didn't cry out. The poison had weakened him. He coughed and tucked into a ball. And then I panicked."

Then? My mouth fell open. *Then?*

"You left the burin," I said. "To frame Keller."

"No. To frame Naomi. I saw the note I'd left and I decided she should take the fall. I wiped off the tool. Then I wadded up the sketches of her daughter that I'd stolen from her tote — I didn't know if Quade was the father, but I suspected he might be — and I tossed them around the room, like he might have been angry with her."

Exactly as I'd theorized earlier.

I said, "Then you washed the wineglass to remove any trace of arsenic."

"Mm-hm."

"And you left a scrap of paper with the

letter *N* on it," Bailey said. "Any more and the police might have been able to compare the handwriting to yours."

Destiny squinted at Bailey. "Yes."

"Blood must have splattered your clothes," I stated.

"I threw on a complimentary robe, waited until the coast was clear, raced to the pool area to avoid going through the lobby, and then on to the parking lot."

"Clever," Bailey said.

Hannah's eyes were wider than saucers. She said, "Destiny, you need to confess everything to the police."

Destiny regarded the three us, then mumbled, "I can't . . ." She wheezed, as if deflated, and slumped against the island. "I can't . . ." She moaned and bent forward. Was she going to be sick?

Hannah rushed to help her.

In a flash, Destiny jolted upright, holding a wine bottle from the wine rack in hand. She grabbed Hannah around the neck and cracked the bottle against the edge of the counter. Red wine splattered everywhere. Pinot bolted to his feet.

Destiny aimed the sharp bottleneck at Hannah's throat.

"Destiny, no!" I cried.

"I can't go to prison."

Don't worry about that, I thought. *You'll wind up in an asylum.*

Pinot dashed to his owner, feet slip-sliding on the kitchen runner.

"Lie down, mutt," she ordered. The dog obeyed.

With her eyes, Hannah pleaded for help.

Bailey whispered, "Jenna?"

"Destiny," I said as calmly as I could with my heart pounding in my rib cage like a jackhammer. "Chief Pritchett is on her way. I notified her before coming here."

Destiny barked out a laugh. "Ha! You're like the boy who cries wolf, Jenna. You've seen one too many dead bodies. She didn't believe you this time, don't you get it?" She nudged Hannah at the back of her knees. "Move. To the front door." She warned the dog not to budge. "Jenna and Bailey, you stay, too!"

As if.

I jammed my heel onto the runner and yanked it toward my other foot. Like the dog, Destiny reeled, trying to gain purchase. Her arms flailed. The neck of the wine bottle flew out of her hand. Hannah lurched left. Bailey caught her before she collided with the island. Destiny toppled backward. Her shoulders hit the tile floor first and then her head struck with a *smack.*

"Jenna!" a voice yelled from the great room.

Cinnamon. About time.

CHAPTER 27

Needless to say, Cinnamon was not happy with us, but in particular *me.* I had to listen to her diatribe for a good ten minutes while Appleby, Ferguson, and Foster tended to Destiny, Bailey, and Hannah. She vowed to lock me up the next time I interfered with one of her cases. I was relieved she didn't plan to this time.

My father was so upset with me he didn't talk to me for two days. He didn't care that Bailey and I had gone to help Hannah. He didn't care that I'd figured out the timeline around the murder and the art thefts.

Rhett, on the other hand, babied me for twenty-four hours, after which he sat me down and said if I really wanted to marry him, I had to be more careful. He winked after his quasi-lecture.

Bailey begged off work for a couple of days. Seeing Hannah with a bottle next to her throat had thrown her for a loop. She wanted to play with Brianna, listen to good music, and eat a bunch of bonbons. All three, I told her, were better than climbing in bed and pulling the covers over her head.

On Thursday, as my aunt and I were preparing the shop for Cinco de Mayo, Flora and Faith sauntered into the store, arm in arm, Flora in a tasteful burgundy sweater dress, Faith in a form-fitting pink yoga getup.

"We're celebrating and going to the Nook for tea!" Faith trilled, releasing her sister's arm.

My aunt smiled. "What are you celebrating?"

"Yardley Alks has hired me to market all of her late son's work. She wants the proceeds to go to an art student fund she has created."

"I thought you were retiring from being an artists rep," Aunt Vera said.

"I've decided it suits me. I love artists. Love, love, love them." Faith spread her arms wide. "But first, Egan Zeller — I've hired him to assist me, by the way — is tracking down any of the forgeries Quade might have sold. Yardley wants us to repay the unwary buyers for their initial expense and subsequent suffering."

I said, "I'm glad you'll give Egan a

chance."

"He's a bright boy," Faith said. "And Flora vouches for him."

"Vera," Flora said, "do you remember when Egan used to help me at Christmas with all the wrapping? He was so sweet."

"Speaking of Yardley," Faith said, "she told me Naomi Genet is moving back to San Jose. She got a teaching job in the art department at the university."

Naomi had called me and told me the same. She was not going to reunite with her husband, but they would go to counseling, and she would allow him visitation rights. I'd told her to be safe and reminded her that Crystal Cove would always welcome her back with open arms.

"Oh, Sis, look!" Flora pointed a finger. "There's that cookbook I was telling you about." She guided Faith to the display table where I'd set a stack of the *Salsas and Moles* cookbook.

My aunt leaned in to me and whispered, "I'll bet Z.Z. put them up to hiring her son."

"Actually," I said, "she was thinking of hiring him herself, to help with the festivals."

"Well, any way the young man can get experience to add to his resume is a good thing."

"Hello-o," Gran said as she swooped into the shop, a to-go coffee in hand, a sombrero on her head, and an oversized tote bag on her shoulder. "Sorry I'm late. I got to chatting."

I burst out laughing. "Why the hat?"

"Olé!" She flung it onto the sales counter. "This place needs more decorations. My husband and I often took cruises to the Caribbean and South America so I have lots of goodies to add." She started pulling colorful items from her purse. A serape. A pair of maracas. "As I said, I got to chatting when I was at Latte Luck. I ran into Edith McNary. She told me" — Gran lowered her voice — "that she and Sienna agreed if Sienna gets into therapy and returns everything she's ever stolen from Sterling's, she will not press charges. Edith is such a darling, don't you think, Vera?"

"A darling," my aunt echoed.

"By the time Sienna's stint is over, that baby will be due. Edith didn't want Sienna to have to give up the child. She believes in redemption." Gran hung the serape next to the vintage corn-and-chili-pepper aprons I'd stocked for this week's event. "This looks nice here, don't you think?"

"Perfect," I said, enjoying her buoyant energy.

"Hi, everyone," Katie crooned as she emerged from the breezeway. "I need a taster."

My aunt, Gran, and I swarmed her. I'd skipped breakfast, too eager to put the finishing touches on the shop.

"These are *mantecadas,*" she said, holding out a plate of mini pastel muffins. "A Mexican sweet bread with a hint of orange zest."

I took one, peeled off the cupcake wrapper, and bit into it. "Yum!"

"About Keller," Katie continued, as if that was a normal segue. Her chin began to tremble.

I clasped her elbow and guided her to the puzzle table. She set the plate of goodies down.

"About Keller," I said. "Go on."

"He's going to continue his art."

"He should, now that he's the official winner of the poster art competition."

"But he's going to give up his ice cream business and take over Taste of Heaven. His mother wants to retire."

My mouth dropped open. "Wow! That's huge news."

"He loves the place. He knows it inside and out. And it will give him a steady income."

"Is Eleanor okay?" I asked. "She's not that old."

"She's in her sixties and says her back is killing her. The shop makes plenty of money. She can afford to retire on her portion of the income." Katie twisted the plate of mantecadas.

Uh-oh. She had that look I remembered from childhood, a look that meant she didn't want to say whatever was coming next. I gulped. "You're not quitting, are you? I mean, you can if you want to be a full-time mother for Min-yi, but . . ." My stomach knotted up.

"No, I'm not quitting. We're going to find a nanny."

"That's great."

Katie's eyes misted with tears. "Do you think she'll hate me for the rest of her life?"

Aha. Now I understood her angst. "Gosh, no. You will be giving her a gift, showing her that she, too, can have a career doing what she loves if she wants. You'll make it work. Taste of Heaven isn't open for dinner, so Keller will be home nights. If you want, you could do the same. If Reynaldo is ready. We'll make it work."

Katie threw her arms around me. "Thank you. I love you."

"Love you, too. Now, go make more of

these mantecadas. I'm hungry and these aren't going to last long."

She scrambled to her feet, hugged me again, and hurried back to the café.

I ambled to the sales counter, where my aunt was sorting receipts. "This has been a remarkable day and it's not even ten a.m. First, Faith and Flora. Then Katie." I told her the news.

"When it rains, it pours."

"I hope it's not going to rain again," Pepper said as she entered the store with her daughter. "Please tell me it isn't. The surf shop's roof leaked in the last storm." The surf shop was above Beaders of Paradise. "If they hadn't been on top of things with buckets and such, that rain could have done worse than drizzled down the wall into my place. Crafts and water do not mix."

"Don't be the prophet of doom, Mother," Cinnamon said. She was in uniform, not smiling, all business. "Go. Talk to Vera. But make it quick. I only have a half hour for coffee before my shift begins."

Pepper split from her daughter and steered my aunt to the children's corner, probably to discuss water damage, seeing as Aunt Vera owned Fisherman's Village.

"Hey," I said casually to Cinnamon. "It's been an unusual morning. Every person who has come in has had some tidbit to share. Do you have anything to add? I feel like Tito should be here taking notes so he can put it all in the *Courier.*"

"I'm not pregnant, if that's what you're trying to find out."

"And if you were, I wouldn't put that in the newspaper." I grinned.

"Listen, you and I need to have a real chat."

"About?"

"You know what about. You, putting yourself in danger."

"Don't go all Dad on me," I said. "I've gotten the lecture."

"I care about you, Jenna. I know you love Crystal Cove. I know you love your friends and family. But I want you to love *you* first and foremost." She grabbed my hand. "Think before you leap." She studied the engagement ring on my finger.

"Are we talking about marriage or danger?" I joshed.

Her mouth quirked up on one side. "They might go hand in hand."

Pepper returned and clasped her daughter's arm. "No more girl talk. I need coffee." She escorted Cinnamon through the breezeway.

Cinnamon glanced over her shoulder at

me and winked.

At noon, Rhett sauntered into the store, a broad smile on his handsome face. "Hey, beauty." He crossed to me. "Are you ready?" He kissed my cheek.

A delicious shiver zipped through me. "Am I ever."

My aunt said, "What's up?"

"We're going to look at three wedding venues," I said. "Let's hope one of them works."

Rhett pulled me into a hug. "You know, if none do, there's always the beach."

I gazed into his gorgeous, loving eyes, and murmured, "I never thought of that."

RECIPES

Asparagus-Gruyere Tart
Gluten-free Single-Crust Dough
(for pie or tart)
Chicken-Basil Parmesan
Chipotle Dipping Sauce
Savory Shrimp Appetizer
Chocolate Mint Muffins
Gluten-free Chocolate Mint Muffins
Wine Cookies
Gluten-free Wine Cookies

Asparagus-Gruyere Tart

(Serves 4–8)

From Rhett:

This is always a crowd pleaser so I keep it on the menu at Intime whenever asparagus is in season. I like my staff to make its own puff pastry, but store-bought puff pastry works well. For a gluten-free alternative, we use a gluten-free, single-crust pastry dough base, with extra butter.

Flour for rolling pastry
1 sheet frozen puff pastry
2 cups Gruyere, shredded, about 5 ounces
1 1/2 pounds thick asparagus, trimmed
1 tablespoon olive oil
salt and pepper, to taste

Preheat oven to 400 degrees.

On a floured surface, roll the puff pastry into a 16-by-10-inch rectangle. Place pastry on a lightly greased baking sheet with edges. The tart will leak. Score the pastry dough 1 inch in from the edge. This will help the pastry rise on the edges. Using a fork, pierce dough inside the scoring. Bake until golden brown, about 15 minutes.

Remove pastry shell from oven and sprinkle with Gruyere. Trim the bottoms of the asparagus spears to fit crosswise inside the tart shell; arrange in a single layer over Gruyere. You'll want to alternate the ends and tips. Brush the asparagus with olive oil and season lightly with salt and pepper.

Bake approximately 20–25 minutes. Check an asparagus spear with a fork to make sure they are tender before removing from oven. Serve warm.

*You may use thin asparagus; shorten cooking time by 2–4 minutes.

Gluten-free Single-Crust Pastry Dough

(Yield: 1 crust for 9-inch pan or 16-by-10-inch flat tart)

2 1/2 tablespoons ice water
1 1/2 tablespoons sour cream
1 1/2 teaspoons rice vinegar
3/4 cup gluten-free flour mixture (*see below)
1 1/2 teaspoons sugar
1/2 teaspoon salt
1/4 teaspoon xanthan gum
8 tablespoons unsalted butter, cut into tiny pieces and frozen for 10 minutes

In a small bowl, combine ice water, sour cream, and vinegar.

In a food processor, mix the gluten-free flour mixture, sugar, salt, and xanthan gum. Add frozen butter and pulse for about 10 pulses.

Pour half of the sour cream mixture over the gluten-free flour mixture and pulse until mixed. Pour the remaining sour cream

* Gluten-free flour mixture: I like to use a mixture of sweet rice flour and tapioca starch mixed with 1 tablespoon whey powder.

mixture over the gluten-free flour mixture and pulse until it all comes together, about 5–6 pulses.

For a pie shell or for tart, turn the dough onto a sheet of plastic wrap and mold into a 5-inch round. Wrap in plastic wrap and refrigerate for 1 hour. Before rolling out the dough, let it sit on the counter to soften up. It will be quite firm. Allow 15–20 minutes. I like to roll the dough between two pieces of parchment paper. Gluten-free flour mixtures can be sticky.

For the Asparagus-Gruyere Tart recipe, roll the gluten-free dough into a 16-by-10-inch rectangle. Place pastry on a lightly greased baking sheet with edges. The tart will leak. Using a fork, pierce dough all over. Bake until golden brown, about 15 minutes. This dough will not "puff up" on the sides like puff pastry will, but the flavor will be quite nice.

CHICKEN-BASIL PARMESAN

(Serves 4)

From Katie:

This is a standard dish that we serve for dinner at the Nook Café. My mother taught me that chicken must be quick fried so it doesn't dry out. Also, you can substitute half and half for the cream, but it won't be as creamy. As I tell any of my customers, when you find a recipe you like, experiment with it to make it yours. No matter what, please use fresh basil.

1 tablespoon olive oil
1 pound chicken breasts with skin on (may be skinless, but cut cooking time by 3 minutes)
1 tablespoon butter
2 cloves garlic, minced (you may use garlic from a jar)
1/2 cup heavy cream, plus more if needed
1 cup parmesan cheese, grated
1/4 teaspoon salt
1/4 teaspoon pepper
1 cup basil, rinsed and chopped

Heat a sauté pan on high. Check to make sure the pan is hot by adding a few drops of water. They should instantly evaporate. Now add the olive oil. It should glisten and shimmer.

Add the chicken breasts skin-side-down into the sauté pan. Reduce heat to medium-high. I cover the pan with a splatter-guard top. Let the breasts cook for 6–8 minutes. Don't try to move them around the pan or lift up to check on them every 5 seconds or the skin will tear and you'll never get a good crisp skin. (Shorten cooking time by 3 minutes if using skinless chicken breasts.)

When the chicken is ready to flip, it will let you know because it will be easy to flip.

Flip and cook for 3–4 minutes. Remove the breasts to a clean plate.

Now, add the butter to the skillet, then add the garlic. Sauté for 30 seconds. Add cream, bring to a boil, then stir in the parmesan cheese. Reduce to medium heat. Add salt and pepper to taste. Add basil leaves and cook for about 30 seconds. Add more cream if you want a creamier sauce.

Return the chicken to the skillet and cover with sauce.

Serve the chicken alongside your favorite green vegetable.

Chipotle Dipping Sauce

(Yield: 1 cup)

From Jenna:

When Rhett and I tasted this on the Pier for the Watercolors and Wine event, we knew we had to recreate it for ourselves. It is so easy and is wonderful for crudites as well as a salad dressing.

1/2 cup mayonnaise
1/2 cup sour cream
1 1/2 teaspoons garlic powder
1/2 teaspoon onion powder
1 teaspoon dried dill
1/4 teaspoon salt, plus more to taste as needed
1/2 tablespoon fresh lime juice
1 teaspoon fresh minced garlic
1/4 teaspoon white pepper
1–2 chipotle peppers in adobo sauce, chopped; save the rest for garnish, if desired
1 tablespoon fresh green onions, chopped, for garnish

Combine all ingredients, except those reserved for garnish, in a blender or in a food processor. Blend until smooth.

You'll want to taste and add seasonings that

you prefer. If you add more peppers, it will get hotter, of course. If you add more lime juice, it will increase the acidity.

If desired, garnish with extra chipotle peppers and green onions. If you want to serve as a salad dressing, add 1–2 tablespoons of water to thin.

Store remaining dressing in the refrigerator for up to a week. It will thicken as it sits.

Savory Shrimp Appetizer

(Serves 4–6)

From Aunt Vera:

What does minced mean? Let me tell you, it matters when it comes to an appetizer. Mincing is the finest amount of chopping. I cannot do it by hand. I typically use a food processor. It's the technique that allows the maximum flavor from the minced item. Chopping or dicing doesn't produce the same result.

1/2 clove garlic, minced
1 green onion, minced
1 tablespoon chives, chopped
1 tablespoon parsley, chopped
1 pound fresh or frozen shrimp, chopped fine
4 tablespoons butter
juice of 1/2 lemon, about 1 tablespoon
salt and pepper to taste
toast points, gourmet crackers, baked puff pastry shells, or salad greens

Mince garlic and green onion in a food processor. Set aside. Chop chives and parsley finely and set aside. (Tip: I like to use kitchen scissors to "chop" these.) Chop the shrimp finely. Set aside.

Melt butter in a large skillet over medium-low heat.

Add the garlic and green onion to the skillet and cook for about 3 minutes. Do not let the garlic brown. Stir frequently.

Add the chopped shrimp to the skillet. Stir until thoroughly heated, about 1 minute. Remove from heat.

Sprinkle the shrimp mixture with the chopped chives and parsley. Drizzle with lemon juice. Add salt and pepper to taste.

Serve the shrimp sauté on toast points, gourmet crackers, baked puff pastry shells, or salad greens.

Chocolate Mint Muffins

(Makes 18)

From Jenna:

Katie gave me this recipe and told me it was an easy one. She was right. It's basically two steps. All the dry ingredients go together, then all the wet ingredients. Then you mix the two. A snap! I adore muffins morning, noon, and night, and adding the mint? Brilliant!

2 cups all-purpose flour
1 cup granulated sugar
1 cup Andes mints chopped
1/2 cup unsweetened cocoa powder
1 teaspoon baking soda
1/2 teaspoon salt
1 large egg
1 cup sour cream
1/2 cup milk
1 teaspoon vanilla
1/2 cup vegetable oil
1/4 cup Andes mints (additional) chopped

Preheat oven to 400 degrees F. Line 18 muffin cups with paper muffin liners.

In a large bowl, combine flour, sugar, 1 cup chopped Andes mints, cocoa powder, baking soda, and salt.

In another bowl, whisk the egg, sour cream, milk, vanilla, and oil until smooth. Pour the mixture into the chocolate mixture and stir until batter is blended. Don't overmix.

Fill prepared muffin cups about 2/3 full and sprinkle with additional 1/4 cup chopped Andes mints.

Bake 15–18 minutes, until a toothpick inserted into the center comes out clean. Cool for 10 minutes before setting muffins on a wire rack to cool completely.

Gluten-free Chocolate Mint Muffins

(Makes 18)

2 cups gluten-free flour
2 tablespoons whey powder
1 1/2 teaspoons baking powder
1/2 teaspoon xanthan gum
1 cup granulated sugar
1 cup Andes mints chopped
1/2 cup unsweetened cocoa powder
1 teaspoon baking soda
1/2 teaspoon salt
1 large egg
1 cup sour cream
1/2 cup milk
1 teaspoon vanilla
1/2 cup vegetable oil
1/4 cup Andes mints (additional) chopped

Preheat oven to 400 degrees F. Line 18 muffin cups with paper muffin liners.

In a large bowl, combine gluten-free flour, whey powder, baking powder, xanthan gum, sugar, 1 cup chopped Andes mints, cocoa powder, baking soda, and salt.

In another bowl, whisk the egg, sour cream, milk, vanilla, and oil until smooth. Pour the mixture into the chocolate mixture and stir until batter is blended. Don't overmix.

Fill prepared muffin cups about 2/3 full and sprinkle with additional 1/4 cup chopped Andes mints.

Bake 15–18 minutes, until a toothpick inserted into the center comes out clean. Cool for 10 minutes before setting muffins on a wire rack to cool completely.

WINE COOKIES

(Makes 36–40 cookies)

From Katie:

What better treat to serve during a wine festival? These scrumptious goodies are easy to bake, and they make great gifts if put into pretty cellophane bags and tied with a ribbon. Enjoy the flavor of the fennel. If you prefer, you could use anise seeds.

1/2 cup dry white wine, like a sauvignon blanc or pinot grigio
1/3 cup safflower or canola oil
1 egg
3/4 cup sugar
1/4 teaspoon salt
1 teaspoon baking powder
2 1/4 cups all-purpose flour
1 teaspoon fennel seeds, crushed
sugar for coating

Preheat oven to 350 degrees F. Cover 2 cookie sheets with parchment paper.

In a food processor, mix the wine, oil, egg, sugar, salt, baking powder, flour, and crushed fennel seeds. (I put them in a baggie and hammer them.) Add water if you feel it needs it.

The dough will be soft. That's how you want it.

Drop by teaspoonfuls on the cookie sheets. Sprinkle with extra sugar. Colored sugar may be used during the holidays.

Bake for 12–14 minutes until golden. Do not overbake.

Sprinkle with extra sugar, if desired. Store in an airtight container.

GLUTEN-FREE WINE COOKIES

(Makes 36–40 cookies)

1/2 cup dry white wine, like a sauvignon blanc or pinot grigio
1/3 cup safflower or canola oil
1 egg
3/4 cup sugar
1/4 teaspoon salt
1 teaspoon baking powder
2 1/4 cups gluten-free flour (I use a blend of sweet rice flour and tapioca flour)
1 teaspoon fennel seeds, crushed
sugar for coating

Preheat oven to 350 degrees F. Cover 2 cookie sheets with parchment paper.

In a food processor, mix the wine, oil, egg, sugar, salt, baking powder, gluten-free flour, and crushed fennel seeds. (I put them in a baggie and hammer them.) Add water if you feel it needs it.

The dough will be soft. That's how you want it.

Drop by teaspoonfuls on the cookie sheets. Sprinkle with extra sugar. Colored sugar may be used during the holidays.

Bake for 12–14 minutes until golden. Do not overbake.

Sprinkle with extra sugar, if desired. Store in an airtight container.

ABOUT THE AUTHOR

Agatha Award–winning, nationally bestselling author **Daryl Wood Gerber** writes suspense novels as well as cozy mysteries. She is best known for her Cookbook Nook Mysteries, featuring an admitted foodie and owner of a cookbook store in Crystal Cove, California, and her Fairy Garden Mysteries, featuring a fairy garden shop owner in Carmel, California. She also writes the French Bistro Mysteries, featuring a bistro owner in Napa Valley. Under the pen name Avery Aames, Daryl writes the Cheese Shop Mysteries, featuring a cheese shop owner in Providence, Ohio. Her suspense novels, including the Aspen Adams novels, *Girl on the Run,* and *Day of Secrets* have garnered solid reviews.

As a girl, Daryl considered becoming a writer, but she was dissuaded by a seventh-grade teacher. It wasn't until she was in her twenties that she had the temerity to try her hand at writing again . . . for TV and screen. Why? Because she was an actress in Hollywood. A fun tidbit for mystery buffs: Daryl co-starred on *Murder, She Wrote* as well as other TV shows. As a writer, she created the format for the popular sitcom *Out of This World.* When she moved across the country with her husband, she returned to writing what she loved to read: mysteries and suspense.

Daryl is originally from the Bay Area and graduated from Stanford University. She loves to cook, read, golf, swim, and garden. She also likes adventure and has been known to jump out of a perfectly good airplane. She adores Lake Tahoe, and she has a frisky Goldendoodle named Sparky who keeps her in line.

Visit Daryl at www.darylwoodgerber.com, and follow her on Bookbub at http://bookbub.com/authors/daryl-wood-gerber, on Goodreads at http://goodreads.com/darylwoodgerber, and on Amazon at http://bit.ly/Daryl_Wood_Gerber_page.

The employees of Thorndike Press hope you have enjoyed this Large Print book. All our Thorndike, Wheeler, and Kennebec Large Print titles are designed for easy reading, and all our books are made to last. Other Thorndike Press Large Print books are available at your library, through selected bookstores, or directly from us.

For information about titles, please call:
(800) 223-1244

or visit our website at:
gale.com/thorndike

To share your comments, please write:

Publisher
Thorndike Press
10 Water St., Suite 310
Waterville, ME 04901

CPSIA information can be obtained
at www.ICGtesting.com
Printed in the USA
BVHW041123090622
639317BV00006B/17

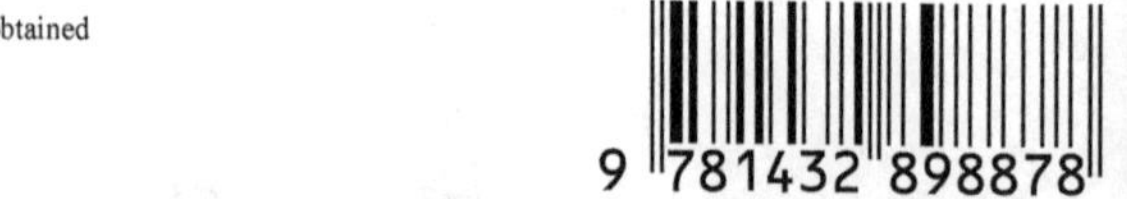

9 781432 898878